THE LUMINOUS SPARK

THE LUMINOUS SPARK

Short Stories

by

DONALD A. GIBSON

"And the luminous spark at the end of the
Equation
observes its hour
and is known

to the benighted traveller on the highroad
to him alone"

ALBYN PRESS
EDINBURGH

Made and printed
in Great Britain
and published by
ALBYN PRESS
(Charles Skilton Publishing Group)
29 Forth Street
Edinburgh 1
ISBN 0284 987379

CONTENTS

For Mary

THE AUTHOR

These eleven stories, each so widely different from the other, started as a by-product from a greater Endeavour which has yet to be realized. When first I had a vision of the task ahead and knew what it would involve, I decided to explore methods of story-telling in eleven tales, although at that time I had no idea what the stories would be nor where they would find their origins. The resolve made, the stories began to come, emerging from layers beneath the Conscious and bringing with them scenes that are real to me now and characters whom I have come to know and love. Nothing has astonished me more than the upwelling of these tales: the chance conjunction of a place and the finding of a forgotten letter which produced the First: the talks I had on winter evenings with the completely fictitious Ian McKelvie, when he told me the whole story of the Fourth: how the Fifth stuck just before the end and I could not unlock it with any key, until I woke at 0250 one winter morning and knew how to finish it.

The stories are not made for absorption in gulps; if you really want to get value out of them, you read them aloud, and if you do it well, you hold your audience captive for the time it takes to read. I say this avowedly because in our times the Art of reading efficiently or effectively is rather rarely found: too often we opt out and leave it to TV which allots us little else of a function than that of the reactive Spectator: or else in our humdrum lives we read for vicarious thrills, nearly experienced in the lives and adventures of others. Here you are invited to read at the pace of Reading aloud, you the narrator, you the characters. The experience is, I think, satisfying in a way that we have mostly forgotten.

Now that they are written, I can see that these stories make some assertions about Life which may surprise or disturb the Reader. In the West whole populations of people have renounced too easily their freedom as patient observers by surrendering themselves to the various religions of our times; religions of God, of Politics, of success or popularity or sensation. And they all have this in common, that they put up the shutters against our freedom to observe and listen and respond simply for the simple creatures which we do not care to believe that we are. Eddie Masters learned this in our times, and Stewart Anderson by becoming blind gained a vision of how things really are.

Who knows, if time or opportunity allow me to create the greater work that is still in the Shadows, I too may have had my vision extended; but it will not be done by study and reading, rather by silence and alert observation. Into the expanding empty room will be placed a Content. That at least is my hope.

Story Number One

KENNY

I HAD reached the far end of the platform for the second time and stood staring into the darkness, sensing the edge of that peculiar excitement which I had always felt, whether coming or going or, as on this occasion, simply meeting my sister off the train from Glasgow. The night was quiet for late September, with only a trifling wind that hushed over the faces of the great Perthshire hills. I thought how often I had stood waiting for this same late Glasgow train, patient, I supposed, with the patience of the country-dweller, who has never ceased quite to marvel that the thing arrived at all.

A squeak on greased trunnions and the metallic clack of a signal announced the approach of the southbound train first. . . then, silence and darkness. A few minutes later with a thin high wail it negotiated the wide curve off the hill and over the bridge; I watched it, coupling rods glinting in the station lights, all steam and smoke, slide to the water point at the end of the platform. Expressionless faces looked out into the dark, enquired perhaps where this could be and why one should alight here. I was so preoccupied with one group in a compartment, watching the dumb show of faces and gestures, that I was overtaken by the Down train clanking past me to a halt, Clan Cameron or McKenzie, some name like that, through carriages from Edinburgh in front, Glasgow portion behind. And there was Ann already humping her small mountain of cases on to the platform, thinking that her negligent brother had failed her. I hurried up to her; there were the usual sparring comments on reunion. She had been abroad, her first holiday abroad. At the homecoming one has always to cast off

1

the glamour and resume the ordinariness, but a considerate brother let her wear the glamour as long as possible. We had to carry all those cases and just managed between us, down the underpass, under a station, as it seemed, crammed with trains, up and over to the branch platform, where one carriage stood with its tank engine, Westinghouse cylinder snorting impatiently. Then the Up train and the Down departed into the darkness and we trundled off on our short journey down the falling single-line branch.

Seven minutes, a short time in which to put an ineradicable thumb print on one's life! Sitting opposite me in the open Third. . . yes, there were third-class compartments in those days. . . was a family of strangers, it seemed, perhaps up for the Glasgow weekend. . . Father, Mother, young sister, aggressively schoolgirl and a young fellow of about my own age. The moment was powered by fate. Ann was in boisterous conversation with a girl of her acquaintance, who had also come off the Glasgow train. The Mother across the passage appeared just a little concerned about arrangements; she leaned over and asked me if I knew where the Tigh-na-cloich boarding house was. I said I would take them to the spot, not five minutes from the station.

"And this is Kenny," (she said). "Looks just about your age."

"You sixth year?" (he asked me with a smile that was to haunt me from halfway across the world).

"Sixth year," (I replied cheerfully). "Going to University?"

He nodded.

"Glasgow?"

"Where else?"

"Me too."

That such a monosyllabic introduction should build so sure and strong I could never understand; it was as though the pattern of the future were arranging itself. Then the seven minutes were up; we were decanted on the platform and the little tank engine prepared to propel back up to the junction, its last journey of the day over. Like a veritable beast of burden I got Madam inside our garden gate, then took the strangers to Tigh-na-cloich. Kenny and I arranged to meet at half past nine next morning.

That late September morning blessed our new-found friendship. The west wind was launching great cloud flotillas over the hillsides as we mounted to a private place which I knew nearly two thousand feet above the village, so far, so high that no sounds came to us, but we watched the tiny vestiges of human activity, the smoke that rose straight into the clear air, groups of cyclists tackling the formidable climb to the summit, the scarce moving beasts in the parks and small fields. First introductions over, we needed all our breath for the climb which was in places not far from the vertical, as we clung to the fading heather and settled our feet carefully on the loose stone. Somehow it was possible for two strangers to share a purpose and a goal and silence and be at peace with the world. Yet our communication seemed effortlessly complete.

Kenny in his Glasgow Secondary school, beside the usual background common to us all, was principally Modern Languages, German by preference. This was a different line from my Latin and Greek, had it not been that I too had an obsession with German literature, though I was a good way behind him in that. He talked of Thomas Mann's Tonio Kröger and I could not help noticing how he rose out of himself at the subject, almost I felt levitated in time and space, with his brown eyes shining and a shock of brown hair that kept falling from his brow on to his nose. I knew I would have to read this book one day, but my six months' acquaintance with German made it a matter for the future. . . would have to read it, if only to discover through Tonio Kröger, that seeker after the ideal, something about Kenny himself.

We did not describe ourselves to each other; somehow there was no need. . . we had already passed that point. For a good half hour we were away, as I remember, on a voyage of mutual discovery, taking as Youth will, the greatest, the ultimate subjects as our most pressing interests. The morning train southbound interrupted us as its shrill whistle on the hillside opposite warned them in the junction of its imminent approach. We watched it in silence. Kenny lay back in the heather, face up to the sky as I was recounting to him the departure of Telemachus in search of his father.

"And all night long they rowed over the wine-dark sea till silver footed dawn. . ."

"Is it really like that?" (he said, interrupting me).

"What?"

"The Homer. Does he really write about the wine-dark sea and rowing all night?"

"Yes. I suppose I am translating from memory. I know that bit well."

"Oh, it's impossible," (and then almost to himself)," so much beauty everywhere you read."

"But at the other end," (I said), the same Telemachus thrills with joy as the arrow splits the suitor's skull. Not very beautiful."

"Yes, but you see what I mean: simple, honest, uncomplicated, not all mixed up with so-called moral values."

Tonio Kröger and Telemachus got on very well together and when they had to go back down for lunch they stood in the road and looked years of understanding at each other. I expect we met again that weekend; and when I got home from school on Monday. . . it wasn't a holiday with us. . . I remember I felt curiously as though part of myself were missing.

Kenny came up and spent a few days with us after Christmas. The weather was cold and damp; the mountain tops truncated with unrelieved low cloud. Our family customarily made little of New Year which was quite to the taste of the Sixth Year philosophers who looked out from their secure eyrie on a darkening world at the dawn of 1938. We explored one another, trying to construct tenuous bridges over the gulf that separates even good friends. But it can hardly have been easy; we were at that stage when, what you were last week, had to be revised, reconstructed, to fit in with what you were to be a week later. Similarities there were, oh yes, and a world of intuitive understanding. But the different standpoint from which we surveyed our common world was already apparent. I with my Classics and an incipient dabbling in Psychology. . . then the science to end all sciences. . . was already in a state of scepticism about Christian belief; was already by persuasion more of a pre-christian pagan and instinctively felt that the solution to Man's problems would not be found in any theophany which disturbed the jerky course of History. Kenny had no religious trappings to free himself from; he was principled and moral in that basic way that recoiled from the sin against the Holy Spirit, if he had known what that is. At the same time he was concerned with his life as a pilgrimage and with anyone else who would follow him on a level of pure and beautiful experience, which was not prejudged as good or allowable. I recall he sat astride the little bridge over the Grudie burn and said,

"Just listen to that. . . that noise of water. I bet you some physics expert would try to quantify and define it. . . a multitude of different movements and directions, expressed in sound and slung across one another. . . a true. . . what was it you called it last night?"

"Counterpoint?"

"Yes, a natural counterpoint. You said that musically people have to train themselves to listen to counterpoint. You would need to train yourself for this too. And look at the visual impression round us, the hawthorn bushes with the uneaten haws. . . blades of grass stiff with frost. . . even the whin and quartz on the road surface. We don't make any effort to contact it."

"Schoolwork isn't concerned with that," (I said with the profound wisdom of my age). "We've got to get places in the Bursary Competition where knowledge is infinitely selected. . ."

"Yes, I know. And we shouldn't be unreasonable about that, because that's the way things are. That's the way life is. But. . . ," and I can see his errant lock of hair thrown back and the triumphant glitter in his eye,

". . . but we've got to win the world for ourselves, the beauty of it, regardless of what life does to us."

Only patches remain in the memory and what I committed to my diary, written in German script so that no one at home could read it. But I must have treasured all this in my heart.

At Easter we went Youth Hostelling, using those hostels which were open so early. We had five days of strenuous bliss, forgetting as it seems now, both Telemachus and Tonio, enjoying that little bit of heroic endeavour and hardship and meeting all sorts of grand people. That's what the hostels were for in those days; it may have changed now. We started from Glasgow up the West Highland line and after a good sixty miles of walking and sixty of lifts, we reached my home where there was just time for a meal and the sorting out of rucksacks before we got a lift up to the junction for the afternoon train. He was a tousled looking Kenny, like me needing a good bath. Together we watched the train from Glasgow come in, all steam and icicles hanging from the couplings; then the south train strode past us with Clan McKenzie second engine. Kenny leaned from the window, gave his wry smile and characteristic twist of the hand and that was the end of that adventure. The train stalked out into the approaching evening.

His father died suddenly the following month. I read the announcement in the paper and nerved myself to write the sort of letter which I thought should be written. Kenny's reply was brief and unemotional. I resolved not to intrude for a while. At the end of June we read our names in the Bursary awards list; only two places separated us. I doubt whether at seventeen I felt realistic about an impending world conflict. It was always there like a fate waiting to descend on us. . . instinctively I thought "us". . . just when we were ready for it. Yet I spent all that summer reading through the books for first Year University. I was in Glasgow in September, the month of the Munich humiliation, and after a visit to the Empire exhibition went to visit Kenny's family in Pollok-shields; they had wanted me to come. I stepped off the tram and was seized with that reluctance, which has become so much a part of me, a reluctance maybe to find a change, to know if we would ever again stand on the Grudie bridge.

Kenny was out for the moment, but I sat with his mother.

"I know he thinks a lot of you," (she said). "He has school friends of course who come about the house, but they never seem to reach the heights you two get up to in Perthshire. I often think of that first evening when I spoke to you in the train."

She had coped well with her bereavement, had taken over supervision of her husband's business and was probably financially stable. I felt awkward though, my seventeen years before her late forties. What do you say that doesn't sound as though you were trying too hard? I was following a track of thought of my own when I heard her saying,

"I've no worries about him. He'll work, he'll apply himself, he'll be careful. But at times there's something so far off in him. . . as though he refuses to take the world as he finds it. I say to him: you've got to be realistic, accept human nature for what it is, not what it might be. I think all this reading of literature. . . Schiller, Storm. . . would these be the names. . . intoxicates you with an idealistic view. I expect you're just like that too, a bit starry eyed? Do you write poetry?"

I could not deny it but I had not realized that Kenny did also.

"I sometimes think the world will let him down; you know, instead of living up to the beauty and the wonder, will turn to nastiness and horror. Is there going to be a war?"

At that moment Kenny arrived. His mother very understandingly (or perhaps because she felt she had been talking about him) went out to prepare tea. We just stood and looked at one another and didn't quite know where to begin. But after tea it came, the torrent of mutual experience which left us sitting on two clouds far above the pother of the world. And as I was staying the night there, it was a late session. Next day I returned home.

What do I remember of the University years? Or rather what of the development of this strange little tale? During the first session Britain was breathing uneasily on borrowed time . . . but war it was to be. We met of course, often, at the reading room, at lunch breaks for our classes were different.

Sometimes we walked together down the wintry blacked-out streets to the city centre where I took the train from St Enoch to my lodgings near Paisley Canal. Yet try as I will, I can find no clear memories of these days. For youngsters like us, and there were no student grants in those days, the message was clear: work, succeed, get a top mark if you want to be selected for the Honours course. At weekends Kenny helped his mother with the family business and I eked out my slender resources with a bit of tutoring of the Wealthy Not-so-able. Came the summer and I was up again in Perthshire while the storm clouds gathered over Europe and a vague sense of shame, that was only to be expiated by our commitment as a nation to the struggle for something. . . anything. . . so long as it meant action. In the summer of 1939 we had the last of our family holidays, to the West Midlands. I still have a confused emotionally-toned picture of lush Worcestershire. . . Elgar's house backed by a cloudy blue sky and the petrol barges moving up the Severn to a secret dump. We were back in Perthshire to hear the announcement of war with the sick renunciation that we had no freedom of action left.

Then Kenny was to come up for a week, the only holiday he had that summer. It was a September morning of the best, chill with a north-west wind that swept the Mealls and the Stucs with a needle sharp clarity. I went up to the junction with my bicycle far too early, filled with an anticipation quite out of character with the times. I stood awhile in the booking office with Rob McNeil, the booking clerk, and heard all the clash of the countryside and more. . . did I know there was to be an explosives dump a few miles down the line. . . maybe this would be a prohibited area with letters censored. How these rumours went around. Then a ring from the East signal box told us that the train was five minutes away. I went out on to the platform and stood as light chased shadow from the great fleecy clouds, racing across the face of the hills like the fluctuating thought of some cosmic mind. Then it came, two black engines, standard types now and an unusually long train, stepping delicately across the crossings, just a wisp of steam at the safety valves, clanking past to a gentle jerk and a stop. I waved to Kenny who went to fetch his bicycle from the van.

That week was a delight. We climbed, taking in several Munros, and cycled and walked prodigiously. One day with the weather set abnormally fair for these parts, I proposed a night walk. The idea was to start after dark, walk several miles along one of the larger lochs, then at a spot I knew to the right of a burn turn up through the birch trees and steer across two watersheds to a village where with luck we would get a lift in the morning or, failing that, one of the infrequent trains home. My parents thought us mad, but with the amiable madness of our age. They saw us both shortly destined for the furnace and did not grudge us an adventure out beyond reality.

So, clad in warm jerkins, wearing our walking boots and equipped with map, torch and compass we set off after dark. My father had arranged a lift for us up and over the hill to the loch in the next valley. The night was ablaze with stars and quiet; the smells of autumn accosted us, damp vegetation, discarded potato shaws, the lingering memory of a bonfire. Probably no one in the village heard us pass through on to the tiny one-track road to the south of the loch. At times we talked quietly; at times we exulted in simple nearness to each other for which there are no words. On the road the going was easy; we met no one, only saw at a distance here and there the lamp-lit window of a cottage where someone was still awake. We turned from the road down a path by the lochside and after two hours we stopped just short of where we must turn up by the burn. Just back from the water and under a fringe of birch trees we rested on a tree trunk. In a world so big and roomy, where people were posturing and making war, we seemed tiny and insignificant. . . at the Still Centre, I remember I kept thinking, though I could not know where I had seen these words.

"Tell me about your Socrates," (said Kenny suddenly). "I was reading the account of his trial. Don't you think that for all his claim to wisdom he was a bit of a fool for not gauging his fellow citizens aright?"

"In a way," (I was thinking quickly), "it was a terrible

denunciation of Democracy, as Socrates believed it should be.
Don't forget that Athens had had a war that lasted on and off
for twenty-seven years; and that she lost it and was humiliated; and that she had her experiment with totalitarian government and was trying to face the future and make ends meet
economically. She probably hadn't the peace of mind for
ideals and noble sentiments."

"You are trying to find excuses for Socrates' condem-
nation. I thought he would have played his hand better."

"Did you read that part of the speech after he had been
condemned to death, where he says that at seventy he didn't
feel that he had much life coming to him anyway. . . and
besides that, his Voice, his Daimonion he calls it, had not
intervened at all?"

"Yes, what about that Voice? Was it something real? I
think the editors always want to explain it away and don't
really believe in it themselves."

"You remember: all his life it had said 'No' to him on
occasions, some great, mostly trivial. But it never positively
urged him to do anything."

Then came the stunning revelation: we never really know
one another.

"I believe in that Voice. When I read that, I knew for the
very first time what the experience of God would be. I can't
tell you how clearly it struck me. Then I went and read the
Gospel of Matthew, but sadly I did not have any positive
impression from that."

"You know, Kenny, I have had the feeling for some time
now that the experiences behind them were one and the
same. . . or maybe part of something continuous that goes on
and on. But nobody had an axe to grind and make Socrates
into a religion. The account of his trial has the feeling of
having been eyewitnessed."

"Unlike the Gospel of Matthew, you mean? It was
written. . ."

"Maybe forty or fifty years after the event, based on some
contemporary matter of course, but edited by the political
aspirations of the writer."

"Do you mean that a true view of Jesus is always obstructed by the political colour and the ways in which the narrative was written?"

"I don't think you get the right picture there if you merely add up the details supplied, which is what is mostly done; somehow you can do it for old Socrates. With the New Testament people are so uncritical. . . downright dishonest too."

"There's a fellow who lives in our street, a medic, a devoted scientist by his way of it, yet he literally accepts everything in the four Gospels. . . especially the contradictions."

"Well. . . that's only possible if you are totally uncritical and switch out the normal processes of judgment."

In the darkness I saw Kenny put a finger to his lips. A rowing-boat came into view quite close to the shore where we sat, two people rowing strongly up the loch, silhouetted against the strange glow that starlight imparts to water. I thought of the fear that would have crept around their hearts if they had known that we were watching them. Then they were past on their hurried errand. . . was it an illicit one I wonder? I looked at the water, an uneven mat of floating glitter, at the fringe of birch branches swaying low in response to some light wind above us. And I thought: water and mountains and sky and birch trees, much as it had always been since the retreat of the ice. Then exactly capping my thought Kenny said:

"And we are the transients in it all. We feel we should be significant but there is little reason to think it true. Shall we get going?"

The next stage needed care. I knew the turn, up past the drystane dyke, but it is strange how dimensions and proportions are distorted by darkness. Once I was sure we were on the right track, we made headway, watching our feet at every step. Then above the fringe of trees we stopped to look down on the glory of the loch and the still watching Bens on the other side. The world was a vast empty room, with only the errant wind and four feet clattering on loose stone. The path was recognizably going somewhere. Half an hour later we had reached a shelf above the valley, where the track must begin to head west. . . tricky going in the darkness, but the compass seemed to say Yes. We stopped for a last view of the primeval magnificence before it was lost to us.

"Do you ever think," (said Kenny), "where we may be in a couple of years' time?"

"You mean this war will go on and on?"

"Of course it will. Maybe like your Athenian war. But nowadays the world could not last twenty-seven years. . ."

"Where we will be personally, you mean?"

"I don't think I really care. . . I haven't enough to lose to care. Only health. . . and a night like this. . . and the hunger after loveliness. Losing these I wouldn't want to be alive. . ."

"We'll be caught up in it, that's for sure. I have had this feeling for four or five years now."

"Maybe so long as our Voice does not block our way or divert us, the future may not be so bad."

"So soon convinced, Kenny," (I said). "Something has been at work on you."

"Something is always at work on us, I am convinced. . . if only we try to be receptive. . . to get the signal."

"And probably "(I said)" old Socrates had seen it all, more than enough, had loved people, believed in ideals, hoped for the best. . . and was about ready to take the hemlock."

And Kenny said strangely, oracularly, as though not speaking to me but to the world:

"Let me always be sensitive to beauty. . . or let me die."

We continued on a south-west bearing, stumbling over heather and blaeberry clumps; the map was of no use now but the torch helped in awkward places. On the south-east sky a lightening suggested the rising moon. I don't remember now the rest of that night. We trudged down to a broad strath, now illuminated by a three-quarters moon; we crossed a plank bridge and climbed up over to the next watershed. Again and again I felt it, the natural world vitally alive around us in the darkness, though largely unperceived; we two so much on the same wavelength that we needed few words. We were tired and footsore when at length we toiled down the last long glen, and at the main road by good luck got a lift for the fifteen miles home.

During my second year at University my family moved to urban Paisley; it was an economic move to make, though I bitterly regretted the uprooting. In the summer after the second year Kenny, being marginally older than I, went to the Artillery; I would get one more session before being called up. We laughed when he said Artillery; it sounded most improbable, but he was going to make a go of it. And so our communication was reduced to letters and the occasional meeting when he was home on leave; but we inhabited different worlds. Then my turn came; I left Glasgow one summer evening for Exeter and the Royal Marines. After that our communication became less lopsided; we were improbably enough Companions in Arms.

We are always celebrating obsequies and last occasions, and never more than in the shifting conditions of wartime. We might never have been on these Perthshire hills again, had we both not retained from our moonlit crossing a sort of yearning to go back. When we knew that our leave periods in winter would coincide, we arranged to get our leave passes made out to a small junction in Perthshire, the spelling of whose name drew grumbles from two Orderly Room clerks. And during our brief leave the day came. It was winter, it was snow, it was cold and black and wartime. But we caught the train from Central long before the dawn; it was hardly day when we descended from the steamy fug of the compartment to the crisp snow of the Down platform. Around us everything was etched in incredible detail, the great round hills and hanging valleys; the sharp air cut us like a knife. We had a word with the station staff, still Rob McNeil and the others, while the train rumbled off up on to the hill.

The sun shone like a blessing on us all day. We took no risks, no amateur mountaineering, just walked and enjoyed the happiness of being home again, where every turn of the road, every snow-filled corrie clamoured for recognition.

Under snow bridges the burns made throaty descent to the loch; there were snow buntings and greylag geese and an occasional game bird eking out a miserable survival in the snow. Out of the corner of my mind I wondered when next it would happen; Kenny did not speak of it; he was radiantly simply happy in a way in which I suspect his companions in the Artillery never knew him. In the afternoon we called, by arrangement, at friends of ours in my old village who saw to it that our creature wants were satisfied. It was already dark when we took to the road to walk the two and a half miles to the junction. Of course we were hopelessly early: when last heard of the train was still thirty miles away. We sat in the cosy Refreshment room. . . oh yes! we boasted that, even in wartime, and had a warm welcome from Bessie Linton at the counter. I found myself slipping back into all the old lore and the new and frightful happenings that took place daily in wartime Perthshire. I noticed how much easier Kenny was in general conversation. Then the Branch train came in and the refreshment room filled up. We went out and walked the muffled length of the dark platform from the water-crane to the ramp and back. The train from Glasgow came in and went. At times we stamped our feet to keep warm and looked up into the heavens where all was as a book. We had reached the water column again when a twang on the wires and a squeak on the greased trunnions and a metallic clatter above us told that relief was at hand. I savoured these moments with an intensity as though I had to remember them: the shrill whistle, the double clanking, the lurch to a stop and steam erupting between the carriages.

For the rest of the war our ways diverged. Kenny went abroad to an area where war was awaited but never came. I had my full toll of adventure and lost many lives in the process. When peace was declared Kenny was back at University by the autumn of 1945 to finish his course; they kept me for two years longer. Once again we were out of phase and letters, when I look at them now, were factual without being informative in the way that mattered. Kenny had now no enthusiasm for University; that he commuted for an Ordinary Degree I knew only later on. He had left to take up some job by the time that I returned to begin a post-graduate degree and professional training. I wrote; I received a brief uninformative reply. But there was a PS: "I often think of our night out in Perthshire." Sometime later I wrote again; no reply came. Kenny's mother had moved to south Lanarkshire and twice I made up my mind to go and find out something. Twice with an utter decisiveness my intentions were frustrated. I have learned to live with this Voice, this "Thou shalt not," and often have wondered if, spanning times and cultures, it was the one which Socrates had known. I have been warned by it in many places, abroad too, once in Hanover when it prevented me from taking the night plane to Berlin. Yes, I was prevented and I knew how to accept the situation. But I wondered.

The manipulation goes on however. I came to know people who lived in Pollokshields and had been neighbours of Kenny's family; they had met the mother recently and she had talked to them about me, then a stranger as far as they were concerned. She had said she would like to see me briefly but did not know how it could be arranged. I arranged it; I took the bus one afternoon in summer and found their house in a village that was strange to me. His mother talked for a while about their move, about the business which she had sold, about her daughter who was in Edinburgh. And all the while I was waiting and she was wondering what to say. Finally I asked outright. She was a courageous woman and told me without visible emotion what she knew. There was some kind of medical condition; doctors had conducted so many tests and had made comforting noises.

"But you mustn't go and look for him. I don't think he could bear to see you. He's out," (she named a farm some two miles away), "labouring, cutting hedges, quite at peace with himself. He comes home at six and we are very practical. Then he goes up to his room and just reads or thinks or looks out of the window. Just now and then he smiles, and I almost wish he wouldn't for it breaks my heart."

I did not want to distress her and stayed only a little

longer; she said she would keep me informed. Some four months later I had a brief note to tell me that Kenny had been buried the Tuesday previously. It had been a brain tumour behind the eye and seemingly inoperable. If he had suffered, he had surmounted it wonderfully.

. . . .

And now many years later people and places have changed. One can be sentimental but I find myself remarkably resistant to it; progress as a description of change has a momentum of its own and we can but keep up with it. I had not been to my old Perthshire home for so many years; anyhow one doesn't go there by train any more. . . that is an episode of the past. We all have cars and roads are straightened out and you get to Perthshire, even to my old home village, in a surprisingly short time. Last summer I went back and, yes! I will admit it, I was almost engulfed with memories. Everything was changed; a new brash young population made noisy sport, motoring and boating with all the sophistications of new found pleasure. Our home was a boarding house; the Tigh-na-cloich was a Rest home. The prosperity surprised me. . . excluded me. I parked my car and walked on a road that is no pleasure to walk on any more. But the great hills were the same and the tormentil and the bedstraw at my feet and an aromatic fragrance in the hot afternoon. After two and a half miles I came off the road and took to the rough ground on my left and pushed my way among the saplings and the willow herb, all but tripping over fallen baulks of timber and odd tiles and bricks. In this scene of desolation I walked along the raised level of the Up platform and stood looking at the shapeless ruin of my memories. Did I imagine it? Did the noisy world respectfully retreat to a distance as I listened down through a vortex of the past to sounds, sounds and voices: warm hearted Bessie Linton in the refreshment room, the endless yarns of the booking clerk in his cosy office. I heard the shrill whistle in the hills, the scrunch of the point rodding in the trunnions and the signal arm clattering down. And a voice so real in my ears, it might have been yesterday:

"And this is Kenny; he'll be about your age."

Story Number Two

ROLF HERRMANN

"AND SO, you see, the larger part of it is technique, or craft, as I like to call it; the smaller has to do with special skills of hand and eye or gifts of temperament or character. You can't altogether blame artists for swaddling themselves in mystery. They find it hard enough to come to terms with the marvellous capacity which is theirs. But I, the artist, will tell you this: if they come clean, they have to admit that it's all got at an enormous effort. . . and there are lots of failures."

We had come in from the painting studio where I had spent a fascinating hour conducting, you might say, the anatomy of genius. But a studio out of hours is a strange brooding place, filled with all sorts of memories of people and locations, crowding in the shadows. We had stepped next door into the living room, or whatever you call it in an inner Vienna suburb, brightly lit, discreetly furnished for comfort and for use. At a glance I took in the Bösendorfer piano, shelves of gramophone records and large folio volumes and on the south wall, most striking of all the full-length portrait of Magda, her hair swept back, her strong face against a romantic atmospheric background; she was carrying her flute, as I had seen her two nights ago at the Musikverein Concert.

"Craft," (continued Rolf), "mostly craft in making animals live or humans speak. You are looking at Magda? Does she speak to you? Yes, everyone says so. Would I be too great an iconoclast if I told you that a slight feathering of the upper lip where it meets the cheek does just that. And eyes that follow you around? Part of any good artist's stock-in-trade."

18

"But it is a very impressive piece of work," (I said). "You think of her romantically still after all these years?"

"Yes, I do. The two of us were bound together in such strange uncontrived circumstances. I sometimes feel as if a craftsman in his own right at some higher level were pushing us into various positions for his own satisfaction. But," (he paused momentarily), "I hear her now in the hall; she said she would be back just after ten. You will have a chance to compare craft with reality shortly."

How I came to be in Vienna hardly matters in this narrative. I had thrilled two nights ago to the playing of the virtuoso flautist, Magda Hermann in the Mahler 3 and other works; I had been to an exhibition in a gallery just off the Ring, of paintings by an artist whom I only knew till then by repute; I had not immediately connected the two. I had met the artist and was invited home to visit him and during the hour we had spent among the sketches and half-finished canvases had suddenly linked the flute and the paint-brush. I was infinitely curious as to how it had come about but, as no part of me is a journalist, had been content to let events find their own course. Rolf crossed to close the curtains on the sights and sounds of the darkening city, which would have no part in what was to come. I noted that he moved with a barely perceptible limp.

"So, you did not connect Magda with me? How should you? Hermann is a usual enough name in the German homelands; but where we came from, the Sils region of the upper Engadine in Switzerland, it was a strange Germanic intrusion among the native Swiss. My grandfather had moved there from Heilbronn last century. Magda too was an outsider: her father, a von Sedelberg of Enns in Austria, had opened a hotel and casino business at St Moritz. After making his pile he fell out with the local worthies and retired in high dudgeon to a large house, some way from Sils. You see, we grew up together."

"And your family. . .?"

"Poor, insignificant by most standards. Yet from my early childhood when my father was still alive, I have strange blissful memories. . . probably romantic and quite. . . unfactual, but something I am always striving to get back to. . . something simple, uninvolved. . . which you might need either no craft to depict. . . or maybe consummate craft, like the stillness of a van Eyck."

"And you lived near Magda?"

"Near enough. A few kilometers here or there was nothing in these mountains. We were children at the same one-room Primary school."

"But surely your art and her music does not derive from there?

Rolf sat down on a backless wicker stool; he clasped his hands and studied his short stubby fingers.

"Do we ever know where these gifts come from? or are they packages of Grace, lent to us, not given? In that case I think we must use them, find how best to use them. But your question: I think my art, but not her music, came from these heights."

He rose and moved across to open a panelled door. Magda came in; they kissed unaffectedly; I was introduced, thrilled, I confess, in a dozen ways to meet the woman whom I had seen in a concert and on a portrait. Her voice was, how shall I say. . . brown velvet; her self-possession was so complete that she summed up the situation and chose the precise key for our threefold conversation. Together she and Rolf spoke Hoch Deutsch. . . proper German for the greater comfort of their guest. Now and then with a roguish smile Magda allowed herself a calculated lapse into the more slovenly Viennese dialect. And later in the evening I realized the secret communication which they held with one another with Swiss or maybe Romansch words of their childhood, which went winging over my head. I had to hear anecdotes of the concert in which Magda had been playing, the quaint posturings of the Secretary of the Verein who still belonged to the "Kiss your hand, My lady" era. I said little; I was happy to bask in their conversation, to steal a glance at Magda still in her simple, almost severe eau-de-nil gown in which she had performed.

"As I expected, Rolf, the pianist did not turn up. " (She named one of the top rate unreliable artistes, all too well known for sudden absences on the concert platforms of Europe and America.) " Josef Meinigen stood in and guess what?... they played IT. I think I had not heard it in years but I lived through every moment of it with rapt attention. "

"We mystify our guest, my dear, " (said Rolf, turning to me). "I don't know whether you are knowledgeable in the minor classics of the turn of the century. It is the Cesar Franck Symphonic Variations for piano and orchestra. Magda always says it is our guiding light, our cloud and pillar of fire. You do know it? "

I said yes; I said that of late we had heard several shock-haired virtuoso young American pianists strike it out of Steinway pianos; I sometimes wondered whether Franck would now recognize the thing as his.

"I wish," (said Magda with her mysterious smile), "I could show you what a certain Rolf Hermann looked like the first time he heard it. "

"Nine years old. "

"Short trousers and prominent ears. "

"I never felt there was anything wrong with my ears. "

"We had it on 78s in our house; one night when Rolf was there, it was played. When it was finished, he insisted on hearing it all again. "

"I can remember that experience yet... or, I think I do. Only some parts of it meant anything then. I was completely certain, or I think I was, that it was about me and the Alps all round. "

"You heard other music at our house, but nothing ever meant so much to you as this. "

"Of course, Magda, I was musically uneducated. I couldn't take your Mozart or Haydn, only bits of Beethoven and a few things. But this was I and the eternal view across the blue Silser See to the mighty Bernina, the ten thousand feet of the Piz de la Margna; it was the mists and storms on these mountains and their fearsome... animateness... that's the only word for it... by moonlight. In the next two years I was to explore these heights and stood once on the summit of the Piz."

"You see," (said Magda) "we were fairly well-off and had a big old house on a track up to the Julier Pass. There was always music; I even had an aunt Charlotte who taught me piano. It happened that Rolf's father had been in the employ of my father when. . ."

". . . He was killed in a mountain accident when I was seven. They say he was a sure-footed mountaineer, incapable of a misjudgment on rock. . ."

"Yes, there was something about a climbing party staying at our house; one of the guests lost his nerve. After that my father had always a feeling for the little fatherless Rölfi."

"But at that age you take everything in your stride. Anyway that's how I came to be listening to the Cesar Franck."

There seemed little need to disturb this picture as it unfolded. But I ventured:

"Do you ever go back. . . to Switzerland and Sils?"

"Go back?" (said Magda, smoothing her hand over her thick brown hair). "We did venture back ten years ago. . . but we couldn't look at the place objectively. There were tourists everywhere and cars and no-one whom we knew. Anyway, we ourselves had changed. So we beat a retreat from Sils and the Maloja pass, which were once our world."

"Now we are content to summon up the past. . . our Past, with the Cesar Franck. What do you say, Magda: I'll put on the disc while you get the coffee; I can't expect you to listen to it twice in one evening."

"Good. But after that, you know, you must tell us about that night in 1937."

She went out graceful, gracious, so that the room seemed less inhabited without her. After making sure that I consented, Rolf put the disc on the turntable. I smiled to myself, for I recognized the American orchestra and the young American pianist.

"My first experience," (said Rolf), "was three sides of 78; you remember the exasperating wait as you turned over or changed needles. At least this is all in one piece."

I felt I had to listen to it with fresh ears, as though it were my first experience of it. There were the dominating, almost sinister, chord sequences at the beginning. . . could that be the Bernina? There was the small voice. . . perhaps young Rolf. Suddenly the thing began to take on a new meaning for me. I heard despair, wonder. . . then the sudden appearance of a new force and drive which swept up the Rolf theme and drove it across the mountains, through strange vicissitudes to success. You might say, the end was confident but never lost sight of its beginning. After the final full stop and exclamation mark, he got up and switched off.

"I'll tell you something which you as a thinker have probably already encountered. What we say about the Arts is often a bit precious. If we care about them at all, without actually being creative writers, painters, musicians. . . and you are a writer and I am a painter. . . we are usually a little unsure of ourselves, in the other arts at least, whether we like what we say we like, uttering our rather tentative judgments. . . from which, mark you, we retreat in the face of someone who gives us the impression of really knowing what he is saying. What shall we do? Shall we treat a poem like a piece of fine porcelain which we turn in the hand as we listen to what it can say to us? Shall we sit in our serried rows in the Concert Hall and listen to our Mozart or our Haydn, unclear, if we are honest, whether we are enjoying them or. . . are enjoying the social experience of sitting with others in order to listen to them. We look for the story in a picture, the plot in a drama, convinced that we are doing what we ought to be doing in front of these artefacts of eternity. Privately however, we may be doing something quite different; we may be using our moments of artistic satisfaction for shameless personal incommunicable ends. Have you ever thought of using music for some purpose. . . some private purpose?

"I apologize for the lecture. Magda says I am too inclined to detailed exposition and claims it as a sign of advancing years. But it really is quite an important point. What are we supposed to be doing as we listen to Brahms or Mahler. . . and what in fact are we doing? That disc which you heard has

been shamelessly used by me. . . Magda too to some extent. . .
both as light source and reflection. At the age of nine when I
first heard it, only a part of it signified, the part that was me in
my surroundings. I heard it again when I was nearly twelve,
when I had already begun to draw and the future looked
bleak. It then reflected my mood. . . but it led me to hope, to
wait for something that should come. Of course I am running
ahead and you cannot fill in the intervening years. I mean that
it not only reflected the situation but. . . somehow. . . gave
light and hope too."

Magda returned with the trolley and all serious matters were
laid aside as we enjoyed the Viennese ritual of the Coffee. I
cannot now recall what subjects we covered but I remember a
conscious glow of happiness and I wished that the evening
might never end.

"Did you listen to the Franck?" (Magda asked Rolf. Then
turning to me,) "But of course you know it? I think that
performance is too percussive, too. . . incisive, though a Steinway suits better than my Bösendorfer here."

"You are also a pianist then?"

"That's what I was to have been," (said Magda with a
chuckle), "if Aunt Charlotte had had her way. But after
taking my school Certificate I went to the Music Conserva-
tory in Berne. . . Zürich too for a little while. Then there were
the war years and after. . . and my second instrument became
my great love. Anyway there's too much competition nowadays in piano playing and the physique factor tends to leave
the field to men. But of course I do play. We do Trio and
Quintet work during the winter."

"I listen," (said Rolf), "but it is understood, if it is something I can't stand, I go next door and get on with some
underpainting or canvas preparation."

"And where," (I asked) "did you two finally catch up with
each other?"

"Here in Vienna" (said Magda). "Rolf had been in Austria
since 1937 but I didn't turn up till '52. And there he was and
there I was and the rest was inevitable."

"We sometimes dispute" (said Rolf) "who married whom; but we usually agree that it was simultaneous. But Magda, my dear, you have mystified our guest, who cannot possibly couple Vienna with the Maloja pass. Yes, I was in Austria from 1937, all through the Nazi occupation and the war and two things saved me from being swallowed up in the Wehrmacht, this limp of mine which you cannot have failed to notice and the strange circumstance of my entry to this country through an unauthorized pass. Officially they never found out that I was here."

"So, you didn't take after your father" (I asked, curious but sensitive in the area of physical incapacity). "You didn't become a mountaineer?"

"I would have done. Already by the age of ten I had been up on the high tops of the Bernina with the men of the valley. I used to go off up among the small... "tarns", I think is what you call them, where the melted water of the glacier pours milky green into the enclosed lakes. For a boy, I was a grand climber; I wasn't lame at that point."

"In fact that's where you discovered your talent for drawing. I remember you showing me your first wild goats and birds of prey... and a fox."

"That was the wonder: I could just do it, three dimensions into two, perspective as the eye saw it. I had no instructor, no text book. I used never to go out without some paper and a stub of a pencil and the shy creatures just stood there and let themselves be drawn. That's what I meant when I said that this Grace is on loan; I can have no complaint if it is taken from me tomorrow."

"Really" (I said), "you had no one to guide or encourage you? How then do you explain the present?"

"Rölfi showed me all his animal drawings and I kept them for him" (I could not fail to note how the memories were cherished). "It was at our house that a Professor from Innsbrück saw them; he did not say anything but he asked to see them again and again; but he never did see Rolf."

"I always wondered what part, if any, he had to play in it. These were the happy days when my mother was still a widow. She was hopelessly poor and just managed to keep the two of us alive. But the eaves of the house were rotting and the floors crumbling; yet, you know, she always kept the balcony gay with geraniums and cared for them somehow all the winter through. That summer I was sent over to stay with friends of ours in Bivio. When I returned there was Matthias, with his cold Anabaptist stare of disapproval. The moment I saw him, I sensed there was to be no room for me."

"Your mother had remarried?"

"I think she was driven desperate to it. She could not face another winter alone. From that day her songs were silent and she never had time to tell me stories of the mountains or of our history. A child of ten or eleven sizes it all up."

"Matthias had a kind of religious mania" (said Magda). "I met him too for he also worked for my father. He was sometimes alright in an off-hand sort of way, but it was almost as though I, being a girl, didn't count. I doubt if his wife counted either; it was always: Woman, do this, do that."

"At first I tried to please him for my mother's sake; but after a few weeks I could see that she would shortly cease to exist as a person and I would have to fend for myself. Matthias made a slave of me, expected twelve hours and more of work when I was not at school. The poor meals that my mother had prepared grew cold as he prayed long and pessi-mistically to his God. We really were hard up; that winter too I was cold. The snow set in early and it froze and froze. Twice, three times I disobeyed him and he thrashed me merci-lessly, the while praying aloud for my devil-claimed soul."

"I could never understand that kind of religion" (said Magda). "He belonged to some South German breakaway sect; it always seemed to me that they were on more familiar terms with their Devil than with their God. I think this made them guilt-ridden and coloured all their lives."

"An eleven year old wasn't going to understand theology; but this was just frenzy. I remember when in a sudden storm a woodshed blew down, one that he had just rebuilt, he stood there, his short legs astride and hurled curses into the wind, calling his God by filthy names. I remember I was frightened; I waited to see him drop down dead. As I say, he brutalized me three times; on the fourth occasion, as he was making ritual preparation for the punishment, I kicked him from behind. He tripped and fell on his face. Then I was terrified, for he did not say a word, did not even reproach me. It was as well I did not know what was at work in that distorted brain.

"Two days later he took me out on the heights above the Septimer pass. . . you cannot know that area. Why we went I did not know; it was a whole day's outing. I was strong for a boy, but still only eleven years old; that day Matthias had the strength of the devil. I had the curious feeling that he was waiting for something to turn up. We stopped on the Storm-rand at midday and ate without addressing a single remark to one another. We saw two birds of prey alight on a glistening rock and I longed to draw them. I thought: if only I could go up to him and say: Aren't these wonderful birds. Wisely I did not.

"In the afternoon I grew tired of the rapid pace and fell behind. At first Matthias would wait for me and when I caught up all breathless, he was on his knees, praying aloud for light in his darkness. Then he stopped no more and there was a good half kilometre between us. I tried a short cut to lessen the distance, for now I was afraid. Suddenly the loose earth gave way beneath me as I scrambled on all-fours up over a rockledge. I felt the earth go: I clutched at the heath and bilberry plants: below me my feet were dangling, above a great bird high in the blue was wheeling over the sharp outline of the ridge. Then it was all giving way and I was so clear in my mind. . . then hurtling rocks and gravel.

"I didn't fall so far, maybe fifty metres. When I recovered consciousness I seemed so far below where I had been, dirty, dishevelled. . . but alive, marvellously alive. The bird had not stopped wheeling above the angular ridge. How long I had lain I could not know, but when I moved, I did know that my ankle was broken. You appreciate, it had never happened before, but I just knew. No one came: no one looked for me. I was terrified and started to crawl, dragging my left leg. There was a mountain stream on my right, the ground hummocky: I crawled, I flaked out, I crawled again. Night came on and I tried to move to keep warm. But it was pitifully slow progress. Finally I lost consciousness . . . and was found by a goatherd in the morning. My life wasn't to end there, you know. He fetched his wife and son and together they carried me several kilometres to their home. With an absurd loyalty, I said nothing about Matthias; they thought I was a foolish boy with a misplaced sense of adventure, climbing alone. They bound up my ankle with what they had and that had to do for several days. When a doctor finally saw it, it was too late."

"And Matthias never came looking for you?"

"I was convinced" (said Magda) "that Matthias rejoiced and praised God that he had rid himself of a piece of stinking corruption."

"Of course my rescuers found out who I was and after three days I was carried back home. My mother wept tears of joy and fussed around. I looked at Matthias with a man's eyes but he turned away and never so much as spoke to me for a week."

"But your ankle healed after a fashion?"

"I spent several weeks in the hospital bed in Sils where they did everything for me that they could. But techniques were rudimentary in these days and it healed as it was. Magda was a great help to me."

"I stayed in Sils with friends and took Rolf out walking. . . so painful at first."

"During that winter I could not go to school. My legs would not carry me. I'm sure, Matthias prayed for my death. I was now an unprofitable mouth to feed and things were pretty tight at home. It was life rather as the animals value it: something that can't support itself is ousted and dies. I sometimes seem to see the sense of it and the awful sentimentality of human beings which keeps every spark of life alive, however distorted. But this way danger lies.

"Down in Sils I could draw and that autumn I spent most of each day drawing. A local retired artist encouraged me and first put colour into my hands. He was astonished when I rejected the yellows and the reds and chose everything muted, the red greys and purple greys and the like. On my return home I carefully hid all these drawings in the rafters of the garret where I lived."

"Did you show them to your mother?"

"No. Rightly or wrongly I felt that she had shared in my betrayal. If she had not been a party to my death, at least she had not asked any questions. But on days when Matthias was away I tottered out on my ungainly legs and drew without asking her permission."

"And Matthias did not discover?"

Magda pushed out the coffee trolley and dimmed the lights in the room.

"We come to that. It was a hard winter. I often went out with a stick to support me, for I was determined to be strong again. One day in January when I was just twelve, I came in flecked with the light snow of a blizzard which had just fallen. Not until I had taken off coat and hat, feeling alive and positive, did I notice my folder of drawings lying on the table. . . open. Matthias simply said: 'Is this Devil's work yours?' And when I did not immediately answer for dismay: '. . . Thou shalt not make unto thee any graven images. . . Is this Devil's work yours?' I replied: 'This is my work'. He lifted his black arm and felled me; I crashed against a chair and was out for a moment. When I came to there was blood down one side of my head. He pulled me roughly to my feet. 'Now watch where this goes!' (He used an obscene and filthy term) 'and think of the way prepared for the sinner who will follow them.' He took the lid off the stove and slowly deliberately stoked the drawings in. I watched, as though I were burning with them and only once cried out when my best one, a Merlin alighting, curled and crumpled in the flames. I cried and choked on my sobs. With grim satisfaction he merely said 'Silence!' and finished the job with a brutal deliberateness. 'And,' he added 'if I could put you in after them. . . but Vengeance is Mine saith the Lord. . . and don't you forget it.'"

There was a silence in the room as we lived over separately and differently this turning point.

"And it was a turning point" (said Rolf) "for apparently I was to be an artist. If circumstances are intractable, some exterior movement is necessary."

"Which year are we in now?"

"It was 1937" (Magda supplied the detail). "Up there with Italy just below the Maloja pass, Austria and Germany further north, we were in an isolated fortress. I doubt if we knew it. Rölfi told me bitterly of the fate of his drawings. Actually he stayed at our house for some weeks while his mother gave birth to a still-born girl child . . . prematurely. That was the second hearing of the Cesar Franck. One day when the storm was raging and we could not go out, Rölfi was so deep in despair . . ."

". . . I thought of Matthias as having tried to murder my mother . . ."

". . . we decided to listen to it again. But you know better how you felt."

"It is difficult after all this time to separate factual truth from the new deposit of imaginative truth. I think I listened to all that first part in the closed luxury of self pity. I did not doubt that it was I and my Alps, the sheer planes of the Bernina, the road that went writhing down the Maloja to the outer world where I had never been; there was a compacted memory of storm and brooding silence and innocent laughing sunlight. Then quite suddenly the music struck me in a new way; there was no more room for self pity. My twelve years had to be twenty: I had to get out: why had I not seen it so clearly before? And while I was carried along in this fantasy, the door to my enclosed life opened. Have your coat ready! Have your satchel packed! your life up here will end. Then I was whirled away by the music to delirious success. I was an artist: I could handle drawing and painting: it was the one thing I could do and the one thing I wanted to do. When the music stopped, I looked at my clumsy leg and wondered momentarily whether dreams might also come from Matthias' devil.

"I returned home but still could not get to school. I made myself useful as I could, co-operating with Matthias and my mother but, so far as I can remember, never aiming to please them. January was grim; February strained me and I was near despair. We had been virtually blocked in for five weeks; the men could get out but not I; no one came nor went up our frozen path, mountainous with snow. Then one night I heard what I was subconsciously waiting for, the cracking, the deep muffled roar and stirred uneasily in my sleep. Next morning everything was etched sharp; villages on distant ledges had come nearer in the night; the blue tarn below our house was black. Every now and then there was a crack like a whiplash. . . you remember it so well, Magda?"

"It used to terrify me, this Föhn wind. I always had a lasting headache till it settled down. I just couldn't practise piano nor read nor do anything. I think we were all a bit like that in the mountains when it was Föhn time. But it was the end of winter; the roads would unblock steadily, every gutter was a torrent. . .

". . . and while you waited" (continued Rolf) "things grew, bloomed, spread. But I am jumping ahead. It was the third of March, 1937. Our house was tense, not only with the Föhn but with Matthias' God and Devil. As a result of something, he took away my stick and put it out of reach. I could not safely go outside now. I tried to work at my neglected schoolbooks but he kicked me out of the way as a loafer. He may have hoped that I would damn myself by suicide; in his reckoning suicides lodged in one of the deeper corners of Hell. But I bit my lip and said nothing. . . and suddenly, I remember it quite well, I heard in the stillness the sound of the music, that dominating, driving, positive passage. . . you noticed, didn't you. It came to say: Hold on!

"That night with the doors barred and the warm wind from the south buffetting our house, we were a silent trio. Matthias was reading in his great Bible. . . it was all he ever read. My mother was darning old clothes close by the lamp. I was reading some semi-religious book that lay about the house. Suddenly out of the wind there were steps and a

commanding knock on the door. I rose to unbar it. 'Sit!',
said Matthias, 'no one does any good being abroad at this
time of night.' I was horrified; it ran counter to all our
traditions of mountain hospitality. Even my mother was
uneasy. The knock came again; Matthias took off his spectacles and folded his hands in prayer. Then the knock came a
third time and with it a voice, deep and commanding but not
as I remember angry. 'Come Matthias, your resistance is
over, your part is played. Open!' Matthias ordered me up to
my garret and stood till I went; so I did not see who entered. I
tried to listen at my door but the voices seemed far off and
low. At times I could hear the stranger, strong and confident
and Matthias reduced to a gibber. Once I heard his voice rise,
with that petulant edge to it only to hear him silenced. After a
while my mother came to the stair foot and called: 'Rölfi,
dress and come down at once!'

"When I pushed open the heavy door, it was as if the room
was filled with light; but I was wrong for there was only the
oil lamp as ever. I could tremble even now to think of that
moment. Matthias stood in a corner, his face screwed up as if
in pain; my mother was in the kitchen; everywhere else was
filled with the presence of him who had come over the
mountains. 'So, this is Rolf,' he said, as though he had
somehow expected me and only wanted an identification. He
was tall and strong featured and fair-haired... this in particular distinguished him from the swarthy mountain folk...
and his eyes were large and grey and laughed a greeting to me.
I extended a hand, as I had been taught by my father to do; he
took it and... maybe I romance, maybe I can no longer
distinguish truth from fantasy... but I could have sworn that
a warm current flowed into me.

"That moment I have no more doubt that rescue was at
hand. It seems crazy now... a total act of Faith... consent,
too, wrung from Matthias and my mother. I would commit
myself to a complete stranger... but what a Stranger! one
who seemed just at that moment to have the twisted skein of
our lives fairly in his control. Who was he? I think you will
understand enough, will not really smile if I reply: Someone

from out there. In these moments I was suffused with light and confidence.

"Events moved: he told me to collect my belongings. When my mother made to do this for me, he forbade her.

"'He must learn to look after himself; he will have all the strength that he needs.' To Matthias he said:

"'Let the boy have twenty francs!' Matthias muttered that there was no money in the house.

"'I am losing patience with you, man. There is money behind the brick over the stove. Give the boy twenty francs!' Matthias cowered and did as he was told. Then my mother set food before us two and he bade me eat; but I found it difficult for excitement and the presence of two terrified persons in the room. The clock ticked; the wind from the South roared round the house and rattled the one window that we had. Then we donned coats and woollen hats and rucksacs, his a bright red, mine an old brown canvas.

"'I thank you for your hospitality,' he said to Matthias and my mother, 'however grudgingly offered. Fear not for the boy!' Then, raising his hand he said, 'God be with you now and in the days to come.' I kissed my mother but she was as cold as a stone. I offered my hand to Matthias, my murderer, but he turned away. Then we were out in the night and the door shut against us. And what a night! The raging warm wind blew us in the direction we must go and the Spring stars crowned my head in glory. For my strength was doubled, my ankle as though healed and the air filled with the only music which I knew."

The room was silent. Somewhere at the end of the street a late tram clattered past. Then Magda said, as though necessarily to break the surface tension:

"In our lives we have known these. . . these interventions, more than once. Somehow they never quite square with the allowable catalogue of. . . shall we say. . . Spiritual happenings. It's much more like the pre-Christian world where ordinary people could meet gods in the woods and mountains."

"Yes," (said Rolf) "maybe these interventions are normal enough, have always been normal enough, only they just didn't figure in the experience of Paul, Irenaeus, Origen and Co and all those other sufferers from spiritual prurience."

I said: "Leaving aside the identity of the stranger, what part did it really play in bringing you to . . . say. . . this evening?"

"Everything" (said Rolf). "The indisputable and necessary link. I could talk of that journey all night; how we came to Sils and there was a sleigh waiting to take us to St Moritz. I was lodged there with people whom I did not know for two or three days, till the storm subsided. We travelled by various means, sometimes by night, particularly in the later stretches, near the Austrian frontier. And always there was a complete certainty about our journey. I was lodged again in a small village, maybe to rest my leg. Then we set out by night and took to the higher mountains. We sometimes used short skis which had been procured."

"And how" (I asked) "were you with this stranger? Was he aloof, formidable. . . condescending to a small boy?"

"It is strange," (said Rolf) "when I was at his side, I could do everything, walk great distances, do without food, oblivious to the cold. He was warmth and strength and put a complete understanding around me and confidence beneath my feet. Yes, we did talk, about birds and animals, about drawing and painting, about climbing and the high mountains. One time I asked him if he knew the Symphonic Variations of Cesar Franck.

"'Why of course,' he said, 'that was part of it too.'" And for once his grey eyes had just the suggestion of a twinkle. "Well," (said Rolf), "the road from the Engadin could have taken us straight into Austria, perhaps to Landeck. But we crossed the Silvretta. . . and you will know how formidable that is. . . at two and a half thousand metres. . . and we came into Austria unbeknown to the authorities. It was a vivid starry night when we crossed these heights and came down by the limitless waters of the great lake there. We came to Landeck; we

came to Innsbruck. I was lodged with a family in the centre of
the city not far from the yellow Maria Theresa palace, if you
know it. And as he came, so he was gone. I never saw my
stranger again. But his eyes have been on me from that day to
this."

There was a profound silence in the room, not the silence of
embarassment, a silence rather that was the outgoing of
thought as deep as existence. Questions would have been
superfluous; intuitively I understood as much as they did.
Could it be that the retelling of the tale at that particular
moment was an "intervention" too? Maybe that too would
be part of it. I thought: What a long way we have come
tonight from orthodox theology, from Faiths and Systems
which that other famous resident at Sils had called "Human,
all too Human". Eventually Rolf resumed the narrative.

"After that the rest was relatively plane sailing. I attended
school in Innsbruck under assumed parentage and address. . .
apparently this too had been arranged. By the time the
Anschluss came, I was an Austrian to all intents and purposes.
But I never was on the Central Police Files because, you see,
no-one ever did arrive across the Silvretta. My lameness got
more troublesome and by the time I went to Art College, I
was clearly exempted from physical effort and Military Service. They did not know of me on official records and never
thought to question, because I was a cripple."

"It was a good deal worse then" (said Magda). "He has done
a lot of exercising and wearing proper footwear; I saw to
that."

"And you studied Art in Innsbruck? That would be in part
during the war years?"

"Yes, Innsbruck. Do you know it? It is vastly developed
now, spoiled with the new functional architecture that makes
a desert of so many of the cities of Europe. Herr and Frau
Pusch with whom I lodged had no children of their own;
they took me to their hearts. Somehow it was all arranged, all
provided for. I had five years at school, the troubled years of
the Nazi occupation. The city was a new experience; a boys'

school was a new experience too and though I could not run around with the best of them, I made friends and under the hammering of circumstance became a person. Did I dream of my mountain home? Yes literally, in my dreams I visited the ledges where the saxifrage grew and the long horned goats surprised you. I realized later that water dropping over rocky ledges lent me some early understanding of Picasso's cubist vision. . . and long before I had heard of Picasso. But Innsbruck was a wonderful place to be, winter or summer. Several times I got up to the Hafelekar, despite my leg. . . or to the Patscherkofel. . . and I was always day dreaming. And you know, it was the same river, the Inn that comes down from the Engadin. In my teens I had mystic feelings about that. . . the drop of mountain water that dashed over the rocks by our home now moving grey-green and sedate, under the bridges of the city. Yes, I dreamed."

"I didn't discover" (said Magda) "for two weeks that he was gone. Then a strange story got about that somebody had carried Rölfi off; I assumed that Matthias had finally got rid of him. But then friends of ours told us of a young boy who had been accommodated in a house in the Pfarrgasse at St Moritz. I too had mystic feelings about the music."

"I wrote from Innsbruck, but we feel that the letter was never delivered. . . whether by chance or one of our interventions, we don't know."

"Then there was occupation of Austria by the Nazis and the frontiers all closed; communication was next to impossible. I was sent to a girls' school in Davos and later, as I said, to Berne, where I discovered the flute."

"And all the time" (said I acting as continuity). . .

"All the time we two were developing our separate lives. After school in 1942 I went to the Art College, the old Institut für Kunst und Grafik. . . it's something else now. When the war ended I felt I could not impose on Herr Pusch any longer, if indeed I was imposing. I got a scholarship to Vienna here to study Art."

"But you kept up with the Pusch family?"

"Why of course. I went back regularly when I could. . .

and in the last ten years attended the funerals of both of them.
They left me all they had."

"But it was hard in Vienna in the post-war years?"

"Hard yes. Cold too. We didn't have enough to eat; and in
a city with three occupying powers we ran all sorts of risks.
But I got on; I met great Masters and Instructors; I learned
technique, worked furiously at it and out of technique came
the power of utterance. I sold my first sizeable picture in
1949, an animal group... and committed myself to that kind
of work, as you have seen... and later to portraiture which, it
must be admitted, pays well, if you have the right clientèle.
One must live and better that it should be honourably."

"And you Magda, were all this while in Switzerland?"

"Mostly. As my gift for flute playing settled into something viable, I had one or two forays abroad, to Italy, France,
to London, to Scotland also. But I too had my intervention...
though nothing so dramatic as Rolf's. I had never been to
Vienna. Probably at some deep level I wanted to go there,
bewitched by the reputed glamour of the place... you only
have to live here to unlearn that. Anyway, I had planned to go
for an extended trip to USA and everything was ready but for
the rail and boat tickets. Then in one week it all changed.
First, I met a friend who had just returned from Vienna and
who told me that there were currently improved chances of
study and concert engagements. Two days later while searching radio Europe for some musical performance to listen to,
there it was... yes IT, you know, the mountains, the atmos-
phere, the Föhn and my long-lost friend Rölfi hobbling about
among it all: it turned out to be a concert from Vienna. Then
on the Friday the Tourist Agency phoned to say that my
travel arrangements had temporarily fallen through, maybe a
strike or an accident with a ship, I don't remember. I knew the
Frau Ahlers at the travel agency well; with a bright laugh I
said: 'Where do you suggest booking me to instead?' And
she, playing this game, this *folie à deux*, said she would open
the Swiss Travel Lexicon at random. She then brightly announced that I was to go to Vienna, train from Zürich at 1440
next Monday: she would make all the arrangements. I said:

Good, go ahead! and fairly took the wind out of her sails."

"And on the Wednesday afternoon in the Marktgraben I in my working clothes, a large folio under my arm, stopped directly in front of a fashionably dressed young woman. I said simply: 'Magda'."

"And I: Rolf'. After that our lives followed a parallel direction more or less. And so we eventually reach this evening here in the Neutorgasse."

The hour was late. I must soon make my way across the quietening city to my hotel. I felt honoured, humble and honoured to have had the vision of their odyssey. I told them so.

"I wonder" (I said) "if any century before has had so many people with their own unique incredible tales to tell. . . if only they had the tongue or the pen to tell it. But your story implies a possible structure to experience; you do not quite believe in chance. . . or, maybe, put another way you really do believe in Chance."

They looked at each other with such an understanding that I would have to envy them all my life. It was Magda who answered for them both in her rich dark voice, her eyes focussed somewhere between me and the cliff face of the future.

"Our interventions? Yes, we know personally on the context of our lives that things do not happen by chance, at least, not the big things. It's a sort of paradox: the great world which impinges at the same moment on these thousands of millions of beings, not to mention the animals, the trees, the plants. . . yet contrives to operate with peculiar concern to us. We agree that to make a philosophy out of this would be complete foolishness, but we live nevertheless from day to day within the parameters of this truth. It is inconceivable as a Universal Truth, simply because the human mind is not up to it. But it is operable as a practical daily faith and it never lets us down. We don't allow ourselves to generalize, to theorize; we don't ever tell this story. But we knew at lunchtime today that it would have to be told tonight, not, I think, for our advantage, but maybe. . . who knows. . . the baton must be handed on to you. You have to do something with it."

"When I remember" (said Rolf) "that moment when I looked at the stranger of the shining eyes, whoever he was, I realize that I was looking at the hidden dynamics of the human universe: that is how it is, that is how it always has been."

PORT MOR

LET US agree to call the place Port Mor. It is not the name you would find on the appropriate Ordnance Survey Sheet. If the integrity of characters in a novel must be protected by a disclaimer at the beginning, I would want to defend this place from the army of the Curious, who would come in twos and tens and hundreds, seeking a vicarious thrill, a contact with superstition or evil or the naked truth. I can see them, the map sheet spread out on a rock, the contours identified, the erosion of feet in their pilgrimage to a spot, where the cotton grass blowing in the wind, the spiky lesser rush and the disconsolate cry of the peewit are very different from what the inflamed imagination hoped to see. So, Port Mor be it, a place you would not visit once in the proverbial month of Sundays.

Here is the port; at one time, or more precisely two centuries ago, a landing place, a small inlet in the red sand-stone and conglomerate rocks where you could land a catch in halcyon weather, or a passenger from over and beyond the open water, or a keg of French brandy if the night were dark and a vessel too large for these parts stood out in the deeper safety of the Sound. All this is a memory on a dull afternoon, when the incoming tide sloshes water round the ribbed rocks and the tresses of weed eddy in endless purposeless motion. That a bare expanse like this, skerries jutting out into the Sound, once echoed to the laughter and talk and cursing of men and women, when lives were lived here and purposes

worked out. . . all this I must try to believe. Lives lived. . . it
is a solemn thought. . . lives with all the striving and mighty
endeavours, with their rhythms and festivals and common
end; lives in motion like the weed, but purposeful motion we
say, because we are human too. But does it all add up to
anything?

Oh, yes! It was a place. In the course of several summer
visits and one at Easter I had become aware of the signs;
changes in vegetation that recalled gardens or small fields;
hummocks of stone that had been gable ends of house or
byre. And, as I researched, distinct mention in old records.
Scotland, and Ireland too, know well the melancholy deser-
tion and abandonment of a settlement; too often the cause
was economic, whether in the enforced Clearances which
scarred the West Highlands with a strange almost ineradicable
misery; or the sheer remoteness and hopelessness which
carried the young off to Glasgow by some newly-constructed
railway and left the old in a dwindling community which
flickered awhile with hard life, then suddenly was extinguished. The roof-trees fell, the houses went under the turf
and the poor sherds of that precarious civilization were
dispersed by the wind or trodden underfoot.

Port Mor was a place of crofts and fishing folk, a Church
too and with it, no doubt, in the best traditions of Scotland, a
school of sorts. The people still spoke Gaelic, I imagine, but
from the circumstance that a bilingual Minister could be
appointed from the English speaking areas, I think that the
great retreat of the native language was already begun before a
tongue more slick and in concepts more suited to an awakening world. But Port Mor was never "cleared"; the great
Cheviot sheep did not oust the people from their homes as it
did farther north. Perhaps the landowner was less grasping or
less impoverished than those in the glens of Ross and Suther-
land. The place simply died out in the mid-nineteenth century; wind and storm and the mould and fungus did their
work and now the casual walker would see nothing at all to
detain him. One house remains, a surprisingly large building
whose front and dormer windows give on to the waters of the

Sound from a safe distance. Built in the early eighteen hundreds to replace some earlier building on the site, it witnessed the total eclipse of the community, the last funerals, the last abandonment; and surviving in a life of its own, it started as an unofficial small hotel and has so continued, welcoming guests if they chose to come, not luring them by the spurious offers of a licence or French cookery. I had known it for years, since a first chance discovery when I was walking this coast; I returned again and again. The official motor road stops three miles away; from there you must trust your springs and your patience to something less than a double dotted line on the map. And then you arrive, and if you are in luck it is North West weather, and the waves are dashing blue and vivacious on the Sound.

The proprietor. . . shall I call her Mrs McNish. . . is the enthusiast you would want to meet, eager to receive you for the person you are, eager to put before you suggestions that will make your stay memorable. But though, as I discovered, she is a mine of information about the history and legend of the place, she herself originally hailed from Northumberland and was thus able to take a slightly more objective stand to all that was around her. The property had been her husband's, but after his early death, she kept it on and lived life to the full. The location of her house ensured that you made one trip by car to it and one back to the highroad and in between you walked or climbed or rowed. Her house could take ten guests, but as I never came in the high season, I never saw it full.

It was on my sixth visit early in June of a deplorable year. I had arrived dangerously down the bumpy road in a dripping fog and in ten days there had been no dry spells long enough for an extended expedition. I had to content myself with memories of the running line of the mountains on the far side of the water; or the rock crests, blue and indented, of the ridge that ran northwards from here on our side and beyond an innocent looking stretch of bog. . . I say, innocent looking, as it was from the house but from the no great height of the Creag Bhreac you saw it laced with silver water, a tumid treacherous mass of undigested vegetation, which broke from time to time like a ripe boil and emptied itself into the sea. My forays that year were small ones. I pottered around the vestigial gardens and speculated on the life that once used that thin soil and rock ledge as its habitat. Herring gulls surveyed the fog bound waters with an arrogant stare while other smaller life pursued their rustling, plopping activities around me. I cannot tell where it came from, nor did I believe that it was more than my own romanticizing at that point: I was seized with a feeling of. . . dread, was it ? . . . no, rather acute discomfort. . . perhaps a great sadness. It could have been my thoughts of the extinguishing of a community, people who had lived and made a fair best of their limited advantages. But no. . . this was no thing of the intellect: it rose, as it were from the soil, up through my shoes, like a damp that made my back muscles twitch. I wondered. Some months before I had read with curiosity and an open mind, the theory that places can have memories, to be sensed or not by the individual. One will feel a vague depression; another catch on to an intrusive train of thought unconnected with his experience hitherto; yet another will quietly claim to see a ghost. All are, it appears, place memories, differently apprehended. I remember putting that idea in the "pending" tray of my mind and had thought surprisingly little of it until at that moment something at my feet transmitted to me more than just an association of ideas.

One morning near the end of my stay I had hoped to go out but was confronted with a redoubled deluge from the West. Angry rain clouds cast gloom on a Sound where no small boats would venture that day. Mrs McNish commiserated in her philosophical way:

"But I'll just be putting the fire on in the parlour and maybe a gentleman like you will be finding something to do with a wet day."

I questioned her about the other houses in the settlement and mentioned my strange feeling of discomfort. She looked at me with a glitter in her grey eyes:

"You will be the unusual one, I dare say. My husband used to say there were those who felt it. . . just by that bit wall which was the gable end of the manse. I think he knew it himself. Discomfort, did you say. . . or maybe some would be feeling dread; but there never was any explanation. I never did hear tell of sudden deaths there."

She paused, thinking back through the years to old memories which she had not shared:

"But I have a suggestion too for a wet day. I will take you up to an old attic, a sort of box room behind the house, where there are boxes of old books. Maybe you will find something to make you forget the weather. And it's going to clear up for tomorrow; I heard it on the eight o'clock news."

So I found myself half an hour later in that box room amidst the discards and rejects of other times. I was directed particularly to a large wooden box.

"I heard tell that my husband's grandfather received that for safe keeping when the Preacher that they would then have was withdrawn. He was to have claimed the books but I imagine he had neither the money nor the opportunity to fetch them. In forty years I have never looked in that box. Maybe you will be doing that for me and let me know what you find. And by that time the fire will be burned up in the parlour."

It would delay the proper account of this story to enumerate the treasures of that box. I rolled up my sleeves, realizing how grubby I was becoming with the dust of a hundred years and more. There was much to interest a scholar, an antiquarian too perhaps, though I have no pretensions as to that. I handled *The City of Dreadful Night* and laid it aside to peruse; I picked up Johnson's *Rasselas* and thought of this volume when it was just a decade or two off the presses and greatly prized. Robert Blair's *The Grave* was laid aside too, as a Must; in the curious spirit of an Age which could combine levity with sombre reflections, *The Grave* had decorated the table on the genteel Scottish parlour; it was, as they say now, the in-thing to be seen to be reading it. I was looking at the quality of the print of it. . . the pages had been carefully cut. . . and was wondering whether an age like ours anywhere produced such edifying moralizing on Man's brief term. . . looking with such a happy feeling of discovery, that I did not notice till I moved my foot, which was cramping a little, the letter in its envelope, yet no letter either, rather a package addressed to a Mr Gilfillan, Preacher at Port Mor. As I write this, I grow cold and tremble to think of that moment; but I cannot think that I did so then when I was innocent of its contents. I had passed so much by, whole bundles of letters, but this one clamoured for recognition, or so it seemed.

In the parlour a good hour had passed with *The City of Dreadful Night* and *The Grave*, while the light outside became lurid towards midday and promised no early end to the storm. Then I picked up the letter. The handwriting on the cover was small and neat, not the copperplate of a Church Officer, but readable for all that; the contents were sizeable, written on both sides of the paper, the work of hours. I do not know whether I expected anything as I focussed my eyes for reading; perhaps I only felt that curiosity which novelty and a voice from the past combined to bring me. But within a few lines a tension and agitation in the writing gripped me and would not let me go. I could tell you about it; but better far would be to let the letter and its eloquent writer, the Rev John Martindale, speak for themselves. To him I now hand over the transmission, paraphrased here and there to suit the modern ear.

.   .   .   .

Methven,
24 September 1782

Mr Archibald Gilfillan,
Preacher, Port Mor,

Dear Sir,

I have not had the honour of your acquaintance and am the

more sorry that we did not meet in passing, that I might have acquainted you with the circumstances of my hurried departure. In this I have no doubt that the wisdom of God is greater than that of Men and that he had His own reasons for giving you an innocent entry into that unhappy parish. Your work will be the more difficult in that the Authority has seen fit for the moment to replace me by no regular Minister. An enquiry is pending, but my suspicion is that it will do nothing more than cast doubts on my sanity and on my effectiveness as Shepherd of my flock. Doors will close : lips will be sealed : the key evidence will not be allowed to come to light. I alone will be lifted high to ridicule.

It is for this reason that I write to you, I an old man though not in years, broken in spirit—to you, a young man filled with the zeal of the Lord, that you at least may not misjudge me, but be warned of the snare before your feet and the pitfall in familiar places and the evil that lurks in the silence. Grant me of your kindness a perusal of my letter and thereafter a profound pondering of its contents.

I was sent to the Port Mor parish in 1773 ; these remote parts of the western seaboard do not operate on the Call as do the more settled areas. I arrived in the May of that year with my wife Meg and my three children, Alastair eleven years, Kirsty ten years and Neal eight years. The sun shone on our arrival and we all lifted up our eyes to the hills around and the blue waters of the Sound and blessed the Lord. With that people I had great work, hard work. I felt somewhat as Jonah at the gates of Nineveh except that I was willing enough to accept the charge. We settled at the Manse. At first the people eyed us as strangers and I did not understand how there could be so much difference between them and us. Shortly after I knew. . . and you too will know. . . that there was but a veneer of the Christian grace over hearts that were rough as the sandstone and darkened by the ancient fairy religion that they had never really unlearned. My children were the first to be accepted and through them I restarted a school, for some time fallen in desuetude. My wife grieved when the women fell silent at her approach and I must daily admonish her to patience as I did myself. For seven years we toiled on our separate stints and I can say that her worth was soon recognized: she was sought in help for family troubles and to set standards for the young queans of the village and the scattered crofts. And she had a wonderful way with domestic management, so that I and my family wanted for little in that tenuous countryside. But the damp and continuous rain were ill for her health; nor was our house as dry as I would have like it to be. She suffered in the winters and on two summers I sent her to the south to recover her health. In 1780 she contracted a congestion of the lungs and when I would have had her sent to the city for attention, we had three weeks of storm and shipwreck, drownings and widespread floods. There was no moving her; she was taken from us one Thursday night when the storm had subsided and the moonlight lay fair upon the Sound. It was the Lord's will but a heavy judgment on us all.

When we had laid her to rest in the ancient graveyard by the Allt Ruaidh, my family showed me what they were made of. They had studied with a learned old man who lived some two miles away; we had often talked of returning to Scotland (as we said) so that they could have careers. Alastair was to have sought the University and made a doctor of medicine; Kirsty was to have gone to her aunt in Edinburgh and Neal was still too young: when he wasn't talking of going to sea he would be a shepherd. Now they gathered round me and sustained me, assuming that my loss was the greatest of all. Alastair worked locally for a year to be with me and Kirsty kept house, cheerfully but firmly managing the servant girls who were only a little younger than herself.

When did it all begin? Why did I not see the signs? Had my eyes like Eli waxed dim? I think now that I was so broken by the loss of my Meg that in some deep recess I had already given up and longed to be away from the sight of her presence and the sound of her voice. But deep, deep it was, deep it must have been. And the doors to my sense were shut; else had I known with the admonition of the Lord what was come amongst us. For life went on, the slow change of the seasons, the attrition of days. There were times of plenty and of hardship; times of storm and of fair weather. My flock, for aught I knew, pursued their ways as before, making their poor best out of a stony soil and a capricious sea. With my years had come wisdom. Mine was not to remake the world, to be pastor, father, judge and censor of my flock, as some will have it. Men and women do not want to be known too closely; their contentment is when each moves in his chosen orbit, predictable to a degree and so able to be avoided. I knew of this and that; of family feuds, of deeds ill done in the outback; aye, of the French lugger that paid its infrequent visits on moonless nights to a spot three miles down the coast and landed there, I will not say what. But it must have spelt danger and a bad conscience to many a peaceful churchgoer who sat under me on a Sunday morning. For Sunday was the gathering point and the general redding up of the week. I tried to measure my words and my admonitions to the reality of their lives; there was little enough in common between the ancient Israelites and the Toilers by the sea. But when the Precentor lifted up his voice for the lead of the flock we sang well and I strove to instruct and inform. But I ask my soul now whether I was losing contact, whether the spiritual world of which I would have them citizens, was all too incredible for a folk struggling for subsistence at the dawn of a new age.

It was the Sabbath nearest to the full moon in the May of that year, and my flock were gathered beneath me, save for the bedridden and the refractory. I became aware during the sermon . . . of something which did not quite strike me then, so intent was I on David and the Shewbread. But I noticed something. And only when we were sat at our meat in the Manse that afternoon, did it come across me like a dream. I said:

"I was aware today of much yawning and weariness among the younger members of the congregation. When I think on it now, there were those who did not seem to have seen the inside of their beds on Saturday night."

I said this as a statement but it struck my family as a question. For once there was no candour in them, only silence and a hanging of the head. Then Alastair said:

"I doubt not that there was some ploy last night, a dancing perhaps or an amusement. Some would not be home till the birds were yaumering."

I said, "You doubt not Alastair, or is that a gilding of the truth?" Kirsty went out with the crockery; Neal was staring at his fingers.

"Is it ?" I asked again.

He replied for the fine courageous fellow he was:

"Och, you know, father, the younger folk have their life that the older do not understand... or maybe they have forgotten. It was, I think, a harmless bit of fun, that did no one any mischief. But that's our thing... and you would not be wanting to make me a traitor and spy on my own friends?"

"And you, Neal, were you in on this" (for I was still unfairly fishing for a clue).

"That I wasn't, father. But I'll no' be saying I don't know anything about it. But Alastair's right. You can't make us traitors: no one would speak to us again."

We dropped the subject and for some weeks it barely crossed my mind. It was a busy time of the year and I was often out helping in the manual work of the crofts where help was short.

Then came once more an indication to jog my too complacent nature. I was rummaging in a shed in our courtyard, when one of the servant girls at an upper window, as I heard, hailed someone on the road. I was in no good position to hear what she said, but I heard her say something about the shadow on Sail Coinich and Saturday next. Sail Coinich is, as you probably know, a rocky mountain of no great height, but the highest point on the ridge that divides the Sound from Glen Dhu... have you come across Glen Dhu, that trackless place, boggy round the Allt Dhu and known to few but shepherds? And as if to wake me from my lethargy, there was a scrap of paper which I picked up in the grate, half burned, with the name of that same mountain on it. The shadow on Sail Coinich? What shadow would that be? I wondered: should I ask Kirsty about it: should I put it to Neal, who was far too honest ever to tell me a lie. Should I say to them, "What is this about the shadow on Sail Coinich on Saturday night?" But I did not, whether from coincidence or a too-easy optimism that it would prove nothing at all. But I did decide to sit up late on Saturday evening, after they were all abed, and venture out on the road, to see if there were comings and goings. I was cheated. An old Mrs McAllistair in a croft by Culkein went that Friday night to meet her Maker; she was hard of dying and it was daylight before I reached home. The Saturday was busy and when I had settled in my study in the evening and rehearsed my sermon. . . which I always did to gain the greater effect in delivery. . . it was only thereafter to fall asleep in my chair.

I awoke to the sound of a click on the outer door latch. It was as if my mind were keeping guard over my slumbering body but must alert me to this. Someone entered: footsteps went upstairs and turned right: it was surely Kirsty. I looked upon my watch; it was nigh on two in the morning and the moon shone bright through my casement and filled the court-yard outside with an unearthly light and deep pools of dark-ness. I waited: within ten minutes, the outer door opened and closed clumsily: I heard Neal say to his brother not to wake the whole house. When they were gone upstairs, I emerged, went out into the moonlight and stared up and down the dirt road. All the world was as if asleep; but I had no doubt that there were those who were not yet in bed.

I was tired, tired and in the deep recesses of my soul perplexed. I prayed for illumination but none was vouchsafed. In the morning service, when I fain would have sat down during the singing of the psalms and slept, I noticed the weariness in the eyes of the younger members. I would have it out with my own at dinner time! But dinner time never came that day. We were all alerted to some building on fire a mile south of the village but when we arrived there was little that we could do for the two young girls who were trapped in the flames. The winds had dispersed the last of their piteous cries and the poor bit biggin was fallen in around them. I said to Alastair:

"You were abroad till a late hour last night?"

"Aye, father" (he replied), "Neal and I had a bit walk in the moonlight."

"And others were abroad on the high road?"

"Maybe that. But we were back by two, thinking that you might find us missing."

"And your sister. . . she went with you?"

"That she did not."

I was perplexed, sore perplexed; these things disturbed the ordinary pattern of our existence, and extraordinary I usually took to be wrong. Tired and dispirited I went to bed.

I was never born to be an inquisitor; but using my native intelligence I coupled Saturday and a moon near to the full and pored over the calendar for the most probable two dates in June. On these nights I sat up like a conspirator and read with my study door ajar, both to hear any sound and to discourage my children from walking abroad for whatever reason they might have. Both nights were silent and unvisited, one dark and cloudy, one late moonlit.

The month of July would bring a bright moon nearer to a Saturday night though it would rise late. I sensed, I know not how, something going on in the young community, something that was to be denied to me. They were silent and awkward at my approach. I deliberated extracting a promise from my three that they should not leave the house; then I considered that that way I would never discover the alien thing that was seducing their hearts. You see, I was far from your canting Calvinist divines who hear the screech of Hell in a fiddler's rant or smelt lechery in the dancing. And that, my dear Gilfillan, was the dreary scope of my imaginings.

That July evening I worked in my study. But late, when none was about, I donned my coat and entered the old coach room off the courtyard. It was eleven of a July night and bright with the eerie light of the Northern summer. I waited, aligning my gaze through the part open door and the gate of the courtyard. I saw people pass southwards but could not distinguish who they were. Then a figure crossed our court and stood at the gate; I doubted not that it was Kirsty; she

was joined by others and they passed southwards. I waited
for Alastair and Neal but they did not come. After a while I
flitted to the gateway, stood awhile then turned south.

If I say that I remember with certainty the details of the
next few hours, the truth might not be in me. Every time that
I think on them. . . and that has been legion in the days
since. . . the dream works on my story so that I now know
not what is fact and what is speculation. Our road ran south
for a quarter mile, then turned up inland clear of the end of
the quaking moss. Diffidently I came to this cross road (as we
called it); I sensed that the night revellers had gone inland. I
followed, looking forward to catch a sight of movement and
backwards in case I too was followed. It is a rough stony
track as you will know, but rougher far in that strange glow
of midnight, for the moon was not yet over the hill; I had to
watch my footing so as not to trip. Now this track leads out
to the wider world, but a small sheep track goes off left, then
up and over to Glen Dhu. I had walked there with shepherd
friends in earlier days, with my fine young Ewan, and knew
the views that you could get if you followed the ridge to Sail
Coinich, an hour's walk to the north. While I thought on
these things in the darkness that was yet no darkness, I was
almost surprised by a group of figures coming up behind me.
I threw myself on the ground and crept behind a broom bush
while they passed above me talking quietly to one another,
perhaps five persons. Again I followed, keeping them well in
sight, till it was well after midnight. Something in my heart
misgave me: here was no social gathering.

The figures ahead were nearing the summit of the track
where it crossed the low shoulder of the ridge. I decided not
to follow them there but ascend the ridge itself and look
down on Glen Dhu from above. This I did and it was no
mean effort in the darkness. Nearing the farther edge I got on
my knees between fallen stones and spurs of rock and was at
once illuminated by the risen moon, a three-quarters moon,
pearly in the clear sky and filling the great waste of Glen Dhu
with a light I could almost have touched. Below me I knew
that the ground would fall away steeply; I went on all fours

and levered myself forward to look down and spy if aught were amiss.

You will excuse me, if I say to you, as I must say to the Commission that I do not know whether what I now saw was Truth or a distorted imagination. I would to God that it were the latter and for my own peace of mind would be happy to say that it was. . . But for the outcome! You will grant me your patience, your understanding and perhaps, if your reading has been wide, an OPEN MIND to entertain what you do not want to hear. So be it; I proceed with my account.

I levered myself forward and beheld some hundreds of feet below me. . . how shall I say. . . a mass of people, perhaps sixty or seventy, moving about on this side of the valley floor. And I saw. . . I think I saw. . . two altars of turf reared up and small fires kindled on them, of which the smoke rose blue in the moonlight. Before the altars hooded persons performed some strange rite. . . not the Romish rite, for I have seen that. . . something so strange and illogical, it must surely be the work of the Devil. I thought to myself with grim resolution: So this is it. . . Playing at Devilry. . . An unreal thing but dangerous for all that. How long I hung there gazing at it, I do not know; my arms were anchored securely around the two rocks so that I could not fetch out my watch. But even as I looked, the crowd stood still, rapt at the strange liftings and layings at the altars. The moon rose higher, the silent spectator of this misguided effort. Then a shout rent the air. The general crowd stood round, leaving a space in their midst. Slowly and slowly they began to circle it, counter clockwise, a silent movement in a silent world. And after some minutes from the midst of the circle there emerged a GREY THING like a low smoke or mist. Time stopped: the moon and the rocky ridges looked on: the sons of Earth circled in silence: and in their midst eddied that awful thing. I saw how it rose, it too revolving counter-clockwise and stretching out maybe twenty smoky limbs towards them. Then a cry: and the Circlers thrust out their left arms towards the thing, some clasping the greyness, some free.

Of a sudden I would have cried: God, make me as one of

the prophets. Grant that I may leap down these rocks and confront this thing and defy it, yes, even if they should trample me and mock me. To my horror, I felt myself being drawn forward, drawn to that evil leering eye, so that I must fight to hold my place, to draw myself back. Sweating and an icy chill chased across my body, as though the forces of good and evil contended within me. I now strove, determined that I should not BE DRAWN TOWARDS IT, such was its attractive influence. The dance below me was now fast, stumbling on the turf with heavy boots and all in a most unearthly silence. Then came a loud wailing cry. I beheld the reeking altars overthrown but I did not see by whose hand it was done. The dance ended; I notice that the Thing had retreated back into the rock and moss of the valley floor. Some stamped out the embers of the fire; some gathered up the hellish implements; while the rest, the great number moved away in groups, ours to the south-west, some few south-east, quite a number toiling up and over the pass north-eastward to Glen Laraig. Soon the light wind had blown away all sound and sight of them and the moon stared up the empty valley from the south.

I waited there, cold in heart and body; maybe I was unconscious. When I was resolved to rise and move away, nothing now held me: the attracting power was gone. I returned down the western side of the ridge still partly in shadow, careful that I should not be seen, stumbling over rock and root as though I were reluctant to return home to my problem. Where the sheep track joined the rough road to Shieldorran, I waited to be sure that no one was behind me. I reached the cross road and the moon stared down on me accusingly as the only one left awake in the slumbering community. I returned home and locked the door; at the top of the stairs I came to Kirsty's door, where I heard the sounds of slumber; the door to the boys' room stood ajar and I could see them as they slept.

With that dangerous ploy the adventurous youth of the area seem to have had enough. I doubted that my children had been part of it. Indeed the younger folk of the parish had a perceptibly warmer approach to me, a willingness to call at the Manse, to listen, to hear the true Word of the Lord. I prayed continuously that my words would fall on a more receptive soil, even if the Plough had been fear and the Ploughman that awful thing. There were no farther excursions by the full of the moon, though I sat up late and went for moonlit walks on Saturday nights. And the warmth and the care of my own family could not be bettered. One thing troubled me, as it would trouble you, my dear Gilfillan: The Lord would not hold them guiltless that had taken His name in vain. Therefore I redoubled my effort. I spent hours on my knees in entreaty that God, who was also present on that moonlit night would of His mercy pity their crazy lust for sensation. Yet I sometimes wondered how far mercy could prevail and how far an inflexible principle of Creation, if that is what it was, be it never so evil, must have its way. I did not have long to wait.

Matthew Abie, one of three brothers who operated a ferry across the Sound some three miles down the coast, simply disappeared on a serene August afternoon when the storm spirits were all gone to another quarter. Long his brothers searched for him, but as he alone had been above deck at the time, they missed nothing until they came up and found the boat driving pilotless with the wind. The sea, if the sea it was that took him, never gave him up. A shudder went through the community. But worse was to follow. Two weeks later as a group of our young girls was returning from Concraig where they held a sort of annual fair, wearing their bits of finery and laughing over their adventures, one of them, Peggy McRae, a big sonsy lass, daughter of a fisherman in Port Mor, suddenly was seized with the terror, so they said, at the top of the Stac Ruadh just where the path is a hundred and fifty feet above the sea. It was, said the others, as though a struggle was going on, something pulling her down and she fighting to retain a foothold. Like the silly girls they were, they all ran to a safe distance and screamed, while Peggy fought and lost her mortal combat. She went clattering down the scree in an avalanche of boulders and was doubtless dead by stoning or by fear ere she reached the deep water. A cloud lay over Port Mor. Even so two might only be coincidence. If there were an explanation, perhaps it was only I who could supply the answer, and I had not yet dared to think of it.

But with Ewan Alexander I awoke to the horror. My heart was warm for that young man, since he was a boy in my school. He had seemed a freer spirit than most of those who toiled in the fields with the cas crom or risked their lives for sea harvest. He was shepherd to the factor and spent long days on Creag Breac and Sail Coinich with the sheep that roamed far. I had walked with him on these hills and he showed me things of beauty, birds and flowers and places that bade fair to be Eden itself in these hills of many corries. Ewan was nineteen and more on that day when they were rounding up all the sheep on the hill. He had risked much to recover a terror-stricken ewe on a ledge, so his friends told me, and had made light of his heroism with a laugh and a kindly remark about the silly old beast. Suddenly, they said, as he was standing on the edge of the Grey Face looking out over Port Mor, he fell serious, staring hard. They called him to come on but he was not listening. They heard him shout ahead of himself, "I wilna come, I wilna, ye canna make me." Then with a hollow groan he fell over the rock ledge. When they found him some twenty minutes later, the life was long gone from him.

Only then was I prepared to realize that there are Spiritual principles of which we know nought. We say: If they are good, they are of God, if not, of the Devil. But should they be as Newton and his Law of Gravity, what does it matter to whom we ascribe them? They will have their way; they would have their way and claim everyone who had been touched. I called my children together, over the evening meal that day of Ewan's burying. They were distressed and frightened. I said:

"You will call to mind a certain Saturday night in July when the moon was at the three-quarters. You will picture to yourselves Glen Dhu and an opening of Hell Mouth that happened there at one in the morning. You will tell me if

Matthew Abie was of that company that night." He was, they said.

"And Peggy McRae?" They agreed.

"And my fine Ewan, was he too so misguided?" The answer was a groan from Alastair whose friend he was. I paused; I lacked the courage to know the truth. But Neal had courage for them all.

"And we were there too, father, that's what ye wanted to know. Are we all in danger? Will it have us all?"

"God alone knows," (I said) "but from this moment we redouble our prayers. We go into no dangerous places. And we must quietly say to those who are in danger, that they look what they are about."

Somehow it was better then; we were at one and no secret more between us. I doubted not that my family enjoyed a greater protection in that I was, shall we say, professional in these matters. But I had to learn what I already suspected, that principles more profound than my science were here involved.

Neal was the first to go. It was a dark October night and we heard his voice shouting from the midst of the bog where no man ever went. We shouted back and encouraged him to keep above water. But the cries ceased and we never more saw him. They say that one day the bog will burst and pour out to the sea and my lovely son will be seen again by the light. . . but I will not be there to see him. Early in December Kirsty cut her hand on a broken crock while she was baking. Kirsty had never once smiled since we lost Neal; I know now that she had surrendered to despair. I bound up the wound and bade her be cheerful. "Cheerful", she said with a wan sort of look, "na, Father, that'll be the death of me." This was foolish because it was but an ordinary cut. But at the morning, when she was not down for breakfast, I went to her room. She was cold and no one could say what had taken her. The factor's man, who had some skill in the doctoring, said it would be the wound that had festered. How could I tell him that she had given up in despair?

By now the whole community was filled with fear. The

people came to me and asked what should be done. I recommended that all confess themselves to God and offer their lives in renewed service. But I knew, I alone knew, that I spoke words of meaning to some, the younger folk, but words of perplexity to their elders who saw no reason for this Jehovah visitation on their lives. The times required that someone remain unshaken and I for all my sorrow and my fear must be that. Fear it was too. Would this thing also claim my last child? Autumn had passed and now it was Winter, and ever the Darkness was waiting to pick off this one and that. It is said that some almost went gladly, such was the grip of the fear that held them. Alastair and I would sit alone at meals, close as father and son could be. For all his blitheness I knew the fear that lay like a canker round his heart; he knew of my fear. But strange to say, he did not know that I had witnessed that event in the misty darkness, only believed that I had learned of it from Kirsty or my poor Neal. In the last days of the year, I decided that we would leave when travel was possible. . . in late February, perhaps. Alastair would prepare and go to Edinburgh to study medicine in the following autumn. I would seek a post elsewhere or become a schoolmaster. . . for, truth to tell, my faith was turning into a raw perplexity, so that only half of me believed what I said to the folk.

It was a hard winter and many were the older folk who succumbed to the cold and the lack of warming food. But there were the others, the younger ones whose life should have been before them, if the Grey Thing had not clasped their left hands. Some came to Church no more, some of the bereft; but worse far for me was it when they reported that a little black bull had been sacrificed in an oak wood by Culkein to placate the spirits of darkness. When I knew that, I surmised that my failure was complete and resolved to be gone. And yet there were mornings of beauty. . . when the frost was hard and the crags on Sail Coinich stood etched against the blue of the sky; or on quiet nights when the Moon (how indifferent to all our concerns!) glittered on the still childlike waters of the Sound.

Meanwhile I made my arrangements, announced to an indifferent folk that I would leave and packed such things as were to be transported northwards up the coast to Inverarnain, the nearest point from which you could take ship to the outer world. Alastair worked on as usual and I counselled him never to court danger or the unknown. February came and after weeks of hard frost the weather mildened and the sun shone. Two more died strangely in that month, the last two whom I had to bury. . . save one. Our effects left by the carrier's cart on the 12th February and we would leave on the nineteenth.

You will not need telling, that by now I had taken the whole guilt on myself. We always hope for Grace; but I could expect none. Deep in my heart somewhere, I awaited the last blow; when it came I was braced for it. The Saturday afternoon was calm and smiling with hardly a wind from any quarter. My son was at work on the farm a mile or so southwards. It appears he had gone fishing with his friends, a pastime which they enjoyed when farm work was not too demanding. They said. . . and it would be so. . . that they were happy to be together though sad at his departing. Then. . . and it would be so. . . he stood up unsteadily in the boat looking out to midstream and said something like : " Yes, I'm coming." And he flung himself into the sea and did not reappear. They searched high and low then came to tell me and wondered when I raised my hands and cried : "The Lord's will be done!" That was a Saturday. On the Sunday evening he came in and we buried him on the Monday.

Nothing could now detain me. I had said Tuesday morning and Tuesday morning it was. I was up early to secure the house and hand over the keys. I walked out to the Allt Ruadh and took leave of my dear ones, my Meg, Kirsty and Alastair. I stood outside our house and looked across the watery flow, thinking of him who was so dear to me; then turned away lest I be unmanned with emotion. The carrier came and we left about ten. There were those who gathered to say goodbye, but others were too hard at work in the poor fields or at the fishing to have time to notice who passed from their midst. A hard folk, only Christian to the depth of their skin. But, as I locked up my house, a strange thought had come to me: You too were there, you too felt the desperate attraction of the Thing; why should it not have you also? If one part of me said: Why not? a desperate resolve steeled in me to win this last battle, when I had lost all others.

I sat in the carrier's cart buried in my reading of the Scriptures, resolved not once to look right to that ridge where I had lain by night nor to the shadowy Sail Coinich, mountain of ill omen. I battled fiercely with the evil around me and imagined I could feel it palpably closing in on me. As we began to toil up the twisted track to the Stac Ruadh, the might of Heaven granted me illumination. I bade the driver stop and jumped down to survey the cart. And not before time. For the pin that held the wheel to seaward on its axle was almost sheared. Wondering much and with some fear, the driver and I toiled to replace the pin and after a half hour we resumed. I concentrated hard confronting the evil that I felt glowering at me out of a smiling day. Just before we reached the top. . . you will know the place as the Fallen Rocks. . . not ten minutes later, I was alerted again and bade him rein in, which he did with a bad grace. But it turned to amazement when a small rock fall just ahead of us blocked the road where we would have been. We stopped and toiled to clear it, then got on our way, making haste for we were now late. Twice more I had to counsel caution, but this may have been of the mind rather than Heaven's prompting. So I came to Inverarnain, unloaded my few belongings and paid the carter, who looked at me as though rejoiced that his association with me was ended. I supped in the inn there and about four in the afternoon went aboard. I said to myself: Hold firm: be vigilant: be strong in the strength of the Lord. Yet as I walked out on the wooden pier, I could still imagine them, the wraiths of darkness, leaning out to claim me in the last moment. There was but a plank between me and the vessel, three or four steps, nothing at all; yet but for the hand of a friend on board I would have slipped. He wondered when I stared wildly at that plank seeing the Grey Thing stretching out weedy hands that had purpose but no mind.

Now I am living here in a sort of silence and isolation, having lost all that a man may lose and more. But not my sanity! Clear and decisively would I have acted, had I been cut from the same cloth as my Presbyterian colleagues: I would have known the Things of Light as from God, the Things of Darkness as of the Adversary. But I am not so made. I ask myself repeatedly, if I have stumbled on a natural Philosophy which the Ancients knew, but we with our secure Science of God have chosen to forget. For of this I become more certain: what was released worked among us as evil: what released it was the massive frenzy and the flight from good judgment of misguided people. As it has been: and ever shall be?

FIONN ALLT

I LAY BACK in the heather and let the late summer sunshine caress my face, observing how, far above, immeasurably far above, two birds of prey tumbled on serrated wings. My world was an upturned bowl, a vast ear listening to the universe; but it was Scotland, Perthshire on a late August Saturday when the general world was otherwise absorbed in football or tennis or show-jumping, whichever was the current attraction. And the Fionn Allt in its rocky valley was mine, all mine . . . I had been to the top as far as the bulldozed track goes, then beyond to the tussocky undulations of wind-blown grass that form the watershed to the great valley through beyond. I had looked at water glittering, gurgling, dripping on its rectangular escalade to the North Sea, looked at the thyme, the tormentil and the lady's mantle asserting their claim to the sunlight. And a great gratitude had come over me to all those nameless people who had made it possible, who had brought me to maps, wild flowers, birds, love of solitude.

About four o'clock I gathered myself together from the great impact of sense that had beat on me all through a morning and an afternoon. The stony path led downwards some distance above the burn, while to my left the frowning crags fronted a cloudless sky. I supposed that I was alone in all these miles of unprofitable landscape; but I was wrong. Rounding a corner I saw someone fishing just where the path keeps company with the burn down to the iron bridge. One part of me would have crept past, making no noise and giving no cause for the complicated interchange of personalities. But only two of us in miles of emptiness. . . it just wasn't possible. So I found the obvious opening:

"Any luck?"

"A bit too bright" (he said, with a good natured laugh). "Anyhow I expect they're watching the tennis as well."

Something in me leapt for delight.

"As a matter of fact," (he said) "I doubt if I'm really fishing at all. . . going through the motions, you might say."

"For some private good reason, no doubt?"

"Right," (he said). "Perhaps I had to do it, like a sort of homing instinct. I doubt if I really weighed it up. . . though I did go to the trouble of assembling all this gear."

I was savouring the voice, standard educated Scots at base, but overlaid with something I could not quite define, maybe a slight trans-atlantic drawl. He seemed wiry, tough without being athletic, thirtyish perhaps but with a face that might have been younger, neat regular features, eyes significantly large and lustrous.

"Presumably" (I said) "there are fish. . . on days other than Saturday afternoons?"

"Well, there used to be. Many's the time I have sat here . . . or maybe in the deeper pools further up. But now I come to remember it, I was usually too busy wrestling away with the thinking and not too serious about the fish."

"So you've been here before; you know the Fionn Allt? I confess this has been my first visit."

"Been before? Why this was once home, workplace, battleground for me. You should see it on a bad winter, the rocks sheathed in ice, snow obliterating even the burn, so that you fall through if you've let yourself get too heavy. But that's it . . . that's why I am here . . . on an unprofitable sentimental journey."

"You make me curious" (I said); "do tell me more. But first let's identify ourselves."

I gave him a thumbnail sketch of myself and the best reason I could think of why I was here at 4.30 on a Saturday afternoon in August.

"Ian McKelvie" (he said). " I don't know what I should say that I am . . . lots of things . . . I was in manufacturing business . . . was in South America, Australia, where I changed my occupation. Yet it's not what I am, but what I am becoming . . . or does it seem a bit pretentious to say that at thirty-two I am still pursuing my destiny trying to discover who I really am?"

"No," (I said) "we're on the same wavelength. Tell me whatever you want."

He unscrewed the fishing rod, took off the reel and packed the pieces away in their receptacles. And all the while I could see him marshalling interiorly the facts which were not usually assembled in order. I was content to wait, considering how the afternoon sun cast shadows over cheekbone and nose and how in portraying him I would specially seek out the asymmetry of the mouth.

"Strange," (he said at length) "it has happened maybe four or five times that I have found myself obliged to give an account of myself. Sometimes it's almost as if the world stands still and I reach a pausing point and have to reckon . . . to myself as much as to anyone else, where I am really going.

He gazed far up beyond the Fionn Allt and the rocky crests into the relatively distant past.

"The early bit is easy. My father was a young bank employee; he was killed early in the war. My mother brought me up in the town down there, very modestly, for even with a job she wasn't well off. My grandparents . . . on my father's side, lived at Gleneich . . . you saw that derelict cottage half a mile down the road; that's it. It was home to them and home often to me, especially in the school holidays . . . a whole world different from that sad sagging ruin you see now.

"When I was at the secondary school, two things happened that were to affect me: grandmother died one winter: and my mother took up with a solicitor, whom she later married. Somehow I understood all that; there never was any of that Oedipus complex trash that filled the novels of the time. I understood that she was lonely and I would eventually leave home; better she should get herself settled.

"During my last three years at school I used to come almost every weekend to Gleneich, where I made myself useful and kept grandfather cheered. He was shepherd and despite his sixty-odd years he was at that time hale and strong. That's when I got to know this valley and the surrounding hills. In my last year and a half at school, when I felt my mother needed the place to herself, I stayed with grandfather. On schooldays it meant cycling five miles and school bus for seven miles each way. . . but there were lots of us who had that sort of effort to make. During this year and a half my grandfather's health declined. . . a heart condition I think. More and more at the weekends I did the shepherding for him and in the school holidays. I can see now that this was very important for me. At school I was reasonably sociable and wanted to be in most things; but I came back each night to endless toil and moil at Gleneich. Then the factor put someone in to help him Mondays to Fridays; I was out Saturday and Sunday.

"Was I sorry for myself? Maybe. But something happened up there, a great easing of the adolescent pain. I learned a new slow rhythm of growing things, a new sort of reasoning which wasn't the limited one of the class room and the text book. And I knew it couldn't go on with grandfather's age and health, with the end of my schooldays and my mother's prospective remarriage. I don't know if you ever had to live with someone so much older, two generations older and measure your pace and your understanding to a totally different view of the world. With him it was so much worth while. I remember as a youngster griping a bit against his ponderous ways, his subservience to routine, his endless persistence and carefulness. I hardly need tell you that I ended by making a lot of that part of myself. But sometimes when we were out on the hills, when my stride was measured to his and the mind was free, I was admitted to the whole world of his thoughts. He hadn't book learning, though he had read a lot. Somehow. . . maybe because he had thought rather than read. . . he was away out beyond modern Science, freely evaluating achievements yet cautious always before the one

Impenetrable, the very structure of Mind, which, as he used to say, imposes form on our thinking and compels us to impose our limitations on what we think. I don't know whether you are with me. It was no accident that I often found him reading in the Old Testament; as for the New one he would say, quietly, that effort was wasted studying the words of that if you did not have an intuitive grasp of what it was about."

"And this was in your last year and a half at school?"

"I got my five Highers and they wanted me to stay on for a sixth year and go to University. But I couldn't impose on my mother any longer; and grandfather, I could see, would not have long to go, at least before he gavé up and became an invalid. I didn't know what was for the best; then my mother's husband-to-be found me an interview with a Glasgow firm in the textile business. Shortly after I was in digs in Mosspark West and commuting daily to the Centre."

"It was languages you were best at?"

"Yes I had French and German. When I think of these Glasgow days I don't know how I stuck it, but, then, I was only beginning to be myself. What I had to do and learn with United Textiles. . . and it was quite a lot with classes on a Friday morning. . . I took all that in my stride, the more so because I knew I would go abroad in about six months. I attended Spanish evening classes in a Mosspark school and I came to know Spanish best of all. But the real joy was the weekends of that spring and summer. My chum Duncan and I had bicycles and made marathon trips to Argyllshire and Ayrshire. You did cycle when you were young? You built something into your nature with the steady plod along the roads of these days. This was the time when I began to keep my red notebooks where I noted down impressions. One weekend we went to Ardgartan Youth Hostel and did the Cobbler and other small peaks. It whetted my appetite for I had never been up a sizeable mountain."

"The Cobbler? Yes, it was one of my early ones too. Where else did you go?"

"One weekend when we were slightly more in the money,

we took a day return by rail to Callander; then you darted out to the booking office and boarded the train again with a new day return for Tyndrum. It was forbidden: penalties not exceeding something or other were threatened but we did it. From Tyndrum Lower you climbed over the spur to Glen Cononish and up Ben Lui which for its modest height was always my idea of a mountain. . . till I saw Chimborazo. What a superb mountain Lui is though. . . so many ways up and down, the Alpine plants and views that left you gasping. Duncan was a great chum on these trips; he was the leader and introduced me to all this. . . and when I left him shortly after to go abroad, it really was goodbye: he was killed in a car accident a year later.

"Well, as I say I got my marching orders and it was to Ecuador. I had about a month to prepare and found that there was little enough in the libraries to tell me about it. My firm was promoting business there in Quito and Cuenca and I went as assistant to an under-manager who really did not speak Spanish well."

"Ecuador? How do you get to Ecuador?"

"Fly to the West Indies, then via Bogota to Quito. At least that's how we did it then. I was three years in Ecuador without coming home. Grandfather had died in hospital and my mother was remarried so I had no real incentive. I worked hard and used leave periods to explore Ecuador and Peru and Colombia too. It was hard work for we were just establishing the firm and I was speaking Spanish most of the day. You remember Quito is 9000 ft up and so it takes a bit of getting used to. But what a place! ringed with hills and volcanoes. . . it has a University too and a wealth of historic churches. Sometimes I had to make the thirteen-hour bus journey to Cuenca, our other centre of operations, up and down over high passes and into fertile green troughs with Cotopaxi behind and Chimborazo, all 20,000 feet of it, in front. One moment you were in the mist and damp, another in the dusty desert and the people crossed themselves for dear life as the bus crawled along ledges on the vertical cliffs. What an experience!"

"I expect Ecuador left a pretty big thumb print on you?"

"Yes, I was coming to that. Even if all the rest were forgotten, even if it were all an episode of years and days, there was one signpost, one door that opened, and I could never go back on it. In Ecuador literacy tends to mean speaking Spanish; the Indios speak one of the ancient less developed languages. Now I had taken the trouble to learn Spanish, to go on learning it, which most British and Americans rarely do; I suppose I had also the Scot's traditional lack of class-consciousness. I got to know all sorts of people and was invited to homes and gatherings where most people don't go. It was during my second year; I managed to do something for a family I knew. . . they were Mestizos and the father was a Catholic priest. I thought it a small thing but they were profoundly grateful. Apart from anything else the old man spoke such beautiful Spanish that every meeting was a lesson. I penetrated a little way into the hopeless longings of an under-educated, disregarded people. The official religion is just frightful, a real opiate for hopelessness on Earth with just a hope in the life to come. You've never been to South America? You should see the horrors of retribution in the cathedrals, the pictures of people mauled, mangled, stung by scorpions; the Christs all stabbed over with the gory wounds, highly glazed and realistic. But old Father Arcadio was deeper than all that; I would say he had a real Grace, a spiritual Gift. In his conversation time was nowhere, patience was endless. . . and he had something which I mistook for resignation. Well, he offered to take me to see his brother who was something I could not make out. . . South American countries have words which are only found in the most comprehensive Spanish dictionaries. This brother lived in Oriente, that is, far down to the eastward of the Cordillera on a small headwater tributary of the Amazon. The prospect of the trip really excited me. I had a ten days leave coming up and agreed to go, without however telling my European sophisticate friends, who would have done everything to prevent me, thinking it lunacy. They never did countenance the Indio population. Our party numbered ten, including the old man, myself and two of his sons and six others carrying various loads as well as food for the three day journey. They told me that in older times you hunted what you could on a journey like that and failing all else you lived on the blue musky flesh of macaws. For half a day we descended the cordillera and entered the rain forest; after that for two whole days we had no sight of the sun under the dense interlaced canopy of leaves. Underfoot it was often damp, some times over the ankles in running water; high above the screeching of birds and the gibbering of monkeys was incessant, exciting at first but strangely oppressive after a few hours of it. We trudged on, each man buried in his own thoughts in that damp primeval paradise. Sometimes our boots squelched through something like North Sea crude oil; and Ecuador has oil there but has not yet exploited it; with their machetes the leaders forced a way through leaves and thickets and scarlet lilies, which almost visibly closed behind us as the vegetation reasserted itself. I had some deep moments of primitive fear but I kept them to myself, for we were never really in danger. Snakes no doubt eyed us from a distance but did not make themselves known; but there were golden salamanders everywhere. Finally it was as if we were moving through an enchanted world, where animals and plants and insects all asserted their claim to life. . . and the plants were quite the most terrifying. Then suddenly we reached a clearing and we were there. Hammocks were slung between trees and under mosquito nets we slept beside a small river. I lay on my back listening to the raucous cries of birds and the night noises of the forest and thought: Here I am beside the headwaters of the Amazon.

"The next morning we went, my host, his sons and I, a short distance inland from the clearing to where there were several circular cane huts; the air had a pungent fragrance of vanilla. My host and his sons went in to greet their relative and for a good half hour I waited, absolutely rapt in the sights and sounds of the place. I knew I would have to think it all out when I got back; here it was sufficient just to be unobtrusive in this marvellous dawn of creation. Then the old Priest came out with his sons and took me into the hut.

"It was a green gloom in there; a figure rose who in that uncertain light could have been a hundred years old. He took my hand and addressed me in the most beautiful cultivated Castilian Spanish I had ever heard. He bade me sit and for quite a time enquired of my origins and my job in Quito and how contented I was. I felt... you know... terribly young and insufficient, but I remember talking to him of my grandfather and the Fionn Allt here. He listened intently as my Spanish, at first a bit diffident, then rattling on, told him of the world he had never seen. Then he spoke to me of the rain forest of the Amazon and its teeming life. Suddenly I realized that we had taken up our respective positions; he spoke to me with the familiar You, the one you use to friends and loved ones while I used the formal You of respect to him. That was apparently right, by the subtle evaluation that these people have so much more precisely than we British. His brother the Priest was with us, but with enormous understanding had said nothing at all. Suddenly the old man spread his arms and said quietly:

"'Oigo tu voz. Como estás de aspecto?'
What did I look like? I wondered if I was momentarily out of contact. Then the Priest, his brother, said quietly:
'Tell him: my brother does not see.'

"Appalled, I thought of the glowing descriptions he had given me of the forest and how he had wanted to hear of Scotland.

"'Since a child, he has not seen,' said the old man. Well, I could not sit here and tell you the whole story and we must get going sometime. But it was the evening which was important. When we left him about mid-morning he said:

"'Juan will come back in the evening alone, no?'
I promised. That evening was one of the great halting places in my life. Later I was to think of it as almost contrived... arranged by some greater agency or other, and for my purposes. Let me think of it again: the utter darkness in that world of leaves and struggling vegetation: the noise of gravitating water, like the Fionn Allt here... I often think it is about the most ancient sound that the ear can hear. The forest

was strangely quiet; they said that a storm was threatening and the night creatures knew it. I went to the old man and sat by him, a tiny oil lamp burning by his side. He wasted no time; spoke with urgency, as though he had a long message and the hours of the night were few. He told me of his earlier life without sight, how he had learned skills and plied them; how he had listened to all who had a message to give him. His brother and others had read books to him and had discussed all the important issues.

"'In my handicap', (he said), 'I was greatly favoured: I learned more quickly, I retained more exactly what I knew to be important and forgot as quickly so many of the particulars that could have no meaning for me. When I was about sixty, it was given to me to break through a barrier: I realized that all the knowledge of particulars never diminishes the amount of what is still not known. So I changed direction, quietly laying aside all speculation about Science and human duties. Others, who could see, could do this, after all, so much better than I. I came apart into this hut and for long years I have striven to increase my inner vision. For, you see, everything that I had understood hitherto, had been understood as it were within the four walls of my human mind. Now I saw that the shape of the walls had determined the way in which I understood. For Science this is no difficulty, as it implicitly accepts the limitation. But now I had to burst out of these walls by continuous effort and by practice and by fasting. You, a young man, will not know fasting. Can you accept from me that it is the ultimate stage in the long effort to gain freedom from the confines of Mind into the wider Incomprehensibility of Reality? I have come to know the one-ness in all things, like arrows of light all directed the same way in Men and Animals and Plants and Trees. You have terror at first as you walk sightless in the forest and feel every plant, every tree and liana filled with the same life as your own. Then I was glad I had no eyes. But there is a rule: once you are out beyond Mind there is no reasoning: you do not classify, describe or make theories. Now when I hear a stranger say: 'What is here?', I think with a controlled terror: Is anything here but

God? Sometimes I feel the great world that must exist outside the Amazon forest; I feel its pressure, its longing to break out and know. But the knowledge is too dangerous: it is only for a few. Did the ancients not say: Can a man see God and live? Are you understanding me, Juan?'

"In that intense moment I understood him very well and said so.

"'But' (I asked) 'what do you say to your brother who is a good man but locked up within the magic circle of Christian belief?

"'My brother knows what I think: he understands it too. But he has eyes and has chosen to be a religious technologist. . . ¡Que juego de palabras!' (he said with a little laugh). 'He gives the poor the best he can give them in the form that they need it. I would not like to be an Indio with eyes in Quito or Cuenca; I would need something to make the real world tolerable. He gives them forgivenness for sins and a Day of Judgment and a hope of Resurrection, for they need these as much as they need clean water or Daily Bread. But my case and yours is different. Do you know when first I knew I would have a visitor? It was five weeks ago yesterday. And all the while you have been coming nearer, first in intention and preparation, then on a real journey till tonight. I will say all that is in me to say, I, José, to you, Juan, . . . because here God meets God and that is a great event in the universe.'

"The hours passed. At times I was aware of a great storm that raged far above the leaves. It was almost as though he knew the condition of the someone inside me who I was going to be and spoke to that one. There were silences, sometimes a soft chuckle to remind me that, though away out beyond Mind, he was a real human person in a cane hut. And, there was the great tide of his beautiful Spanish. I knew that I could not remember all that he said: I knew also that the other Me whom he was addressing would hear the words as mandate and instruction. Next day, I slept through to the afternoon and in the evening we made preparations for departure on the following morning.

"At the end of my three years I returned to Glasgow; I had

done a satisfactory job, or so the manager hinted when he said that they would be sending me with promotion to the Manchester branch in a month. I found Manchester like Glasgow, a bit dirty and wet and the English habits of life and of speech took a little getting used to. But the people were great; there was a warmth and honesty about the place and I never seemed aware of the class divisions which friends told me were such a feature of the South. I was three years there and lived with a very decent family out in Ashton and commuted daily to Victoria."

"So now you would have a new hinterland to explore."

"Surprisingly I fell in quickly with a young group that went Youth Hostelling and walking in the Pennines. . . Kinderscout and up by the Snake Pass and Dovedale, all very different from Perthshire. Yes, that was a fine time and sometimes we went climbing in North Wales or in the Lake District as your Mancunian generally does."

"And what did Manchester add to your Red Books? Presumably it wasn't a sterile period?"

"Sterile? No, it was the next step forward."

Then changing his tone Ian looked at me in a hopeless comical way.

"But see, I feel like the Ancient Mariner here, obstructing you on your way home to tea or dinner. Can we meet again this evening and I will finish the story. . . no, not finish it, for there's lots to come that I don't know. Could we do that?"

It was soon arranged.

"Well, suppose I tell you the Manchester bit and leave the rest to our evening session. Or am I really being terribly self-centred? Do you really want to hear?

But both Ian and I knew, he that he had to tell, I that I had to hear. We looked up the rocky valley where the shadows under bush and stone were perceptibly deeper. And still not a soul had passed up by in all that heat as the Fionn Allt prepared for another evening of untroubled quiet.

"They were three hard working years . . . don't let me give you the impression that my firm did not get the effort out of me that it paid me for. Frequently I did not have evenings to

myself or even weekends, if something was wrong with
production or labour relations. At the beginning of the second winter . . . I was just 23 at the time, a friend suggested
that I accompany him to a class in Social Work, a sort of lay
participation that was just a little more professional than it
was amateur, if you take such an Irish way of putting it. I
didn't know at first if I wanted, for I had not been aware of a
nagging social conscience; but I let myself be persuaded. The
first winter it was Youth Leadership and quite a remarkably
good course. I learned all the way, and when, by the spring,
we were going out to Youth Centres at evenings or on to the
hills at weekends, I found that I relished the struggle. Naturally it was the problem youngsters who were the struggle.

"Did you find you could strike common ground with
them?"

"We were warned about wrong approaches, particularly
sentimentality or anything that highlighted their different-
ness. Some of the others basically felt sorry for their deprivation or had left-wing socialist consciences. I was more ready
to admit the reality: they had often ugly anti-social attitudes,
immature characters which were desperate to create an identity by any sort of self-display; occasionally they were un-
washed and looked undernourished. And there was always
the danger that one might spend one's time staring at the poor
then go and write a book about it. I tried to take each one at
his face value and said to myself: Here is a youngster, trying
to claim his right to life and sunlight, obstructed by various
unattractive habits and attitudes but to be won, if it is at all
possible. I remember writing in my Red Book: 'but not by
reasoning, rules or principles, by sheer warmth of contact.'
Does that sound rather pretentious? I sometimes think that I
come to crushing decisions for myself which any qualified
social worker could have told me in ten minutes."

I said I thought the discovery for oneself was of far greater
importance.

"Well, I was now living a double life and a very exhausting
one too. I remember I took two weeks holiday in the summer
in the Prescelli hills of Pembrokeshire, all on my own with a

tent, just trying to get things in order. You see I felt . . . I felt
as I have often done since . . . that I was unwittingly taking a
step towards an unknown future. I had been offered a place
on a Drug Dependence course . . . one of ten places . . . for
the next winter and I wanted some certainty that this was to
be my way. It was on the train on the way home to Manchester, on that marvellous Central Wales line that I found that I
was all enthusiasm for it."

"So you studied Drug Dependence? That's very interesting. I have read much about it but always in a purely amateur
way. Did you find it hard going?"

"Three evenings a week for most of the winter. The Physi-
ology or the Chemistry wasn't too difficult nor too important either. But what pained me . . . if I don't sound too
arrogant . . . was the immature attitudes of so many of the
subject experts. You were invited to choose a unique
solution . . . understanding Chemistry or Society or techniques for rescuing from chemical dependence, as they called
it. Mind you I learned everything that was put in front of me,
though it was woefully thin in places. Some of the Big Names
just didn't want to know and selected their statistics to
comfort themselves and the people at large. When we went
out to the Centres, as mere helpers, I was fascinated to watch
the doctors and trained personnel handling the cases . . .
fascinated and sometimes so angry that I said to myself: They
had better get me transferred from Manchester before I blow
up."

"What was your problem, then?"

"I hope it wasn't arrogance . . . or some childish idea that I
knew better than the experts. I think now, it was a deep-
seated frustration. Drug Dependence could have been tackled
as a social evil, but no one was prepared to do that. It could
also be treated like symptoms of an illness, rather like schizophrenia, and people deluded themselves that by getting rid of
the symptoms by one kind of withdrawal or another, that was
enough. Yet the statistics, poor as they were, suggested that
there was very little permanent cure . . . for some other
reason. Was there a drug-dependent character type? . . .

that's what I wanted to know. I asked everywhere, I had correspondence with various people and found that the whole of this area was in the same state of basic non-knowledge as was Psychiatry, though your psychiatrists wouldn't agree. Basically we did not know whom we were curing of what. But don't get me wrong; I learned a tremendous amount."

Ian turned to look at me intending to be apologetic; for he was really a very modest fellow. But his eyes had a depth to them that presaged a good deal more of a story. We walked together over the iron bridge and past Gleneich.

"No tears," (he said), "it was one of the building bricks in the edifice that is still growing. I carry a bit of my grandparents around with me, which is, after all, as much immortality as we have any right to expect. Grateful though, very grateful."

.   .   .   .

The few hours that elapsed before we met again in the evening brought to mind the old-fashioned theatre of my youth, where the curtain came down between scenes, and if you stayed in your seat, you heard the hashing and bashing as scenery and props were dragged out and reassembled. Somehow that interval gave the illusion of time passing, but it could also allow you to reset your mind for the next act with questions and speculations to be answered. Ian had been visiting his mother and her husband and their family.

"Do you really want to continue?" (he said). "I feel rather awful about dominating the conversation this way."

"I just could not bear not to know what happened next. Maybe it is an elaborate disclosure of yourself but it has a value for me that I can't begin to tell you. Please continue!"

"I finished that course and continued in the textile post till the next autumn, when I got a posting from my firm to Sydney, Australia. But before that I had a reckoning inside me. I guess it was coming, just had to come and chose its own unique time. I had a fortnight camping in the Lake District. My salary didn't rise to a car for I was saving hard. I camped up Wasdale, not exactly off the beaten track, but at least away from Ambleside and Keswick and the day trippers. The first ten days were dry and I plodded up over Great Gable and by Sprinkling Tarn and sometimes over to the valleys, leaving me prodigious distances to cover to get back to camp. Maybe you know that part of the Lakes? One cloudless day I made straight for Scafell, not by the tracks round and about but keeping south of Lingmell and straight for the blue crest with several hundred feet of scree at the end. It was quite frightening, steeper than the scree on Ben Lui. I remember disciplining myself not to turn round in case I lost my nerve and got stuck. I started about 6 in the morning and was up on top among the massive ankle cracking boulders about 9, maybe earlier, anyhow before the crowds grew to fairground proportions. Sitting out of the wind by the cairn, I suddenly had the strangest feeling of being enclosed in a translucent globe. Of course it was purely a construct of the imagination. In that moment I was struck with the thought that, while being human and sharing in the common limitations of Mankind, I had at the same time a sort of Physics and Mechanics all of my own and that success would depend somehow on my power to observe them and follow their promptings. I thought of the early events of Fionn Allt valley and I could see how these had pushed me in a direction and I had put up no resistance. I saw the Ecuador episode, most of which was just broadening of experience and growing up, except for the descent to the Amazon; that hung about me like a cloud which I could not yet penetrate. Then I was waiting for some catalyst. And with a strange anticipation I knew that my penetration into Drug Dependence and the Amazon episode would in time explain one another. How long I was caught up in this way I don't know... like sitting on a thermal high above the Lake District... for there was no-one about. The whole Lakeland massif was thrusting up around me and out to sea was the strange silhouette of the Isle of Man. I remember I laughed aloud and said solemnly: You'll be all right, boy: just be alert and miss no move. That autumn came the instructions to proceed to Sydney and in a sort of reckless way I was prepared to say that the decision was only in part the responsibility of United Textiles. I arrived there in all the heat of Christmas and wondered what had hit me. Have you been to Australia? Of course it doesn't tell you anything to go as a tourist; you have to live there to know if you fit in."

"I've heard of quite a number of emigrants who returned, because they claimed they did not fit in."

"I was glad to have an enormous back-log of work to catch up on. . . my predecessor had had a long illness. . . and for months, for a year, I lived for work. Gradually it dawned on me that I was working to justify myself, because I just did not fit in. Don't mistake me: there were loads of fine people, cheerful, good-humoured, who could teach me everything about enjoying life. That was the one thing I could not do. I thought of the Amazon, of Manchester, of Scafell and wrote it all down in my Red Books. . . which has been very interesting to reread, for it describes the increasing bleakness of that first year.

I was trying to think of the next move, for you would be sure to ask me; then I remembered what it was. I joined a group of younger people of my age and we went trekking in the hinterland of Sydney. . . the Blue Mountains and the Hunter Range and up the Macquarrie River. That saved my sanity: I just lived for it at weekends. But it has little to do with this story. Quite casually one evening in a forest clearing above Portland we were resting after a long day. I think everyone was tired, even these irrepressible Australians. The talk was quiet in the cool air, in small groups rather than all together. I was talking to two of the girls, real tough mountaineers from Sydney, and in one of those wandering conversations they told me that they helped in the Downtown Drug Dependence Clinic.

"Just skivvy work, of course and womanly compassion. . . holding hands and wiping up the vomit. We're not qualified to be allowed to do any more. But it kinda does something for you to make a bit of effort that is neither satisfying nor rewarding."

"I went all cold as I felt the plate glass doors revolve to wave me in. But I was guarded. 'Is it a massive problem in Sydney?'

"Endless," (said Naomi) "and not at all nice. You should see the running sores and the hepatitis sufferers."

"I often think it's just hopeless" (said Margaret). "Even if you gave your all for these kids, the've just nothing to go back to."

"Would you like to come see sometime" (chipped in Naomi, perhaps mischievously wanting to hear the Scot back out). "Tuesday's our service day."

"I'll come."

"So began the next leg of the flight. Of course I went and found that in basics it was only worse than Manchester. I was qualified and soon enrolled as a voluntary helper.

"And was your experience as frustrating as the Manchester one?"

"No, I'll give it to the Aussies, there's no wool in front of their eyes. Sometimes decision was harsh, almost brutal, but it was measured against the realities of the time, not some infinitely distant Utopia. The team leader, a tough professional of 45. . . we called him Jake. . . had a prominent jaw and an equally prominent determination that no-one could break. The first time I was shocked but only briefly, when he drew me aside from a case I was labouring hopelessly with. 'Let him die' (he said) 'and be at peace. There's nothing in this world for him'. And right enough when you saw the pathetic efforts they made to kick the habit, you knew they had to have some fitness left to do it. The piteous cries, the stench, the filth, the utter collapse of personality. . . no, I think I never saw anything so bad in Manchester. If a kid was hooked on heroin and maybe had hepatitis and possibly VD and could eat nothing. . . well, they had mostly signed their own death warrant: and the numbers who did were far greater than the Government statistics. Governments don't want people to know that a thing is out of control.

"Well, there started that exhausting double life again. I took two evenings a week and got away to the hills at the weekend and all day worked in a respectable suit and tie. I knew it couldn't go on but I was always waiting for the hint. . . or the kick. After six months I was learning to cope with myself better. A magazine article featuring us called us sentimentally Angels in Hell. . . and I agreed about the Hell bit. Sometimes even yet, if I have a nightmare, it has the sounds and sights and the stench of the Drug Dependence clinic. People sometimes said to me: What a kick you must get from tackling the impossible! No, no kick, just a steady draining of pity until, if you're not careful you become as objective as I imagine a Harley Street Psychiatrist must be. Objective in Hell. . . can you imagine it; but that's what happens if you take too much.

"Actually I did have a spell off, about three months, on medical advice, because I was beginning to be unable to find words when I wanted them. . . a real disaster for me, you will no doubt agree. It happened quite suddenly, and fortunately the Centre Psycho knew just what was what and put me out to grass. I went to a place up the Hawkesbury River and walked about in the forests all day. . . and gradually I returned to normality. But while I was walking and talking to myself I began to get hold of the problem at the right end.

"You see, Jake was right in a way, though it's a dreadful thing for a man to play Jehovah. In effect the effort spent on eighty percent of these cases was all waste, gratifying to us do-gooders who were sacrificing ourselves maybe, but just an extension of the torment of the sufferers. We say they are hooked; but if you unhook them, what do you do with them? Mostly they had abandoned home or been abandoned by home, burnt all their boats, squandered their health, their reputation. . . their self-respect too, that was the most important. And we did not know how to remake them. During that three months I thought a lot about it. What sort of effort would it be to dry someone out, to remake him and return him securely. . . perhaps to a simplified environment? I wondered. I read anything I could find, maintained a correspondence with two experts, one of whom helped, the other not."

Ian emerged from his long memory and looked seriously at me.

"But is all this interesting you? I haven't thought about it for long enough. Now it's like the incoming tide."

"Yes," (I said) "go on. I am interested in your struggles here.

And besides your Odyssey is not yet up to date."

"I wonder if Odysseus ever does get back home to Ithaca in my case. I wonder. . . anyhow I was restored to health and returned to the punishing routine, but I took more care this time not to burn myself out with hopeless sorrow."

"The problem really was endless?" (I said). "I want to know, for I am really out of my depth."

"I don't know how it compares with the States or France or London for that matter. But they came endlessly, the youngsters, more boys than girls. . . somehow the girls are tougher in the fibre. . . people older than me too, hard cases, but they usually didn't have long to go. Bronchitis, pneumonia or the river, that was the usual end of the tale. They just stopped turning up and we never knew whether they had gone away or just finished off. Now the question was always before me: Why? Had they been doomed at conception by some irreversible weakness? Or was it some basic lack of security that they had picked up on the way through? But in either case it was almost impracticable to turn the dials back and remake them.

"Then a strange thing happened. . . you'll be thinking all my things are strange. I was asked by the DD authority to become a full employee of theirs, which financially wasn't really on. But it threw me into a bit of confusion. However the very next week. . . I forgot to tell you that United Textiles had recently been the subject of a takeover. . . Well, I was informed that my department in Sydney was to be merged with the takeover firm's in Melbourne."

"And you. . . ?"

"I was virtually out of a job. At least I was offered something in Manchester, hardly promotion. So I resigned and became whole time DD and stayed at it for another two years, amassing technique and knowledge. But still there were the unanswered questions."

"And had the Ian McKelvie of Manchester days significantly changed under the impact of all this experience?"

"Strange isn't it how one self merges imperceptibly into another. I am sure someone said it before me; we are the complex survivors of our former selves. I would sometimes delve into the past. . . stand with Duncan on the horseshoe corrie on the top of Ben Lui, and look at myself progressively down through the vortex of these years. Something was happening to me though. Unlike the billiard balls on the table, when there was a collision, I felt that the other person was deflected but I just gave. . . and didn't move very much. Or put another way, I felt continuously called on to be an implement for the need of whoever bumped into me; almost a renunciation of personality. I wondered. . ."

"And did you ever get your chance. . . or maybe challenge. . . to reconstruct somebody? I could see terrible problems, terrible dangers. . ."

"Dangers?"

"Yes, of playing at God!"

"Didn't I, too? It was the one thing that would have stayed my hand for ever. We are talking, you know, about people who, despite their equal claims to humanity and recognition, are physically the flotsam and jetsam of society. Once hooked they have no motive force but the desire to maintain their dependent state; if you unhook them, they become flotsam once more. To society as represented by Economics and Politics they are about as valuable as the contents of a trash can. Yes, I did it once."

"Success?"

"I think so. At least I have a letter every month or so and they ring hopeful."

"Tell me!"

"It was a young fellow of eighteen of Norwegian origin; his name was Erik. He came into us one September in about as pitiful a state as I had seen, apathetic, dirty, suppurating sores from infected needles, wanting to die; mercifully there was no hepatitis yet. We had a procedure for new cases, unemotional, matter-of-fact, dealing with their first needs, medical, basic nutrition, cleaning up. That was routine and he was like five or six who had been through our hands earlier that day. He was put down to rest and was in my office while I got on with the day's paper work. I was, you see, about the

only one on duty about two that morning. Every now and
then I took a glance at him lying under a blanket on a pallet.
He was often racked by hideous spasms of trembling and a
nasty cough. I made no effort to speak to him; we always
waited for about twenty-four hours before we made a brief
psychological inventory. I continued to write my reports,
formal reports on the ghosts of real people. I glanced over
again and found him half sitting up on the camp bed, his fair
hair all wild and dishevelled, his pupils dark blue staring from
deep sockets. He was staring at me. I confess I got a shock,
almost of fear, as though he had risen from the dead. And I
realised that I hadn't spoken to him, didn't know how good
his English might be. . . and I did not know what that stare
meant. Then he just said in a low voice,

"'Mister, save me, save me before it's too late!'

"In a flash all systems cleared, mountains moved out the
way and the impossible became. . . well, accessible. I heard
myself say,

"'Do you believe you can be saved, Erik?'

"'You can save me, mister.'

"Well, the long and the short of it was, I took him on. At
that moment the DD could only have offered reinforcement to
self-help. About 10% of bad cases like his made it. . . the rest
succumbed. I installed him in my flat; contacted a friend who
could cover any periods when I was out. Fortunately I
happened to have a week's break beginning that day, a Saturday. I reckoned: ten days to break the worst of it. I really
would not like to tell you of that ten days. . . it would disturb
you unnecessarily; I wouldn't like to recall it in detail myself.
Suffice it to say, when we first got home, I and the pitiful
Erik, we had a quick change of roles. I found that I had
already thought it all out. To be able to go through Hell in the
next fortnight as he was to do with me as his guide, he had to
be totally under orders: no free will was left to him, no
decisions, no choices, not even any masking of the pain. Just
one task and one goal. . . and it started that Saturday morning. I tyrannised over him: his life was reduced to meticu-
lous routines; keeping himself clean, doing things to order,

domestic chores. . . and even when about the fifth day without heroin he filled the place with cries and moans, I had to be inflexible and show no pity at all. All this I explained in advance to him as he sat with his pale apathetic almost hostile face that Saturday morning before we descended into Avernus. And he believed me, that's what saved him, believed that I could do it and was prepared to put himself totally in my hands."

"That must have been a frightful ten days. You would not really know what was happening to him, nor what you were doing. . . all in the dark. . . Avernus, yes. Your worst experience yet?"

"I don't know which of us suffered more. Maybe if I had been trained as a psychiatrist I would have been able to be more objective, taken less out of myself.

"But who ever said to a psychiatrist: 'Save me, mister?'

"I set him up a bed in my room with the instruction that if ever the horror came on him in the night he was to wake me. It did on nights one to seven, several times at first: I held him tight as great tremors racked him from top to toe and he was icy cold: then after a half hour it passed over and he would sleep."

"Did you get any relief during that week?"

"Yes, I had a young friend who was an assistant instructor in a gym in the north end of the city. He came in on afternoons and let me get an hour or so in the fresh air. He was prepared to hold Erik down if there was a trembling session, though I saw he was shocked: the fit don't really want to see human dereliction. I walked in the open or down by the beach and counted the slow days. On Day Two I said: I'll never make it. By Day Seven I wondered at the buoyancy and confidence that sustained me.

"It was the morning of the ninth day, I remember. I had Erik up early; the taskmaster gave the orders, washing himself, making the beds tidying the room. . . I kept him at it for a good two hours. There was no way of telling whether he was willing, or hated me or just did not care. Then he did some simple physical exercising with me. . . I had done that each day out of a conviction that a physical build-up was more necessary than anything. Well, I had him prancing around like a cart horse; but the lad was so weak and could not take too much. At one point he tripped and rolled face down on the floor and I picked him up. I couldn't believe it; he was laughing, the first sign of personality I had seen, laughing and his eyes were a lighter blue in his pallid face. He grasped me round the neck and said so wearily:

"'Oh Ian, God, Ian, you've saved me: I'll never do it again.' I was happy. . . yet shocked. You see, I hadn't looked at it that way, not for a minute. I had thought: If only I can be the means of discipline, the brutal implement, showing no mercy and no pity, he would have the strength to recover on his own. He wouldn't do it without someone, but the Someone was only the means. And here he was believing in me."

"But I expect" (I said) "you have long since coped with that, understood it in human terms. After all, a youngster of 18 has never come through a thing like that before."

"Of course. And later when he was home and dry and I was building him up and reconstructing his zest in life, I heard all the details, the usual things. The family had emigrated from Norway to Australia, to Fremantle; the father deserted, the mother tried a marriage on the rebound and it was a disaster. All this he took. But when his mother to whom he had too much of a fixation became emotionally entangled with a thoroughly deplorable character, Erik left home. . . and drifted. The increasing gulf of insecurity in him was beyond his strength and he just rattled down the ladder to the bottom. He was really doomed: most of them are in that situation. . ."

"If Mister hadn't saved him?"

"Oh don't. My heart will always miss a beat when I hear these words; for, you see, I'm almost terrified that some day I'll come to believe it."

"And Erik was a success after all?"

"In my last year, I got him to a college where he upped his educational qualifications; then I got him in where he wanted, as an apprentice auctioneer. He's doing fine. There's a letter I had last week."

Ian handed me the airletter, written in a neat backsloping

hand. The sentences were well formed and sounded like the utterance of a real living person. He showed a concern with what Ian was doing and where he would go next; he never alluded to the Hell they had been through. But I could not help noticing at the end the 'Love, Erik'. . . I suppose you are bound to love someone who goes through Hell with you. Ian looked at his watch.

"I had better hurry and get up to date. You see, there is one more episode to tell you. . . to retell to myself. In the end I was faced with a decision. My work permit, originally negotiated for United Textiles, was going to run out: to stay I would have to apply for Australian nationality. I cliff-hung, as the saying is, and something decided for me that I was to return to base in Britain. . . not maybe logical nor reasonable nor in my own best interest. But that's how it was. My passage home had been paid for by a deposit two years before and I decided to make the most of it. The first leg was by cargo steamer from Brisbane to Calcutta calling at the most romantic places, Surabaya, Djakarta, Singapore and Rangoon. What a voyage! In Calcutta I had the address of an Indian I had known in Sydney and went there. They held on to me for three weeks till I had to get a flight home. You haven't been to India, you said. Three weeks is long enough only to make you curious about that strangest of all worlds."

"What about your social conscience in India?"

"Switched out! I made that quite clear to myself that I was in transit and would not be tempted to meddle. My hosts were charming in a way that made Scotland seem rather rough and heathery. They took me everywhere brought me to meet people and allowed me to ask endless questions."

"And three weeks were too short a time to make a significant impression on you?"

"It might well have been so. But I was always waiting to make the response to anything that happened. I had read Borgès in South America and was waiting, I think, for gardens filled with moon-coloured hounds, circular stone towers, assassins and the general stench of death. Instead of that it was one old man sitting in a booth off a side street; through a bead curtain was the rest of his dwelling. How I got there is a story in itself, but not for now. I was standing outside in the late evening, watching a flight of birds in a golden sky, when a voice in English called me in. I was taken aback, nervy a bit, but when he said: 'I have waited for you all evening,' I accepted the condition and went in. He sat cross-legged on the ground but indicated a stool to me. With a wry smile which I could still see in the dusk, he said:

"'Friends from the West do not sit comfortably as I do. Please seat yourself!'

"Then, as you are going to guess, I found myself at one of my review points. He asked questions of me, displaying an almost clairvoyant awareness of my life to date. I suppose he could not really visualize the Fionn Allt or Oriente or Ancoats and Openshaw or Sydney. When I had given him much information, there was silence as he abstracted it somewhere out beyond Mind, I supposed. In these silences I heard the strange cries of the city, voices across the street, a dog barking. . . all at a great distance.

"Young Man," (he said), "I waited this evening for one who would need light. I did not know you nor which light you would require. Therefore, I will speak as the Great Spirit moves me. I will not know your light but you will recognize it for yourself. When you do, take it and go and do not thank me.

"'You seek the Truth as we do but yours is a Truth realized in action, for you are of the West; contemplation comes not easily to one like you. You are seeking for Truth far out beyond the reasoning of the human mind: know that you will never grasp it, only learn to respond to it, work with it. You could never be a child of Mother India as I could never understand the restless noisy West. But I see that you have been tried to the utmost, labouring to reverse the signs and symptoms of things when the only possibility is to remake lives. In your next existence, the one you return to, you will learn that we may seek to be used, hope to be used, but must never become the User. But as we approach Enlightenment the function of Implement and User is blurred.'

"He asked me more, particularly about the condition of

the Poor and Rejected in all the countries where I had been. And I became filled interiorly with radiance and buoyancy. I told him of this and he knew what I meant. . . precisely!

"'Look for it at every hour' (he said). 'You cannot say when the Kindly One will lift you clear of the world, clear of all worry and unresolved decision; you are filled with the radiance which is the promise of the future. Then gently you are let down and returned to your heavy body. For you it comes differently than for us but it is the same.'

"Then he said, shocking me by his penetration:

"'You have a decision to make about your next direction: do not make it. Wait until you are desperate with waiting; it will be shown to you. Were I greater or wiser or nearer to Ultimate Bliss, I might help you. I am however just what I am, an implement of the moment.'

"We did not talk much longer; it was hardly a conversation anyway. I felt almost as though I might gaze through that bead curtain and see for myself how Reality really is. His last words to me are printed on me for ever. In a moment of valediction he said:

"'One claims nothing, no rewards, no praise. One is at the least an arrow moving down the great shaft of light that is God. Our task is so little: at all times and in all conditions to wear one of the five thousand radiant faces of God.'

'He bowed: I stood and did likewise, murmuring the word that is used on these occasions. Then I was on the street and navigating through thick darkness to where I could get a conveyance back to my home.

. . . .

"And that," (said Ian, turning the blaze of his dark eyes on me) "that's it for now; end of report; but the file is still open."

I said: "The only possible comment is a profound silence."

He said: "I have been in Britain for four months now, mostly in Manchester, as it happens. It was easier to make a

temporary home there. I have been waiting... probably you
are the only one in the world who will understand it...
waiting for the next direction."

"You are, then, under orders?"

"That's what it has come to. Free will serves for daily use,
for the little local problems; for these other things you've got
to... shall I say... unwill it. I heard the words once and they
were just words; now they are the mainspring: Humility is
endless."

"Tell me," (I said) "if you dare, which discovery lies to
your hand like flaming sword?"

He looked at his upturned hand on the table for a measur-
able time.

"Two, I think... this first:
'Truths that are built on human reason are no truths: Truth
always enfolds the possibility of its opposite.' And this second:
which is the first reversed: 'All philosophies, theologies, en-
quiries into the Nature of Things are like a little portion of the
Truth screwed up in a child's small fist. The way... is to ask
no questions... work out no systems; you wait for orders.'"

We walked together down the quiet streets where the douce
citizens were abed or absorbed in late-night TV. In the station
the last train had come and gone. I too had my orders and
would receive mail and business communications for Ian
McKelvie Esq., when he disappeared once more on his next
assignment. We stopped outside his mother's house and
shook hands. He said:

"It never ends."

"Never!"

Story Number Five

THE REPRESENTATIVE

WHAT REMAINS in your imagination is the tick of the second hand, moving inexorably onward, punctuating the continuity of silence. Then your eyes focus, adjust from the winter darkness outside and you find yourself high up in a sort of Visitors' Gallery in the Transit Hall. It is, you think, like nothing that you have ever known, hence the difficulty in adjusting yourself, identifying what is going on, even grasping momentarily that you too have been here but had lost all memory of it. You are high among the steel trusses which bleakly support the roof; several floors below you are galleries, archives and offices which at this late hour are silent. For the work of this Transit Hall proceeds by principles which we may not immediately grasp, but not at such urgency that research need continue after set of sun. It is midwinter and the sun has set early.

At this late hour all the activity is concentrated on the ground floor of the hall, where the misty darkness is patterned by circular pools of light where shaded lamps illuminate the working desks of officials. The pattern is irregular for some desks are unattended. Up here the sound is diffused. . . the hush of footsteps coming and going, the broad glass swing doors on the left which open from time to time to admit on a tide of laughter, jubilation and feasting some unidentified figure; the narrow door too on the right with its strong piston spring through which from time to time a figure disappears into the bleak night wind. And all the time the second hand of the clock above you is sweeping out time in the human universe.

You surmise: travellers waiting to cross the frontier are dining, talking to friends, enjoying the warmth of each others' company in the lit hall to the left: when the time comes they bid casual farewell, enter the Transit Hall and the doors close on the warm secure world they have left. We watch them move unhurriedly to this desk or that; in coat and hat, scarf and gloves they are prepared for the cold. Their documents are scrutinized by an official whose face we cannot see; he may initial various entries or on occasion lift a telephone and ask some question of a controlling office. Sometimes too, shockingly unexpected, a loudspeaker among the steel girders crackles into life; a message of general or particular import booms down through the shadows; officials and travellers stand to attention to receive its tidings. The process is inexplicable, unlike what we have known at frontiers elsewhere, unhurried, yet intensely purposeful.

From this height we see no details of scutineers or scrutinized. We fall, as people invariably do, into the intense contemplation of an enigma, unable to impose a meaning on it because, as we said, we have been here ourselves only once before and recognition will come only when we cross the Transit Hall floor on our return. But we will try once more. A figure has just been wafted in from the right on a gust of warm identity. He goes to a desk and places his documents on a tray; there is a leafing through his dossier, a checking of his documents in order. The official speaks with the Controller and we guess that it is now time to leave. The official hands him an illuminated card of final instructions to read. We would like to read it also, but no matter, the same message will stand above the exit door and will be illuminated as he leaves. Of a sudden the loudspeaker crackles: officials and travellers stand; the Voice, to which we cannot ascribe any other quality than authority, says briefly: "27TGE 4XZ departs with our commendation and good wishes. We await regulation accomplishment." There is a shaking of hands, a buttoning up of documents as with a curt nod our traveller turns to the exit up right. Now as he stands formally before it we read the lettering glowing in red:

"To achieve 1% success, 100% effort is necessary."

Holding his lapels together and pulling his hat down over his brow, he pushes on the door and goes out into the darkness.

. . . .

Braced against the wind that buffeted him from the west and made him clutch at his hat, he turned at the end of the building into a drab road that led between high fences. Potholes filled with water mirrored the racing clouds. This was no man's land indeed, no man's business to keep it efficient and in order for travellers newly arrived from the neighbouring country. Tall buildings came towards him and he fancied that some of them were but façades with the luminous sky peeping through glassless windows. He presumed that this way, the only way, would be the right one and in any case he knew his first venue; he crossed to the other side to avoid the jeers of drunkards round a café door. But the experience was faintly disturbing so that he felt himself already insecure of the friends he had left behind . . . only the message on the card and above the door still burned in his memory.

He woke up late in the run-down hotel which was his first stop; outside curtainless windows a yellow-grey sky hung low over the façade of what seemed a neo-classical building, pillars, capitals, architrave and nothing behind it. It was far too late for breakfast and his train did not leave till late afternoon. He leaned over and fetched his documents from his inner pocket to check them through; his travellers' cheques and immediate currency, international driving licence, trading licence, his membership of societies. His passport presented to him his photograph as the camera saw him, not as he knew himself. And beneath was his name: POYNTON, MICHAEL, age 27, business representative, hair brown, eyes gray, mole on left side of cheek. "This is me, I suppose", he thought and smiled to think of the quaint convention of describing much longed for, much loved babies in terms of kilograms. Later he was to trace back to that moment a curious feeling of split in himself. As far as this country was concerned, he was a business rep come to work for the home firm, to make contacts, to enroll assistants and to push business in a country that was strange and by methods about which no-one had been able to give him any advice. Privately within himself and growing smaller every hour he was Michael Poynton of such and such an age, such and such physical features, something that was totally personal to himself and the friends he had left behind. He lay back on the pillow and pondered the eternal question: how does an alien establish himself in a new land? He thought of the thousands who had emigrated and found just this problem, of the thousands of refugees and displaced people to whom it had been a central anxiety. One thing was different for him. . . but in a sense it was always different for the individual. . . he was on his own. No face was ready to smile for him here, no hand prepared to reach out and grasp his own. "I am an intruder," he said aloud, "my first task will be to change that." In the back of his passport lay a plain white card headed with the name of his firm. He had seen it a few days ago when he was given his business documents. It stared at him now like something hostile. In the firm's print stood the words in small black (Helvetica medium?) capitals:

SHOULD ONE METHOD NOT SUCCEED, REVIEW
AND TRY ANOTHER

Below in typing which certainly had not been there before last night:

To achieve 1% success, 100% effort is necessary.

He looked at it with a momentary indignation, wondering how a good rep like himself expected to make. . . what was it? . . . 10,000% effort.

Now he had been for some weeks in his first destination, a considerable town in the interior and, thinking over it, he decided that he had not wasted time. There were people to meet, business conferences to attend, helpers to recruit (he had only had one success so far) but above all to decide on the type of promotional scheme he was to adopt. This, of course, depended partly on an assessment of the business climate and opportunities, partly on his sizing-up of the national characteristics and of the sort of effort which would impress. He liked to think that his decision would have nothing to do with the sort of person he remembered having been in his homeland. The assessment of his surroundings was surprisingly difficult. From the first moments of his train journey hither. . . he remembered comparing it with train journeys from Lima and La Paz. . . he was oppressed by the drabness and apathy of people. It was not national poverty, for needs seemed very basic and some sort of social security cared for perhaps sixty out of every hundred; nor was it that the life of the population seemed joyless. . . he saw adverts for all sorts of social events, but many were spectator sports or gambling activities or something akin to community drug-taking. But, he thought, the alien must go carefully and have no opinion at all until he is sure of his ground.

He wrote:

First appreciation of the situation after one month:

The principal obstacle to successful business promotion is the apathy of the people and the routine course of their lives. Plain business logic and favourable propositions do not wake a spark of interest.

Resolution:

People must be released from their "unimagination" which imprisons them. I must use shows diversions displays. . . anything that will bring them together and give them mass release. At that point business promotion begins. The whole effort must be in low key, the initiative couched in simplistic utterance, which will effect a delayed suggestion in the minds of those who are genuine clients.

Caveat:

The process may be wasteful in resources; many will be contacted, few affected.

With this resolution firm in his mind he set about arranging promotional meetings, sales drives, charity performances. Each began with a showy display, a vaudeville, a firework show (these drew huge numbers), the employment of conjurers or magicians (also very popular). With satisfaction he observed the stolid resistance breaking down, the light in the eyes, the vivacious talk, even the immediate and profound silence when he came to address them. Business was done; his order books received healthy lists of names and with the self-suggestion which he stood so much in need of, Michael felt he was making distinct headway and reported it to his firm; which however made no response. Not to lose impact, he stayed only for a limited time during that summer in any one town.

He wanted, as we all do, to believe in his personal success; he had however what we do not all have, an uncompromising estimate of things which was prepared to tolerate happy euphoria only for a short time. It was in a run-down seaside resort in the latter part of summer that the candy floss colours gave way to a brilliant grey assessment. He was walking as he often did in the evening, muffled against the stormy sea wind past closed kiosks and ice-cream huts and pier amusements which had not opened that summer for lack of sponsorship. Suddenly he stopped and spoke aloud into the wind: "Effectively it's all a failure. The crowds are there but the business is minimal. I must write express to the firm explaining my predicament." We can only guess how he felt in that cold wind on a rain-lashed promenade, if we put ourselves in his shoes and imagine ourselves the chosen rep, chosen perhaps out of hundreds, two-thirds of a year past and virtually no impact made.

He brooded in his lodgings; read this and that; frankly enjoyed himself in the company of young friends of his acquaintance. In self defence he expected no reply from his firm; when the envelope was there his heart leapt. But the buff card within it fell to the table as he read. . . yes, he almost knew what he would read:

Should one method not succeed, review and try another. Bitterness, that was the first reaction and a hollow laugh. Then came the necessary second thought: they are not surprised: they still trust me. He lay face down on his bed and thought awhile then wrote down:

Second appreciation after eight months:

Mass efforts are a dead loss. Unless I am prepared to be such a one as a politician and use the meretricious attraction of an assumed personality, I cannot reach the rank and file who assemble in large numbers. The best new deployment of my effort will be to cultivate individuals, as many as possible and by a kind of entrepreneurial Osmosis or Contagion (neither metaphor seemed quite respectable) to transmit successfully the fundamentals of business.

Resolution:

All spurious displays, mountebanking, fireworks discontinued forthwith. A new effort to approach people must be mounted. No cult of personality!

Caveat:

Beware of overpowering people by making them think you expect too much of them.

It was a relief that autumn to be done with the hollowness of showmanship, his face bright and laughing before and behind the set lips the mutter: Failure again. Poynton gathered about himself friends, some older, some younger, of both sexes, people who were real people, not just occupational ciphers; and he felt the genuine human warmth as the delicate bridges built between him and the others grew stronger with two-way traffic. Soon the groupings of his friends made a new world that was purposeful and creative beyond the sum of its members. He was later to remember long evenings when they wrestled with understanding and sought to build the picture of a new-structured world together. The slant of the times was different: logic, reasoning, computer talk were all left behind as irrelevant, playing no useful part in their plans. Only sometimes there was the uneasy jolt when they returned from their iridescent euphoria to the chill workaday world. But the magic wove its spell and Michael felt the weeks pass like an endless sublime fantasy. But when Michael was doing that, Poynton was sometime just mistrustful.

One bright winter day after the turn of the year, the group hired a bus and went to the hills. There was ringing frost on the low ground by the streams fringed with delicate ice and rimed grasses. The slopes were snow-clad and those who cared could ski and enjoy the exhilaration of sub-zero temperatures. Wrapped up in gloves and mufflers Michael climbed with a group of his friends to a view point, from which they looked inland to range upon range of snowy peaks, the delicately shaded violet and blue as the planes faced away from the sun. They were all silent with the beauty of it, none caring to demean the moment with a substandard comment. Then they sat around in a little log observation hut and fell to talking. Michael and Poynton were both there sitting side by side in the centre of the group; much was said, other things were implied, but these did not surface till later on.

Someone said: Had they never thought of going to X. . ., naming the capital city; surely the best opportunities of all would lie there? At the mention of it, immediately the temperature dropped. Simply and in broken sentences different people voiced apprehensions: the State Police, the Authorities, the arbitrary Law system, the well known xenophobia of the population there, the frequent disturbances, uprisings and ritual murders. Somehow it did not then seem so attractive, as all sorts of hindrances came to mind and the fear that they might just make no headway at all. Michael. . . or was it

Poynton? . . . recalled a momentary lull in the conversation when his imagination suddenly and idiotically screened: "100% effort is necessary". But they went back down and joined the others in the bus and spent the evening dining out at a country hotel.

During the next few days he slipped away to an upland village, where no one knew him. He. . . or they. . . had to get things in focus. Some internal tension. . . he felt it in his hands. . . troubled him about transfer of activities to the capital. You could weigh it up quite rationally, he thought, even making allowance for the reluctance to come into contact with the worst excesses of the National Character. A crazy economy had reduced most of them to dependence on the state dole: that he knew. Huge numbers of underemployed males always spelt trouble; at these times the veneer of civilization wore thin. As the authority of the state increased over a dependent population, laws were superseded or changed, justice was a summary and inexplicable procedure. Whole categories of people were proscribed, the unfit, the senile, mental cases, criminals, orphan children and any alien who fell foul of the Law. The names of voluntary suicides were mentioned with honour on the radio at midday. Everything in reason suggested the futility of a transfer to that location.

But there was this nagging "100% effort". Would anything less be 100% effort? Could he recross the frontier in the knowledge that he had shied before a challenge? Could he move alone to the Capital? (Answer: No way!) Would his friends go with him (he felt that some would). Whom would he contact there? Or would he return to firework displays, and conjuring? (Poynton said a very definite NO to that.) Or in the end was it a mere question of courage? He might be arrested on a misunderstanding on a dozen counts, not least that he was alien. What about his passport: would it be valid or treated with contempt? Here he remembered what he had never thought of since his arrival. Sewn into the seam of his jacket, just below the breast pocket was a plastic disc. He now felt it through the lining and ascertained that it was there.

That, the official had said rather vaguely, was his last resource and must on no account be lost. These thoughts occupied Poynton all of two days as he walked endlessly in lonely woodland paths. He wrote urgently to his firm for advice.

But all the while Michael was waiting his turn. A line of thought had started with him as he sat (with Poynton) among the young friends in the wooden mountain hut. He could not escape one appraisal. All were looking to him as a person in his own right, not merely as the firm's representative. Could it be that he had been shirking this issue too long? Could he be wrong to allow himself to be known as a person who was outgoing and had a sort of dynamic authority among them? The authority, of course, was not his own, rather lent to him. Was this the advice that his firm would now give him? But he was troubled: to cross from the secure limitation of being a representative to the vulnerability of a person in his own right, was an enormous step, perhaps an unauthorized step. When you are a person and a leader (he thought) you gather the hopes and expectation of others around you; you believe that you take your own decisions, but more and more you are a prisoner to their expectations. How strange is it then if, by being a Nobody-in-particular you are free to steer your course; but by being Someone you must inexorably live up to the expectations of the others around you!

Perhaps, if he took to himself the personal illumination of leadership, it would prove the release of. . . not so much power. . . imagination rather. He had tried spurious attractions, Poynton had, and the deep pervasiveness of personal friendship among equals. Was Poynton now admitting a total failure and Michael suggesting a new initiative? Somehow the city, if he approached it as a person, a leader, a lighthouse beacon that streamed forth imagination rather than reasoning. . . this way the city was tolerable; as a Non-entity never. That night he wrote again urgently to his firm outlining his new ideas. Then for a few days he was absolved from thought and simply enjoyed the articulation of the body and young blood.

He returned and his friends were soon around him. Where had he been? What had he been doing alone in that one-horse little village? Michael Poynton smiled and gave non-committal answers which left them wondering if he had another side to his nature. Two days later the firm's envelope arrived. He was speechless as he stared at the card. They must have a stock of millions of them:

> SHOULD ONE METHOD NOT SUCCEED, REVIEW
> AND TRY ANOTHER

It was, you would say, a shocking let-down. Yet, yet... as he pondered it, he knew that his letter had been received and read, his predicament understood. Perhaps even his suggestion had been approved... yes, approved. The more he thought, the more the card burned with authority in his jacket pocket. So he wrote:

Third Appreciation of the Problem After 14 Months:

Unrelated display and intellectual reasoning have proved unsatisfactory. The gulf of incomprehension between one person and another is basically not to be bridged by either method. Only when imaginative enthusiasm reaches such and such a "temperature", so to speak, does the requisite creativity take off, creativity that penetrates all impossibility and makes the fair vision a reality. The fundamental issue is: how to raise this temperature from nil to functional level; if not by logic and reasoning (and definitely not by logic and reasoning), then by imaginative effort. Why then did the original displays not succeed? Answer: because they were directed to those in whom it was not possible to raise enthusiasm. Question: do I not therefore know to whom I am directing my effort? Answer: that too involves reasoning and you must deny yourself the luxury of that security. Further question: how does one raise enthusiasm-temperature in others?

Michael decided to allow a few days to elapse before he committed himself to an answer to that question. When the smoke and dust of irrelevant hopes and fears had cleared, he wrote down:

Resolution:

I must henceforth see myself as a personal representative: the Personal is the spearhead to the Representation. Those who are concerned (and I will not always know who they are) must take fire in their imagination from my performance as a Person. Anonymous non-identity is finished: in the next episode I am the firm. Thus only will I have strength and confidence.

Caveat:

Humanly I am apprehensive because I do not know whom I am addressing nor in what direction I am going. This will be the time for self-discipline and personal decision.

From that point onward a change came over the group. The matter-of-fact business procedure gave way to a pyramidal organization, something Poynton ruefully thought, like a way-out transatlantic religious sect. The eyes of all were on the Leader who provided direction, vision and inspiration. Straightaway some friends returned home, not to reappear. They left sometimes without announcing it, without at least a cheerful good-bye, probably out of confusion and uncertainty and a true feeling that they no longer belonged there. Michael was vexed at their lack of candour, though he was the first to assert that active involvement was infinitely preferable to mere human loyalty. Those who remained fell in with the organization of the group and their own personal role. Many would not have their Leader's commitment to the extrapolated Vision and were more and less assailed with logical doubts and questionings from time to time. But the fire in them burned hotter and the moment came when the move to the capital seemed to them less of a risk and more of an imaginative enterprise which most were glad to undertake.

The Poynton half felt that the arrival in the city was just a little ridiculous, if not embarrassing. They had hired an old General Transport bus which had seen better days, with

Michael at the wheel and adverts and posters stuck all over it. All were in a state of high enthusiasm, even hilarity, but the few early morning pedestrians who were about when they arrived either did not turn to look at them or curled the lip in contempt. Michael looked curiously at the scene, the towering flashy rectangular modernity of the streets, the garish and tasteless displays in the shops, the cartons and rubbish that blew about in the cold north wind. They had an address to go to and soon settled in.

The group had resolved to avoid all excessive behaviour and draw no attention to itself, for the first few days at least. The place was filled with sightseers, cultural folk whom you could tell by their earnest looks and the official guide book in their hands; and proletarians who seemed to have no internal purpose of their own unless they were marshalled in queues at bus stops or outside the (to them) incomprehensible monuments of the past. It soon became clear that wherever the friends went there was always the seedy-looking middle-aged man in the offing with trilby hat, tashed raincoat and down-at-heel shoes. Heinz, a young German friend, called them Zopiloten and the name stuck. Nevertheless they too went about and queued before the cultural monuments and in the meantime the two administrative secretaries arranged public meetings. These passed off, you might say, satisfactorily with even some show of fervour from the audience; but the presence of the Zopiloten cast a blight on the proceedings. As Heinz said, you could just about smell them. They could not know that their every move was being monitored in a room on the tenth floor of the Police Presidium, while the authorities maintained some irresolution about them. Perhaps they might even have lost interest in such a harmless bunch of people (Mayflies was their name for people of that kind) knowing that a whiff of disapproval or danger would send them back to the stupid towns in the provinces from which they had come. Perhaps. . . but this is to assume choice and no accident.

An outdoor meeting was scheduled for a Tuesday afternoon in a great open concrete square where in summer

everyone paraded in the evenings in something like the Spanish paseo. The day was bright and cold : a large audience was
expected : the friends were excited and happy. Only Michael
conning his facts and figures in a small room, felt irrationally
gloomy. He remembered the 100% of course. . . it was almost
the only thing Poynton had to say to him now. . . but so
many disturbing stories had come to his ears about this
Government. It was wrestling with intolerable economic
problems and with a population several times greater than
could support itself or be supported. It had given up in
despair its historical heritage, the co-operation of all classes
and conditions of people and had replaced it by a brutal
subdivision into Essentials and Expendables. Michael felt
vaguely that he could stand only so much of this before
something in him broke. At this moment when he was
conning his facts and figures, he was nearer that point than he
knew.

When the time came they sallied forth to an area of the city
where he had not been before and reached the assembly place
well before time. Organization was good ; microphones and
pot plants decorated the platform ; old faded placards of the
State Leaders had been temporarily removed. Michael's enthusiasm had returned, as he felt a great compassion for
people who lived such an undervalued existence. They stood
before him, their dull dog-like faces looking up for something
that might signify that they too were after all significant. He
looked at his watch and longed for the moment when proceedings would start. Momentarily he turned and stared at the
building behind them. He recognized it at once from descriptions in the guide book, the former Cathedral which had once
served the religious function in the city. A footnote in the
book had told him that religion had been declared irrelevant
and, while not forbidden, was cultivated by a minority of
elderly and immature persons. Michael recognized the cathedral, romanesque in style with tall pillars and a processional
stairway. But what rooted him to the spot was the red neon
sign (the 100% had been in red neon also) slung between and
in front of the pillars, announcing

KUMFIDEATH

In a blinding second he knew he was standing before the State Institute for voluntary suicide, the practical and ever more popular solution to the problem of excess and unwanted population. Perhaps you have forgotten, perhaps never known the impact of a totally new idea. In our lives thoughts follow as a glittering chain, every one linked somewhere to something formerly experienced. Then comes something new, the experience of the earthquake, of total solitude, or, as here, Man's final assessment of the basic worthlessness of his fellow Man. Later Michael had a little time to think things out in order; at that moment something went up in fire within him. He turned, on being invited to speak, and spoke as he had never spoken before. In a blazing eruption he denounced a system that sacrificed everything to politics and economics. His friends gasped: the crowd swayed with emotion: the sleazy men slunk for cover into doorways. Turning he pointed to that building, the symbol of their slavery and defeat. They were with him, surging around, bellowing. Then suddenly it happened: something was thrown: and with a crash the letter D was hanging crazily down, its glass smashed and all the neon display extinguished. Who had thrown the missile was never quite clear; two of his friends later told Michael in fearful whispers that he had slung a water decanter at it in the climax of his address. At that the crowd melted away and the friends beat a hasty retreat along lesser streets back to their hotel. Late into the night the debate raged among them, whether Michael had not now become a liability and that the city project should be abandoned at once. Michael and Poynton met alone in the upstairs room.

Poynton: That's torn it.
Michael: I don't care.
Poynton: They will blame you.
Michael: I'm not sure but that's the way it goes.
Poynton: Your friends? What about them? Are they to share your danger?

Michael: If I were a naive idealist, I would say, yes. But I'm not.
Poynton: You mean, they'll leave you?
Michael: Put yourself in their shoes, wouldn't you?
Poynton: It's hardly success to allow events to take over.
Michael: Who knows? I just had a thought, like a flash of sunlight on a cloudy day. Maybe even this is the 100%... even all that's going to happen.
Poynton: Is it?
Michael: I think... maybe I see the way back to the frontier.

The events of the next few days were confused and took on a dream-like quality. We are accustomed to keep order in our comings and goings by calling on the logic of events, mistaking the limitations and structure of mind for the true face of reality. A century or two of popular Science has imbued us with the faith of Cause and Effect, the inevitability of beginnings and ends, illusions which the mediaeval alchemist or the hermit in his mossy cell would have found alien enough. We are like inexperienced swimmers who fear to cast away our floats; we do not dare to face a reality where nothing is inevitable, where EITHER.. OR can sometimes read BOTH... AND. In what were, after all, the few days till the adventure was over, Michael never ceased to wonder at the improbability of things, never ceased at each turn of events to look for the less logical more invalid consequences.

The events of that disastrous afternoon in the square filled all with apprehension. They went out little on to the streets, their talk was subdued, unemotional. At night there was especial tension when from their apartments they could look over the vast city burgeoning with lights; it murmured with human activity, was sometimes punctuated by cries, sirens or shots, then the silence soon filled again with the great polyphonic murmur. They feared the hammering on the doors at four in the morning when people are at their most vulnerable and compliant. When two days had passed and the authorities had shown no reaction, Michael became aware in himself of a strange feeling of cynicism : that business of the smashing of the D in the sign, had it been but a meaningless gesture, the heroics of a small boy cocking a snook at authority. . . and authority simply disregarded him. And there was another thing. From the moment that he had resolved to don a persona. . . and they had all consented to it. . . he felt himself distanced from them. Before that point they had all been together, sharing a vast imaginative enterprise, all of them looking to him for a lead, for guidance, for commendation. Now they still looked to him, but there was a distance. The look of incomprehension often visited their eyes and the questions on their lips were not those of people who actively shared in decision-making. In principle this was an unhappy development. Poynton broke his silence to comment that by implication their Group was finished, unless some return to their former togetherness were achieved. Michael agreed gloomily. . . and set about thinking how he should manage a return to the situation where the cell as a whole, not merely himself, decided its movement and direction.

It all seemed too improbable. The world of the city went its way and paid no attention to them. Even the greasy Zopiloten were not much in evidence. Some of the friends began to enjoy the heightened tempo of life, the raw garishness with which human needs were underlined and catered for. So long as you did not look up or peered at the rubbish in the corners, it was a brave new world, a decided advance on the inhibited standards of the provincial towns. Then one evening the bubble burst. Michael and a few others were strolling along Victory Avenue with the cherry trees in bloom and a fresher green on the grass plots on the pavements. He was suddenly hemmed in by half-a-dozen citizens while two police vans, sirens screaming, closed in on his other side. Handcuffs were snapped on him and a hard object thrust in his back. Over by a shop window he saw one of his friends desperately torn between an act of martyrdom and one of flight. He winked slowly at him. . . and the other turned to the shop and feigned indifference. Then he was in the van and they hurried off, he could not tell where. Presumably the little tableau in the

Avenue was of too frequent an occurrence to arouse any interest and anyway it was better never to appear interested.

The van door opened and Michael found himself propelled down several flights of steps and pushed into a pitch-dark room, filled with breathings and human sounds and the stale emanations of bodies. Events had outdistanced him and he was left to catch up with himself. He slumped on a bench beside someone and allowed himself to return to a state of relative calm. In fact he nearly fell asleep until he found a hand exploring the contents of his pockets; he thrust it away in disgust and remained in a state of semi-wakefulness.

His first examination took place next morning before a group of city magistrates who enquired civilly about his name, address, nationality, and provenance; they examined his passport then returned it. They informed him that while he had been found guilty of sundry offences, he would be examined next day by the chief Prosecutor who would pronounce sentence and subsequently read out charges and produce witnesses. Was he not, asked a genial magistrate, ashamed of damaging State Property and casting a slight on the kindly provision of the Great Leader for all superfluous citizens to do their patriotic duty? Michael was silent, not, be it noted, from a resolve to give no further offence but out of a strange awareness that his world was coming unstuck at the corners. There was, after all, if you looked at it one way a kindly provision in KUMFIDEATH and his own behaviour (if he really had thrown the decanter) quite inexcusable. Seeing that he made a sorry figure and could find nothing to say, the magistrates dismissed him and the guards took him at the frog march down three flights of steps, turned to the left and thrust him into a little cell of which he was the solitary occupant.

The day passed slowly in the darkness: food was handed in twice; he slept soundly at the beginning to make up for the broken night before. Then he awoke and thought long about events, the arrest, the imprisonment in the mass cell and the first examination. He had to wrestle hard with it all to align it in a sensible way; and he did not quite succeed in doing this.

He thought of the friends and hoped vaguely that they were on their way out of town by now. Oddly enough (Poynton suggested that "heartlessly" was a better word) it was as if they had blown away from him as irrelevant as the night rubbish in the windswept streets. He fancied that he weighed less, was thinner or smaller but this he knew to be false. In the darkness he checked over his passport and other documents and almost as an afterthought felt for the disc in the lining behind his pocket; it was there. But realizing that he had never handled it he tore at the lining until he could insert two fingers and fetch it out. As he held it in his hand he was aware of a strange tension which filled him not only with a marvellous confidence but also the edge of a certainty that present events, however unpromising, were aligned on some track of purpose which just escaped him for the moment. He slept and was still asleep when the door opened and the guard thrust in a tin basin of water, instructing him to wash and shave as the Prosecutor would arrive presently. He had peeled the disposable razor and soaped himself with some difficulty in the darkness, when the door opened again and the guard carried out the basin and razor, leaving him unshaven and vulnerable. He struggled to put himself to rights before the guard was once more jerking him up three flights of stairs and into the Presence Chamber.

Proceedings began with a lengthy recital of his misdeeds, his anti-People attitudes, his failure to accord sufficient praise to the State leader, the formalism of his approach to State problems and his general rejection of the State Ethos. For this he had been condemned. Had he anything to say?

Here Poynton took over rather abruptly and was prepared to challenge anti-democratic proceedings (strange how one always assumes (theoretical) democracy to be right for every occasion). After he had uttered two words, a State Guard, standing to his right, took two smart steps forward and struck him down the right side of his face with his rubber truncheon. "What you did not know," said the Prosecutor, "is that all petitions are pronounced in terms of (it sounded like) 'Your Extravagance'".

Poynton hastily reprogrammed to include this input in his performance. "Your Extravagance, my Passport, which I see you have in your hand freely negotiated by the sovereign state of which I am a member, grants me safe conduct in situations such as these. I demand. . ." Here the guard on his left side struck him with his rubber truncheon. "Incorrect procedure," said the Prosecutor. "In any case, Demand refused. Do you think Life is a game to be played at like politics? In any case, how do you know who you are?"

"Your Extravagance," said Poynton with painful memories on each side of his face, "I have a disc here, an identity disc. . ."

But even as he spoke and began the search for it, he knew himself defenceless, discless. After a futile search, he smiled, threw up his hands and shrugged his shoulders.

"You see," said the Prosecutor.

Then a small man, red-cheeked like a crab apple, who had been dozing at the far end of the hall repeated, "You see", then "Call the testimonies."

In filed a group of persons shabbily and uniformly dressed in Poverty Clothing.

"Is the Prisoner guilty?"

And they replied like schoolchildren reciting a poetry lesson, "Mani-fest-ly guilty".

Michael and Poynton both looked at them, miserable proletarians, and while the latter turned away in disgust, the former looked again to make sure that it was two of the friends who were in their number.

"And you are guilty?" asked the Prosecutor, posing a self-incriminating question.

"Your Extravagance," Poynton replied, "by your reasoning, not mine, I am guilty. I am still under your protection."

"Pish!" said the Prosecutor, "is this a University debate?"

"You will be removed forthwith and deported from these territories."

With a kindly smile he dismissed him and the guards hustled him down to a waiting room on the ground floor.

Michael Poynton (his official name though only he could vouch for it) sat in a waiting-room like many another from which he might have been summoned to a dentist's chair or an interview. The wall clock pursued its scheduled activity with a particularly loud tick and at the quarters uttered asthmatic groans, as though it would have chimed had it not suffered some ectomy of its joyful parts. Somehow time no longer mattered; he was effectively out of time. He felt too a strange dissolution. Reasoning and systematic argument has all become a part of what the Prosecutor had styled University debate. Trailing consequences and causal action no longer gave any grid reference to the Present. Above all the True and the False had merged so that he kept seeing the one through the other; there was no sure ground. Strange, he thought: this must be the experience of those who look for the first time on their portrait; the world calls it well done, praising the angle of the head, the jut of the chin and the penetrating arrest of the eyes; but the Proteus within us, the Saint and the Sinner that is most of us laughs drily in a corner. . . only movement discloses him.

"Who am I, anyway?" he said aloud, extending his fingers before him. "I have been several socially acceptable people in the last two years; am I one of these? Or am I my function seeking the 1% achievement by the 100% effort?" These thoughts occupied him on that still morning but grew increasingly academic and remote.

At ten by the clock a working citizen entered and greeted him civilly. He wore the badge of solidarity, the faded Poverty Clothing, and carried a wooden case, no doubt filled with the tools of his trade. He sat and smoked a wicked-looking self-rolled cigarette, but apart from a muttered, "Sorry I can't offer you one, mate," he stared apathetically now at the floor, now at the dust motes that danced in a sunbeam. At exactly twenty minutes past ten he muttered something like "We'd better be going" and got up; Michael Poynton did likewise. "You carry that," said the man, indicating the tool case. So they left by a back entrance and made their way through hopeless streets where dirty washing hung in the gloom, and barricaded windows may have spelt unoccupied houses. Michael was all the while trying to orient himself. He could have been in the gloomy hopelessness of a back-street in Bogota or Chicago; or one of the shrill lanes in the University district of Naples. What few people were about either paid them no attention or stared as if their passing did not register as movement. In one street, broader but no less squalid than the rest, two women, busy devouring some bit of scandal together on an open staircase stopped and stared and said almost simultaneously, "Oh, the poor soul". Elsewhere an apple core dropped on his head. Michael realized that he could not now find his way back to the Palace of Justice and followed meekly, carrying the tool case.

In twenty minutes they reached the Railway Station. Since his original journey Michael had seldom patronized the State Railways, which were one-class and only used by the more immobile proletariat. Here were hundreds waiting on the concourse, camping amongst piled up boxes and battered cases, children squalling, snivelling or sleeping everywhere, their mothers enthroned like lesser queens and their shiftless and unshaven husbands who grew more hopeless and desperate with each hour that passed. No trains were visible. A brightly painted signboard announced that: A TRAIN WILL DEPART FOR. . . but it gave no hope of a destination.

"Are we going somewhere?" Poynton asked the citizen; he gave a curious crafty look and said, "You could put it that way", then switched out and became anonymous once more. They went across to a sort of buffet, where, despite the crowds camping on the concourse, there were few customers. Michael surmised that you had to have some official status to use such places, and this his citizen had. They sat at a chipped plastic table and looked gloomily at the scene. As there seemed no possibility of conversation, the two of them gazed all round the place, without ever allowing their glances to meet. People from the platform, unshaven men and blowsy-looking females kept flattening their noses against the glass of the windows and staring into the buffet. In their existences, so empty of incident, anything that focussed attention even for a second or two was abundant life. Michael felt vaguely that he knew some of these faces, knew them quite well but he was too far from them now in time to summon up a name. They stared with a shameless curiosity and he felt himself increasingly naked in front of them.

When some point or other had been reached, the citizen asked him for money to buy a coffee. Poynton had only a large note and handed it over, saying, "Get me one also". The citizen stared at him, then said something like, "Better not for you. . . better if they don't drink". He shambled across to the counter. Poynton felt that the contours of his world were crumpling. Reason had gone out of it and human values. Now his identity was so far gone that he felt himself only a rude sketch of what he had been. The world outside, that world of the concourse, was a thousand miles away, a procession of grimacing puppets which had no more to do with him. He tried to think back over the two years he had spent in this land, the high hopes, the constant reappraisal of his task, his preoccupation with his identity. All these struggles had been real in one set of dimensions, yes; but in the end the reality which he felt himself drawn to had a totally other set of dimensions, that made of his life here a series of bubbles, dreams, nightmares. . .

(the citizen was esconced on a high stool at the counter, drinking his coffee no doubt and in animated conversation with the coffee woman)

. . . And this business of the 1% success: what a cruel charade! Back home he might hope for an understanding appraisal of his difficulties; he had been given absolutely nothing to go on, no advance briefing, no back-up, no special facilities. If one method proves unsatisfactory, try another. . . so read the firm's unfailing advice. But truly (he thought with momentary grimness) if he were the assessor, he would have pronounced: Failure, total and utter, not even a fraction of a percent success. Poynton (for Michael appeared no longer there) felt the edge of bitterness, resentment, self pity, but he was far too disciplined for that sort of thing and quickly oriented his thoughts on the main problem. What after all is

1% and 100% even if you translated them into 'infinitely small' and 'total and complete'? What did they signify? And even more so in terms of success. What would success be? Would it be obvious, self-disclosing, the cheering crowds, the warmth of engulfing smiles? Or would success never be able to be estimated here on our terms, but would be discernible only through the diffraction of another sort of reasoning? When he got to that point he suddenly felt time stand still: it was as if he were on the end of the axis of something, turning soundlessly, effortlessly.

"I think we'd better get on with this," said the citizen, suddenly recalling him from his preoccupation. "Don't you?"

"I suppose so", said Poynton, with him in several ways but still gloriously turning, moving without going anywhere. He smiled at the citizen. "Anything you suggest?"

The citizen had opened the tool-box and to Poynton's astonishment it was filled, crammed with all sorts of dreary adolescent rubbish, studded belts, comics, a marshal's hat, motor-cycle gloves. The man rummaged in it, emptying it all on the floor until he found an imitation Luger pistol (a good imitation, maybe even not an imitation). He waved it about, pretending to be some sort of Storm Trooper.

Meanwhile Poynton, seated metaphorically on his revolving spindle of necessity (but actually on a bentwood chair), saw the window of the buffet all steamed up by the crowds of peering faces, children sitting on the shoulders of men, even a few women. He suddenly thought:

"I have in effect died: I can expect death in a few moments. There is nothing left to do, but go."

The citizen then came forward, held the Luger to Poynton's forehead and squeezed the trigger. It clicked. The man threw it childishly away on the ground, swearing loud and long by some defunct deity.

"Let me have it", said Poynton, holding it carefully so that the barrel pointed at no-one. He broke it open and fished out the remains of an old cartouche from a chamber of it. He checked it over, handing it back and nodding to the citizen. By now the time for words was past, spoken words or thought words. There was only the still revolving axis, the unconcerned environment and the crowds staring through the glass with a hungry lust for sensation.

The citizen tried again. There was an enormous explosion which rocked the building and disproportionate volumes of acrid smoke billowed forth. Reverently he stowed the remains under the table, gathered up his bric-à-brac, and went out on to the anonymity of the concourse.

. . . .

You are standing once more in the gallery of the Transit Hall, whether you or your surrogate is immaterial, for life is endless and the continuity of personalities is ever being twisted into a new beginning, woven in time and unravelled. If you were there on the previous occasion you have doubtless been preoccupied at a deep level, deeper than worry but well above forgetfulness, by the enigma of the percentages.

Travellers who fare forth are always invited to read and memorize this message and rumour has it that the wiser of the Civil Servants far below will estimate the success of the journey then being undertaken by the response that the travellers make on reading. What after all is the point of confronting a traveller with a ludicrous criterion of success? Is nothing due to happiness, to pleasure, to the service of others and friendship? Do we travel on business only, not, say, to inform ourselves, broaden our horizons and stimulate wonder? You have pondered this and have maybe felt that like an incomplete psychiatric dream you must repeat the circumstances in the hope that the dream will utter itself in completeness. That is why you will not have been able to rest until you returned, you or your surrogate, to your lofty perch among the steel trusses and the cliff of galleries offices and archives.

It is again night, though at what season we have no way of telling. Behind and above you the clock with its shuddering tick marks time in the human world. Far below where the pools of light punctuate the darkness the curious ritual of arrival and departure enacts itself. You watch the double doors on the left, the small single door on the right, the door with the strong piston to keep it shut. Officials are busy in their unhurried way. We see the outgoing clients in coat and scarf, men and women, present their documents; we note the officials who communicate with Head Office and are occasionally alerted by the crackle of loudspeakers up in these girders and a definitive pronouncement. On these occasions all stand and listen with solemnity. We see the neon sign burn red above the small door and no longer need to strain to read its bizarre message. Elsewhere arriving travellers push through the small door and go to a desk where they present their credentials.

In a quieter moment a traveller arrives, stands a moment to orient himself, then walks shadowless and foreshortened beneath us to a desk. The official shakes hands; the traveller presents his documents; there is a telephone conversation. Then comes a crackle from the loudspeaker at which all the officials stand.

The Voice: Which traveller has returned?

The voices: (hushed and like the responses in a cathedral) The returning traveller is 27TGE 4XZ

The Voice: What have we to report of him?

The voices: He has made one percent success.

The Voice: Quote then the rubric;

The voices: (uplifted and jubilant) To achieve one percent success one hundred percent effort was necessary. We await the statement of elucidation.

The Voice: (terrifying in its echo, swooping around us and filling the shadows, but at the centre so small) And the secret of it all is that one percent is all that is required.

SEONAIDH

AND THE DREAM is alive: only with waking comes the sorrow. You have surely had the experience: wakened warm and happy with voices of the past still ringing in your ears, loved ones, distant ones. You knew the cadence, the laughter; you were so much at home in their company that you took your relationship for granted. When the curtain came down, when the boat pushed off from the quay, there they were happy as you had known them, with the characteristic stance and the little gestures you recognized so well. Only with the waking did you realize that you were waving distractedly to them, but they took no notice: they saw you not. Only then were you aware of a relationship that had snapped and a sorrow succeeded to the warm happiness of the night. So I found it one October morning. What fantasy had passed the doors of my perception or where or when or how it did, I cannot know. The face was a face I had never seen, but it was sun-browned and laughing, with the innocent laughter of a girl against the sparkle of sunlight on the incoming tide, her black hair loose to the wind and the light of triumph in her eyes. And the lovely life of her in her seventeen years of sojourn in the world, forged in a silence that she had not chosen, laughed to me strong and confident from the dark eyes. The waves danced and fingered their way among the ribbed sands of the Traigh Mor. Only with waking did the eyes stare at me lustreless from the waves and the hair woven with sand and tangle was the only moving thing in the inching waters. She receded from me, the light and the life gone; I was no longer with her or about her, but barred and banned as only real life can do it. The sorrow came and imparted itself to me.

Old Mrs Macdonald says:

I well remember the year when Calum Morrison came back from the fishing and brought with him the girl from Lewis. He came back long after the other men had returned to their crofts in our township facing the Minch. They had wed, so it was said, in the Registry Office, he a grandson of Alexander Morrison who had wrought great things among us, she not even a Lewis girl, no, that she could not have been . . . from Perth or Glasgow or somewhere down in Scotland. And they wed in the Registry Office. You can imagine that caused quite a stir; but Calum's croft, that he inherited from his father, lay beyond the township towards the moor: and for some days they kept to themselves and no-one knew what they were making of it. Some felt that the hand of friendship should be extended to them; but the Church Members were affronted and it was said that with the Minister and much praying they were directed to have nothing to do with folk who had so insulted Jesus by marrying in such a place, and she not even a Lewis girl who had learned her Gaelic at her mother's knee, but in some school or college.

But it goes hard not to speak or to make a civil enquiry and you passing the house on the way to the peat banks; and there were some who did . . . I was one of them . . . and a friendlier creature you could not find. But it was difficult, you understand, for the folk looked over their shoulders at one another, wives at husbands, daughters at their own mothers. And it was said that the chief Elder . . . Alexander McColl of Fawbost it was . . . interceded mightily against this thing that had happened, and prayed that such folk should have no issue or if they had, that it be as the fruit of the accursed fig tree. I thought that terrible, not being one of the elect myself and reckoned that after all God would have a more liberal view of things than Alexander McColl of Fawbost. So bit by bit there were doors opened to them and the Lewis girl was seen at the store and the Post Office; and rumour had it that she and her Calum were wondrous suited to each other.

They were with us in these years but were blessed with no family. So that the Members made bold to say that the arm of the Lord was strong to reject the malefactor, and they were not a little smug about it, which I thought, and not I alone, showed little true Christianity. In the season Calum went to the fishing with the others . . . always well-liked he was, a strong gentle fellow and he never swore. And the girl minded the croft, worked with the cattle and the oatfield and you often heard her singing in her house as you passed, so that folks said she could not be all that unhappy. And she just lived for her man's return. Then on the third year she was with child. There was much talk in the township and some of the women defied their men and went to her to see how they could help. I don't know what the Members thought; but I was in my place that Sunday morning, when the Minister . . . I will not mention his name . . . preached from Exodus, how the righteous God would visit his wrath on the unborn children of the first, second and third generation of them that obeyed not his ordinances. If this was not the calling down a curse on an unborn child, I do not know what his purpose was, for the text had no meaning else for us. I did not go back to the Church for many a long day and I was not alone.

Roderick McEwan, old Roddy to his friends, now a bit stiff and arthritic puffed on his pipe: he called to mind the days of the fishing, the long haul, sometimes to Yarmouth or Grimsby. So much had changed as the Western Seaboard tried to keep its footing on the shaky European economy. I listened fascinated; then asked about Calum. He thought long, so that I imagined he had not known him. But it was only the uneasy process of sorting out impressions which had been flung like old rope ends in a corner.

A strange young man . . . he said at length . . . one of us, but different: he never touched a drop nor swore nor blasphemed. He would sing and laugh like the best of us and he was the most honest worker I ever knew. But then he would

fall silent and the others just knew to let him be. I never
understood what he did with his great silences. His father,
you know, had had a drink problem and had driven the
mother to despair . . . she ended her life in the deep water by
the rocks of Innisdougarie. Calum inherited that old man as
his problem and I'll not be saying it wasn't a mercy when
pneumonia following a drinking bout in winter carried him
off. Of course there were voices raised . . . you know the
people . . . And after that Calum never came to the Church.
Nor did the Lewis girl whom he married in the Registry
office. But they made a good life of it together and Calum was
a grand fellow to know in the night at sea or when a storm
bore down from the north-west. A grand fellow! I wonder,
do you know where he is now?

Mrs Malloch clearing stones from the outfield near the gate,
straightened herself and looked down through the years at my
question:
  Our croft was next to Calum's, you would say a hundred
yards or more up the peat road. In the three years since the
Lewis girl came among us, I had been in her house quite often
and she in mine less often; for my mother that lived with us at
83 was rigid in her views and a Church Member all her life.
Especially when Calum was away at the fishing we would sit
together at our work and I would tell her of Uladale and
Fabost and who was married to whom and who was in
America; and she would tell me of the grand places in
Scotland and the easy unrighteous lives of the folk in these
parts. We were quiet friends together and understood each
other. And I knew before all the rest of the child that would
be. As it was her first and my three were all growing up I
could advise her and help her . . . women's things that you
would not be wanting to know. The birth was to be in
September when Calum was home again. But one day late in
August I saw her queerly and would send for the midwife.
She did not want her; I insisted but not too much. And well it
was because that woman was elsewhere . . . you understand
she had a little drink problem, her life had been hard and

unrewarding. So I cared for the girl myself and many an evil look I had from my own mother. Then when Calum was still a week away it came on her and there was no avoiding it. I sent for the midwife but she would not come. "God would not be wanting to find me in such a house," she said. So I made the preparations and with my twelve-year-old daughter to help, we delivered her safely and the little daughter lay in a small cot beside her. And when she was through the worst, we prayed together, she and I, and gave thanks that it had gone so well.

Then they all came, folks who had not stooped under the lintel before and brought things for her as only Highland folk with the big heart will do. But the Members were wroth; you could see it in their faces; I believe they would have been more charitable had she been a Hindu or some South Sea Island pagan woman. Then Calum came home and mother and daughter did well and Calum went round and thanked the folk who had been so kind. Then in November when the weather was bright and calm they went off for some days to visit her friends in Lewis and there the child was christened Seonaid. Not, mind you, as far as the Good Folk of the township were concerned; they would have it that the child was never christened and was fallen into the clutches of the Adversary.

Meanwhile my mother had relented and went one afternoon with a little gift to visit the woman and her child. I was out helping with the peats and found my mother at home again in her chair. She looked at me queer-like and said: That child is either of God or of the Devil. She had sensed something and I'll not be saying I did not sense it myself, though I have not the second sight. You see the child lay so still and happy and with round dark eyes; she made not a sound. I sensed too that the girl was worried but we did not talk. It was just after Christmas when Calum told me, one day of a westerly gale: She's deaf mute; the doctor in Stornoway found this out. But don't be saying anything in the township. Then turning to me with a sort of despairing look he said: Those ones will know why that is.

So the years passed and there were no brothers or sisters for her. Little Seonaid was a lovely graceful child who walked and did other things so early, but never a sound came from her when we were there. Somehow her mother spoke to her and the child understood with her heart if not with her ears. I think she made sounds, queer animal-like noises but her mother taught her: never when anyone else is about. Seonaid loved her father and mother and when we came about the house she made us so welcome with her laughing eyes and little outstretched hands. I heard many a one say that it did them a service to be in the presence of that child, which was maybe daft, but maybe just a way of saying something else.

I am Angus McEachern, Head teacher of the Junior school on this island; I was the sole teacher of the Primary school of Uladale and Fabost in these years. I remember Calum coming to me one evening after work was over and telling me of his child. Some months later I was able to attract a Child Guidance doctor to the village and he spent some hours studying the little one. It was a classic case, he said, and short of the family moving to the populous south, he could offer no solution, no solution that would be realistic, that is. She could get no help from school and the other children, imbued with the wickedness of their elders might make her life a misery. Better that she be brought up by her mother to habits of industry than crushed in the social millstones of the school playground. He went away; he was a realistic man; but I felt that this must not be the whole story.

I used to go round to them on a Thursday evening, when Calum was at home . . . for propriety's sake, you understand. The child was four, not yet of school age and together with the parents, especially the mother, we worked out ways of contacting her mostly through the eyes and by her movement in response. I became absorbed in this problem and corresponded with experts in Inverness. I had a recorder and could play quite well. One evening I played and the child sat upright watching me and, you would say, listening with her body. When I changed my rhythm her eyes danced and when

I made a funny little squiggle of sound, she laughed, a deep throaty laugh. I taught the father and mother how to use the recorder and the mother came on quickly for she read music. When Seonaid was just five, we gave her a little recorder and incredibly she watched my movements and began to make my sounds. How she did it, she with no hearing, was the wonder of those days but her parents besought me to say nothing of it in the community. Alas for me, when she was still six years old, my career took me away to this island and I but seldom heard of her. But I thought: what would it be if a man learned no words but experienced only music? I think we use words as the hand-holds, building our personality, giving us something sure . . . something we can return to, as the climber rams his pitons into a rock. But what would the world be like that came largely on the wings of music? But we won't ever know. I heard all about it and I was grateful for the little part I had played.

I sought out the sister of Seonaid's mother; she said:

I visited my sister in Uladale when little Seonaid was maybe eight years old. Oh, it's easy to romanticize: Western Isles and cloudless skies and the sparkle on the water and all that. I did not really like it. The crofting life is all right, I suppose, if you are brought up to it, but I thought it just . . . nasty . . . and so terribly limited. Of course I did not say so. I helped in the house and went out only with the little girl, for the folks would turn their back on me and stop in the middle of their conversation as though they did not wish to be over-heard speaking the Gaelic. Oh, they were civil enough if I spoke, but I just had the feeling that my being my sister's sister was just too much for them to bear.

But, mind you, the visit was worth all the trouble only to be with the girl. She was sturdy and strong and led me over the moor and along the shore, pointing out things that a townie like me didn't really understand. She would nudge me and make little grunts, little quiet sounds that were different and meant different things. She would sit on a headland with me just out of the wind watching the birds . . . fulmars or cormorants I think . . . sometimes absorbed watching a wild bee nuzzling up to heads of the sea pink. She had the most intense observation and interest in everything; I thought one night as I lay in bed that it was as if the daylight and the tide were shining through her eyes. Only the silence was uncanny. Most of us need to be talking, I think to reassure ourselves that we are what we think we are. She simply was and needed no sound; except of course her music, and that made my flesh creep. She played on her recorder so beautifully and making correct notes and keeping time. But how was it possible, she who could not hear the waves crashing on the shore? Or could she? Could she hear with some other part of her? I never did make out. But I think it was well for her that it was just gulls and waves and the folk trundling carts from the peat banks and not the city street. She grew up a fine girl but strangely alone, except for her mother who had instant communication with her. I often wondered what the end of the tale would be, when she grew up. Well, well, things have a way of sorting themselves out and so it was with little Seonaid.

John Murdoch of the Forestry Commission said:
Our house, Camus an Righ, stood back from the village about a mile. My job was the charge of the forestry over an area twenty miles by eight . . . not all forest you understand, but plantings of different ages. We had crofting labour and a couple of permanent men. My two children Jack and Janet went to the Secondary school Monday to Friday and always came back by the Friday evening bus for the weekend. They were in the school orchestra and played recorder besides their main instrument. That was how their acquaintance with little Seonaid began. Somehow they heard this fine playing one day coming from a croft in Peat Road and . . . well, at their age they were not over shy and went in and found this little girl; they realized in two minutes that she was deaf mute but somehow that wasn't going to make a barrier. They spoke to the mother, a very civil intelligent woman and said they would come back next day with their recorders. And were as

good as their word. When I came for them in the evening, you know I just could not believe it; there they were, the three of them all playing together and making up music.

The father and mother saw that they and I understood and were glad to give their child a chance to have friends. Sometimes she was brought to Camus an Righ, sometimes mine went to Peat Road and this was a great joy to them all. I watched that child, so shut within herself yet here displaying her personality to us all. I spoke to her parents too who were humbly glad that so much had been granted to her in her infirmity. But they were plainly worried. "It's not the problem how she'll get on when she grows up," said Calum to me one evening in the still darkness outside the house: "I'm thinking of the day when she awakens and asks who she is. Then she will notice what she never notices now, the dull fear in the eyes of those who think of her as different". "Is she so different," I asked, "apart from her infirmity?" Calum stared out over the Minch, then looked steadily at me with his dark eyes caught in a gleam of light from the house. "Sometimes I think a great fire is blazing at the heart of her. If it cannot out, I do not know what she will do. Now the recorder is her tongue; some day it may not be enough."

"But you are hopeful?"

"I am hopeful. When you are out on the high sea fishing you must always be hopeful, so I think it is my nature. Only my wife dreads that it cannot last." So the years of Seonaid's childhood passed, happy in their way, full after their kind but only the dread of the woman came between me and my sleep sometimes.

Mrs Malloch had more to tell me: The strangest thing about her was her fearlessness . . . you know, fears of the dark, or the way lost in the sea mist, fears of the sharp stone on the road or the effort that is too great for your strength. Seonaid didn't seem to know these things. Do you think it would be that she did not know them because she did not have the words for them? I often wondered. At twelve she would roam the moors and the rocky coast; she would carry a message that her mother had written to a croft three miles away and think nothing of wind or rain or darkness. I said so one time to her mother; she replied: "Oh, don't you see she has the inner strength." And true, the happiness that showed in her dark eyes looked as though it could be a match for all the forces of Nature . . . or the wiles of the Devil! Of course our district was a safe place then, safer maybe than it is now. I would not let my grandchildren run about as Seonaid did. But maybe you are safer when you don't know things, don't hear what people say . . . or when they stop talking as you pass. I think little Seonaid was sure in her world and had no idea of the strange and terrible things that lurked in dark places or cowered in the fold of the wind. I often spoke to her mother and knew that she was anxious about something, nothing physical you know, nor the long thought of her distant future. I think she was waiting for something to move on and bring a sort of awakening to the girl. It happens to us all, but we have words to name it and control it. What do you do if you have few words?

But fine I mind the 26th of February . . . a year later it was. A full week of gales and storms was no stranger to us; this one had been particularly black and a boat, not one of ours, had gone down towards the western shore. We knew that but there was no other information. Then a ship's boat and some spars came ashore on the Achellary strand and we waited. Apparently . . . and this is all you can ever say about her . . . Seonaid was round the far point after some cattle that had strayed when she must have seen something in the water. You try to imagine yourself in that position, seeing something rolling over and over in the waves, no swimmers these for the limbs moved as the water directed them. We with our knowledge of the Bible might have felt it our part to pass by and prefer not to have noticed. Or you might wade in . . . as Seonaid surely did and fetched them unresisting on to the dry sand. She was a strong girl . . . or maybe strength was lent to her, for they're not light when the sea has filled them. There was an elder man and a teen-age boy in their sea jerseys; they were later identified as from the sunk boat. What happened next? We can only guess. I think that Seonaid had never seen death before; maybe she thought they were cold or asleep for she seems to have tried to revive them. Then, as the afternoon was wearing on and there was no response, she seems to have been frightened for the first time. For this was the state she was in when she found her mother and conveyed to her something of the truth. Together they went back round beyond the point where the tide was going out and the bodies lay forlorn on the drying sand. Her mother told her to stay there at some distance while she went and fetched the men; but I think the girl would stand by the bodies and stare long and hard trying to work out a meaning for this new thing in her world. We say: Death . . . and what a lot there is when we say that word. But she would have to work it out for herself.

I don't know. But this I can say. From that day there was a change in the girl. Not that she was unhappy or anything like that. She just grew quieter in her ways and you would often come on her sitting on the stone dyke and watching the cattle, but far, oh so far away. Or standing barefoot in the Traigh Mor as the tide rolled in gently around her and staring in the water after the reflection of herself. My eldest daughter, now married, the one who helped me to deliver her, would visit me at times and always went out with Seonaid . . . she just talked to her as if she could understand. She said to me that she felt it like the full tide in the girl, turning and beginning to ebb. But I could not see it that way.

A cousin of Calum had a son that was a Divinity Student at New College, Edinburgh. He came to the croft one summer; Seonaid would be fifteen. He got on wonderfully with Calum's wife and because he was a relation by marriage and a very upright young man, no one said anything; for Calum was away at the fishing. He had a tent pitched near the lee of the dyke and seemed quite comfortable, though it looked a bit near the ground and rough for my liking. I think the woman was happier that summer for she never liked it when her man was away; and besides she was glad of some help about the croft and the chance to repair some winter damage. They were always talking and sometimes, when the girl was there,

you would have sworn that the three of them were at it
together. For this lad too seemed to have the knack of getting
through to the girl. He had a little battery transistor radio and
when there was music he would turn it up loud and she would
hold it between her hands and I'm thinking she could hear it.
For she was still like as if a great water was running over her
and she only moving her eyes as she felt it in her heart. Young
Malcolm would search the air and find music on the programme and she was content so long as it lasted.

Then he found a new way of getting through to her. He
would draw simple pictures, St Columba landing in Iona, St
Patrick, John Knox too and stories from the Bible, especially
the Old Testament. Then he would act out the story for her,
getting her mother as second actor. I am sure Seonaid learned
from him. And he invented head and hand signs for her . . .
there was little use in the usual language of dumb people,
because she had not even the words. Then she fetched picture
books from her childhood, Bible stories they were, and now
she seemed to understand them. What's that? Did she understand them? It's my guess that she knew their meaning in a
way that we will never know. Often you would come on the
two of them sitting down by the skerries, where the waves
boil and fret at the flood tide; or on the heathery knoll by the
standing stone, where you can look across the Minch on a
blue summer's day and see the distant mountains. And it's
brother and sister you would have thought they were, so
complete was their communion. And I would have sworn
there was a fire in her, a great consuming fire that filled her
comings and goings with heat and light. She would put her
arms about her mother's neck and play with wispy bits of her
hair and she would look at her . . . oh, I could not tell you how.

Findlay McGregor had been at school with Calum and they
had come up through life together. He told me:

The fleet was out beyond the Flannan Isles; we had weathered a force eight gale, which is not so unusual in these
waters, even in summer. I remember it was night: we were
heaving at anchor somewhere off the Lewis coast, the water lit

by the fitful gleams of light between the rushing cloud; for it is never really dark up here in summer. I came out on deck for a smoke before my watch and found Calum there staring across the Atlantic as if he would have seen St Kilda. He didn't mind me sitting beside him; we had our own private thoughts and hopes and worries and just sat as comfortable as we could on boxes and gave ourselves up to the movement of the sea. He sighed deeply, I mind; I took my pipe from my mouth and looked at him. There was only the strong silhouette of his profile against the floating glitter. I put my hand on his and said: "Come on man, Calum, out with it. Better to share it . . . it's lighter that way." He turned to me and the eerie light fell on his eye sockets and round his mouth and lit, I remember, the whites of his eyes. "Och, I'm fine," he said, "I've little to complain about."

"Seonaid, then," I asked, for I guessed that this was always on his mind.

"Aye, that would be it. You see . . ." and his voice trailed off; I waited till he caught the thread of it again.

"You see," he said at length, turning intimately to me, "she's no' like the rest of us."

"Aye, aye," I said, for we all knew her affliction.

"But it's not just that", he said, "not just that she can't hear or speak like the rest of us . . ."

"Folk say," I replied, "that she can hear and speaks with you and her mother in her own fashion."

"With her mother: I have not the same gift of understanding. No, it's not that. She might have been like a dull beast of the field, but . . ."

I waited patiently; the wind was changing to the south west.

". . .but I think the fire of God is in her. Or does that sound awful blasphemous? She knows things, she understands, she can read your heart as if it was all glass and she could see through it. It is wonderful . . . but I wish she were just a girl, like your Moll or the others."

I said: "I think she's done wonderfully, though many of the folks don't understand that she can do so much."

"You know what they say," he said, his face strangely lit
by the midnight, "you know what they say, the so-called
Elect, that she is accursed because of the sins of her parents
who married in a Registry Office and would not breathe the
air of the Church. You know what they say: 'Child of the
Devil, a great and thunderous proof that God will not be
mocked'."

"Easy on, man," I said. "This is only some of the folk who
see the world through the spectacles of the Old Testament.
But the rest of us . . ." I did not complete the sentence, for I
knew too well that most of the others were superstitious too,
like their Celtic forefathers, and all too ready to believe such a
thing. I think Calum knew why my words stopped there.

"Thanks, Finn," he said, "it's good of you to stand by me
and try to understand. But you know and I know how it is."

"Are you worried about her, then? How she will make her
way among the folk?"

He gripped my arm suddenly and fiercely. "I don't have to
worry, for I know that she is too good for such as us . . . and
will be taken early."

I was shocked. "But she's well and strong and seems to
love her life."

"No," he said, as the clouds parted and the light of midnight
encircled us . . . "No, she has been lent to us and maybe we
will never know why. Folk say, she has the mark on her
because she came as she did, a reproach to her mother and me,
a victory for righteousness. I think she will be taken from us
when we least expect it and how we least expect it. And" . . .
he paused, gathering bitterness from the depths, "the reproach will be against Uladale and Fabost. She came and her
own would receive her not."

We talked only a few minutes more, as I recall, before a
message came through on the wireless and Calum went in to
rest awhile, as I kept my watch. I had strange thoughts that
midnight: there are those who make it all sound so cut and
dried, part of a great movement from Creation to the Day of
Judgment. But Calum troubled me with this mystery of who
we were that inhabited these bodies of ours and why we

came. I thought of the certainties of the established Church where man's end was defined and his duty clear . . . then I minded a night, just like this one, when I was up Loch Roag, just over there on the Lewis coast and I woke in the early morning to see these stones of Callanish looking at me; ancient they seemed and full of knowledge and indignant at the mess we got ourselves into.

It will always seem astonishing to me that even in this present century, admittedly more depraved and desperate than those that have gone before, there was no imagination, no joy in the extraordinary to welcome Seonaid's steps into the community. We may look for obvious explanations and point to the guilty parties. The whole history of Scotland has been lacerated by struggles for domination, often under this religious banner or that: Celtic and Roman: Kirk and Popery: Episcopacy and Covenanter: the Saved and the Damned: the Elect and the rest. It may be religion but it knows nothing of the love of God. The arrogance of Mankind knows no bounds and is at its most dangerous when it is fanatically spiritual or pseudo-spiritual. Yes, one can point the finger, and it was done, but too late. Even more surprising, in this century we have churned out books on psychology, churned out Graduates in psychology, collected and processed data . . . but still we could not understand. My own hunch is that the split between Scientific method and Imaginative method . . . and the easy and arrogant rejection of the latter by the former, explains much. We have enthroned Intellect and sent imagination below stairs. The truth probably is that in any attempt to understand Imagination and Intellect are mutually necessary: separate them and they produce the disasters of our times.

The folk in Uladale and Fabost, had they had another history behind them, might have accepted the unusual and surrounded it by the indulgence and kindness they could so often show to their unfortunate folk. But intellect had warped imagination . . . or shall we say, religion, (human all too human), had blinded them to the love of God which sent her among them, so that first the Elect and the Devout, but later also the Unconcerned feared her because she was different. In most of the Christian world an almost exaggerated cult of care for the handicapped, the mentally disturbed, the deviants helps to absolve mankind of its guilt feelings. But Uladale and Fabost, townships on those Isles at the sea's edge, was hardly part of the rest of the world: by their way they were more purely Christian, by another reckoning not that at all. Alas, Man's arrogance works out the schemes of God for him and decides what is to be. In my more bitter moments I often say that had Creation been structured as the Theologians would have it, nothing could have prevented the tragic error from suffering a sudden angry obliteration: the slate would be wiped clean. That it does not so happen suggests that we are so far from the truth that our misconceptions do not even offend.

Voices in the wind, chattering, searching their souls, seeking a justification and finding no rest:

"I think they should be more shamefaced than they are and not let that girl be wandering about the hills and the shores and driving her cattle across the Traigh Mor. If she was mine I would be keeping her in the croft and not exposing her to the folk."

". . . It could never come to good. What with them never darkening the door of the Church and marrying in a Registry Office . . . and we don't know anything about that girl before she came to Lewis. I could be sorry for Calum, but he must bear his share of the blame."

". . . Well I know just this. I would not have that child in my house. I have two little ones and I would not take the risk . . . what she might do to them . . . you know, mark them, or mutter a strange spell over them . . ."

". . . What I say is: there must be some reason for it, something terrible I do not know of. Children are born with defects, of course, but nothing so great as this . . . and her walking proud and happy through the township . . ."

". . . Vanity of vanities. We need look no farther than Exodus 20 and 5 . . . and the sins of the fathers shall be visited upon the children. And fathers means mothers too. Some of the folk waste their time talking when the answer is there for them in Scripture . . ."

"I'm sorry for the girl. I try to imagine what it must be like for her, seeing everything and wanting to know and her not able to ask, not knowing words and books. She helped me reap my oats when my man was away and I had hurt my arm. She didn't make a sound, just worked and when it was all done just took a glass of milk and smiled so big and happy that you would think it was I who gave her the favour by letting her work for me . . ."

". . . Her parents were foolish, that is what I say, foolish. They should have cleared out, gone to Perth or Glasgow or somewhere. They can do things for children like that in the cities. But it was wrong in every way for them and wrong for her and uncomfortable for us to have such a one going about among us . . . "

"It's frightened of her I am, with the great dark eyes of her looking as if she could see right into your heart. Not natural, I say to the folk. Where did she come from, for I feel sure it wasn't Calum Morrison was her father. And if not Calum, who, that's what I would like to know . . . "

In my dream I seemed to see the long summer days with the bees in the thyme and hot aromatic gusts blowing over the hillside. Seonaid was happy then, in her element, for she was, as the poet said, made one with Nature. The broom about the rock crests, the lazy trails on the summer sea and the birds of August, swooping and wheeling that did not seem to feel her an intruder. I dreamed too of the black northern winter, the

short thin daylight and the endless procession of storms that
blew from north and west. Outdoor work stopped and the
folk shortened their lines and clung to existence with the
tenacity of their fathers. But even then Seonaid was often out
and about, happy to be toiling up the hundred steps in the
teeth of the wind or scouring the headlands and the infinite
horizon in the pale light of a winter's day. Some doors were
open to her; some greeted her with a wave of the hand and a
bright smile; and she cared for sick animals with a devotion
that was not known in these utilitarian places. No-one will
say why it was that, when she was sixteen, tall and dark-
haired, weatherbeaten, with strong hands like a man's, the
climate in the township changed, the human climate. Was it a
great wave of ignorance that had its origin in the minds of a
folk, imposed on by many cultures, not their own? Was it the
reaction of a simple people living on the edge of a complex
world, learning at last like the rest of us to be objective about
suffering? Or was it simply, as the old Myths asserted so long
ago, that Man is at heart inturned and selfish, ready to reject
the weak and any that are different? I wish I could think that
it was none of these things.

Suffice it to say that smiles became fewer, doors were
closed to her that had been open; on her approach there were
some who turned away or rudely stared, their silence out-
matching hers. She would notice it; she had, as some had said,
eyes that could look right into your heart. She longed to
discover blitheness there, generosity and giving, but she saw
the response to nameless fears, black fears out of the childhood of the race. I conclude that the day came when she knew
that she was that fear. It is hard to collect evidence: lips are
sealed and a surprising forgetfulness has come over folk. I
think it took several months to dawn on her; for a while after
that she stayed about the croft; she never again went through
the township and her mother never required it of her. She
would go to the Cnoc and play her recorder hours on end as if
she might plumb the physics of the human heart that way and
understand. In the end it had to be failure: there was no
understanding. The rest of us with our words can make

something of an illogical universe, she in her prison could not.

It is hard to research that day in September, a cold clear day of the north-west wind, when the foam broke over the skerries and on the far horizon you could see the isles of nearer Scotland. The day was not marked in any way as special: most of the men were not home from the fishing: the women and the older men and youths, were busy in the crofts, what with the winter ahead and the short hours of daylight. Seonaid and her mother had cleaned the house till it shone and the girl must have known that her dad was soon to return; for if she was close to her mother and could communicate with her, it was her father that her eyes looked for. When he came home, she would be his girl. In the early afternoon she took a letter from her mother to an old woman who lived a mile or two away, that and some eggs, for the hens were laying well. At the gate in the wire fence, she held it open against the wind to let Ewan McDonald bring his cattle through and she smiled big and bright, so that he had to smile back. She bolted the gate and went on her way. Some folk down at the peat banks saw her stride up the hill, her lithe figure rounding the crags till she showed her black mop of hair blowing against the blue sky. Old Mrs Stirrat was crouching over a low fire when she arrived; Seonaid set herself to work tidying the house and carrying in peat for the fire and water from the pump that she had. Mrs Stirrat knew her well and appears to have set scones and milk before her and talked away to her the while they ate; for she did not need an answer and, who knows, Seonaid understood her well enough. Later some folk from the township passed her as she returned but they gave no greeting.

And later still, before dark, she went to fetch the cattle that had strayed across the Traigh Mor to where the grass was sweet. The tide was out. Old John Levan, whose fishing days were over but who never missed a good afternoon on the Cnoc to stare across the Minch and dream of summers past. . . he saw the girl cross the Traigh, her bare feet leaving a narrow line of prints on the ridged sand. Awhile she stood there staring, so it seems at the rock pools and the crawling

fingers of foam far out at the ebb's edge. He saw her turn with
the cattle, leading them, not driving them, for they came
when she bade them. But it was getting dusk and he went
home before she got to the wire fence.

In the evening her mother went to help a neighbour who
was sick and bade Seonaid keep the house. But after that the
trail disappears. At first her mother was only a little worried;
then with mounting apprehension she went out into the
darkness of the moonless cloudy night, calling her name
(though she knew that was in vain). She went and told her
neighbours and together they wandered about, knowing that
there was nothing to be done. For very weariness the mother
slept at three in the morning and woke to daylight and a
knock on the door. But it was some of the men come to
enquire if the girl had returned. They went to her usual
haunts but they found no trace. The tide had been full in the
night so she would not have crossed the Traigh. At ten the
mother let the cattle out on to the shore; and it was only in
the afternoon when she went to fetch them again, that she
found them lingering strangely out on the edge of the skerry
beyond the Traigh. They did not come to her calling as they
did for the girl; they would not come until she came right
over where they were. Then she saw in a deep crevice of the
skerries with the water of the incoming tide already washing
over, agitating. . . the limp hands, hair, weed. We don't know
what she thought, whether she cried out or wept. The mute
beasts clustered around her and she did her duty and brought
them home.

And no-one knew and no-one could know. But Calum
when he returned on the next day and looked at her, now dry
and free from the weed, made no comment, whatever he may
have said to his wife. Only later he said after the enquiry: her
time had come: she had had enough. And who is to say that
she did not come to him for a last time, his own daughter,
when he was out on the Minch in the deep water, between
one and two in the morning?

SGEIR NAN FADH

For the first four months the unreality became more marked each day. That was, of course, after the hospital episode, after the physical deprivation, when decisions were not so much made as taken by others. A curious loss of identity began and the feeling of some endless retreat.

When he allowed his memory to return to it, Eddie found himself trying to disentangle what he had really felt from the layers of subsequent experience. One moment it seemed he was crouching across the steamy paddy field, aware of the muddy water in his boots, his flak jacket sticking to him with the sweat that lubricated every movement. Bryce and Chopsticks and Boyo were up front . . . that was the regular order as they left the perimeter and made for the first abandoned ville on the patrol route. It had been raining and the slabby drops, a massive condensation rather than rain, pattered in the mud terraces. A bluish smoke hung about the acid green foliage. It was all so vivid, always so vivid. He remembered running over in his mind the risk points, the covered ground and the ragged hedge where you showed a silhouette to any Gook sniper. It was life narrowed down to a single moment where the only question was: which of us will be here tomorrow. But you never saw yourself dead, nor your mates . . . it was always the nameless others. Without fail in that memory too he saw a scarf, a cheap gaudy thing that some kid had thrown away and he remembered it should be his step-sister's birthday tomorrow or the next day. And just at that moment came the end of the world, a sound so loud

136

that it ceased to be audible, a brilliance that lit his way to unconsciousness. After that what with the morphine and the pain and his transportation as freight, there was a long break in the corridor, no memory of Da Nang or Okinawa . . . then the slow rebirth in a hospital in Japan. The two halves of his life did not fit and the link between was for ever missing.

At first the improbable comparison between an ultra-sanitary hospital ward in Kobe and the surrealist hell of the Vietnam paddy fields was curious, interesting as a temporary phenomenon providing you held on to it as that. Festooned with tubes and dressings on his abdomen and left leg, his right leg in plaster and both hands muffled in bandages, he accepted his thingness with a wry resignation and co-operated with clenched lips in all their probings and searchings. The Japanese doctors and nurses were good and he had a relationship with them; but when Major Barker, the American MO, came round, they confined themselves to the usual cheery patriotic slush on both sides and Eddie never had the nerve to ask the damage. But he wondered. Still curable it seemed; people were always stopping mortars and returning to their unit. Somehow nothing else occurred to him, nothing else was possible and he found himself sometimes dreading that so much must be happening to the platoon and he out of contact. If only he could be allowed to be on his feet again, be mobile, be with the others. The healing process was protracted, particularly his hands with the phosphorous burns . . . he saw them while they were being dressed . . . and besides some of the shrapnel was not yet removed from lower down.

Memory foreshortens, Eddie could not remember reaching an awareness beneath the threshold, that his next posting would be homewards not south to the . . . he smiled at the word . . . theatre of operations. Theatre? The greatest show on Earth. But he was ready for it. So that when he asked the new MO, a quiet-spoken middle-aged man from Ohio, when he could reach for his flak jacket again, the doctor said almost absentmindedly:

"Say, don't you think you've done your share, son? I think it will be home for you. Where's home? Georgia, I guess?"

The kindly intuition that had been growing within him rose to meet the authoritative word, and he just knew that things were a sight worse with him than he had cared to think. From then he began to hold firmer and firmer to his memories. His fellow marines, so many of them drawn from the tough fringes of American society, from all the States black and white, brought down to their irreducible limit, men battered by their training and whatever length of experience they managed, into fighting machines, in whom privately survival was paramount. And the dirt and the flies and the red dust that covered everything, the endless improvisation and the making do without everything that was not there. Was he really romantic about that? Eddie felt that there was something that would have drawn him back and it wasn't just the strangeness of that oriental world with its smells and rainbow colours, something . . . but he was still too weak to pursue any thought to its limit.

Then the day came. He knew the extent of his injuries, recognized the finality of the moment in the paddy field. He wrote to a couple of the fellows, but even as he wrote was embarrassed to feel himself years out of date. He posted; and cut the link with the past. And with the flight back home it began, the terrible sense of unreality, that he did not belong to this dude world of shallow contact at one's finger tips. On the flight across the Pacific he said nothing; from San Francisco to Dallas, wedged in between a fat man and a strident woman, he fought to keep conversation away from himself. Even in Atlanta, Georgia, that he knew so well, he stared at its streets and its crowds with something like a hostile rejection; on the bus journey to Madison he got a grip on himself and came back to his mother with a wry smile.

It would have been better had he been able to turn the page and apply himself to the new chapter; but it took an age, four months to be precise, for him to walk freely and not feel pitiable in the vigorous sport-loving society around him. About one thing he was clear: his new status put him under a threat . . . of wallowing in self-pity or taking a header into a wilful sort of schizophrenia and being thought of as a poor

nut. Faced with limitation, deprivation, and the curious stare
of polite folk who did not always ask but surmised why he
had so abruptly returned, he determined to build a life that
was independent of all that, justified by its own activity and
usefulness, as we all do most of the time. The Vietnam phase
was to be private to himself, never discussed, not even with
old stagers who claimed kinship through their experiences in
World War 2 or Korea : points to be lost for any day when he
was betrayed into talking about it. His own family, his
mother and step-sister, quickly got the message and let him
be; with Mr Average outside it was often more difficult.

In these months, as the reality retreated and became a
moving picture, he wondered how much of it was true and
how much the perverse creation of his own imagination. He
saw the terraced villages with their tree-lines and haze of
growing rice; the basketball flares that extinguished themselves in the night like huge candles. A chance smell or sound
would transport him in an instant. He imagined himself in his
bivouac, high above a grey oozing river; it was a quiet
afternoon and the hills stretched endlessly to the north. Or at
times it was the tension of a night patrol, when you strained
your muscles to keep between the glimmering tapes where it
was thought to be mine-free. Or deep in a weapon stand
peering into the uncertain dark and peopling it with moving
shadows of men; how the night grew darker and courage
waned; then before the east was barred with grey, improbably in all that world of devastation, some old rooster up and
hailed the dawn of a new day. Then the watch was nearly over
and when man could see man again, there was the staged and
careful withdrawal to the perimeter and somehow life was
turned on again. Eddie spent afternoons in woods outside the
town or in the public park; by night, when the suburb where
they lived was relatively quiet, then there was screened for
him films out of the archives that he hardly knew existed.

After about a month the scenes and events retired to their
true position as backgrounds, backgrounds for men. Out of
the roseate fog he would see faces and hear voices and he
knew of a sudden that this was where his heart was lost. There

they were glistening with sweat and caked with mud; or lying about at ease on a hot afternoon, fingers busy with domestic make-do-and-mend. Or faces contorted in laughter . . . how different one from another, or fear or flat with apathy or despair. Once he began to list the many he had known with a thumbnail sketch of each; but he gave it up as he perceived that the luxury of personality disappeared, volatile as a gas in the brutal ultimates that they met day in day out. Some were just reliable and you committed your all to them, where you had to . . . Boyo and Tingletoes and Sambo, a black marine were that, totally and unquestionably reliable till the day they were eliminated. Others were individualists, always kept something of themselves back that they would not let you share, and they were not reliable. There were the indomitable few to whom laughter came easily who transmuted the ugliest situation with their epiphenomenal character, Birdy and Digger the Blue, both of them long since silenced. By the time he was walking easily and active again, Eddie had begun to define the problem that was to live with him in the years ahead.

Through one of his mother's acquaintances . . . she seemed to know a wide range of people who had nothing in common . . . he found a job in a transportation office in Atlanta. With some relief he closed the chapter of the dependent ex-hero on the shelf and began to earn his keep. In a bedsitter in a drab street with a view of freight yards and railroad tracks he settled in and prepared to explore the preface to his new life; for he was clear that transportation was not his career. From eight-thirty when he left his room to half-past five when he returned, his day belonged to his Corporation and left no time for anything else. He mastered the work easily and caught himself sometimes putting the same desperate drive into it that vaguely recalled paddy fields and perimeters. If the work gave him no qualms, relationships with others did. Not that he was morose and inclined to keep to himself, not indeed that at all. But he wanted to be without a past, wanted no-one to ask where he came from and what he had been doing, or why he had not aimed higher than a transportation clerk. But people were endlessly curious; the less he wanted to talk of it the more they asked. But, he reminded himself, it's quite the usual thing and no reason for me to throw a neurotic fit. With some of the others in the firm he went about at the weekends, enjoying what the season provided. One of the girls, Cathy, in the audit department took sort of pity on him . . . or so he interpreted it with a wry smile when he was alone. She was a nice kid, superior to lots of the others who just lived like mayflies from day to day. Cathy had long serious talks with him; she got him to go out dancing. She was the one person who accepted him and did not demand to know all the details. In fact she was much more of a catalyst to him than Rik and some of the other fellows who simply lived out the various facets of their manhood without being aware that they impinged on others at all. Eddie often found himself rather envying the ease with which they handled life: they never asked questions. But Cathy, good kid that she was, by trying to understand him and bring him to life, only hastened the day when he would stand at the cross-roads and choose the solitary way, knowing who he was. For there was always the feeling of a great world between him and them, even more between him and her. He knew that nothing could come of it. He did not want her as a mother, a nurse or a worshipper but he could not say so. His first year passed with work and modest amusement . . . a bit of travel too, for he made various journeys as representative to transportation departments in other States. As he thought of it afterwards there was surprisingly little time for memory . . . and in the wider world the Vietnam adventure was turning sour and would be recognized as futile before long.

One year, one year and four months and all the while the process was going on in the depths. It surfaced one evening in October when they were in the cinema. The usual corny-porny mixture kept the audience laughing like a one-brain moron till it was brutally interrupted by the Pathetone News. There they were, marines in regulation outfit preparing to leave the perimeter on a night patrol. Eddie became aware that he was watching with quite different eyes from the rest; he had seen these official video units and how they staged it:

the determination, the heroic look on the faces, the mystery of the South-east Asian night. "Perhaps Mom will see it back home" was the usual carrot, but you couldn't smell the sweat, the overflowing latrines, the perfume of fear. These men were processed through the perimeter fence knowing that one or two of them would probably . . . stay out, maybe whole, maybe in pieces. Heroes? Maybe from the point of view of these cushy birds in the plush seats whose dirty work they were doing. "Heroes by proxy". But to themselves, the abandoned, the neglected, human projectiles and expendable. Outside in the glare of the street he said nothing, not wanting to discuss it. But he had no need to worry: the Pathetone News had not even recorded on his companions; he doubted if they had seen it at all. Back in his room, with the view across the freight yards where shunting went on all night with the clash of buffers Eddie knew not what to feel, rage or despair or self-hate. He sensed that the grid of his life had softened into wavy contours; but he went on trying for a few months more.

What emerged surprised him: it felt like an uncertainty about himself. He wanted to be alone, to stay mostly in his room after dark (where not even the clash of freight cars disturbed him), but he could not put a name to what was wrong. Not, that is, till one evening when he was at a friend's house in an out-of-town suburb. They listened to some new tapes this fellow had got, classical ones. He played the Mozart Requiem, which Eddie had heard but did not really know and modestly . . . for it might have been well known to everyone there . . . the fellow gave the usual spiel about how Mozart composed it, the Dark Stranger, the failing health and the romantic tradition of the pen falling from the Master's hand as the choir in an ascending scale reached a shout of climax in the word "Guilty". Thinking of it afterwards, Eddie could not remember anything that was played after that word. The shout echoed down through the chambers of his being. All that weekend he was on his own calmly confronting this new thing. He was surprised not so much at the word which had been flung in his face, as by his immediate intuitive acceptance of it as a hint from somewhere that would lead him out of the maze.

Sometimes he was back south of Da Nang, living again the terror of the forest darkness, the feeling of encirclement by hostile figures . . . fear, don't call it anything else. He looked at the marines around him, all well-known to him more or less, but each slimmed down to a basic phantom of himself. Scenes flashed before him, the revolting onset of decay, flies and congealed blood; the inhabitants of the villes reduced to the few basic survivors of themselves, some shot at point-blank range in a moment of rage. Somehow the beauty was all gone from it now, the romance and the fundamental nobility of those around him. They were not the Selves they were born to, nor was he. He wrote slowly and carefully on a small sheet of paper: "Guilty". "But," he argued with himself, "I was caught up in a moment of history. If it wasn't to have been World War 2 or Korea, it would have to be Viet Nam; it was there and I was there." For a fleeting second he thought of far away Scotland, of the father he had never known, how his mother had come to New England, then to Georgia. "No, stupid," he thought, "it wasn't all designed so that I would be shot up in a paddy field, you can't think of things in that complexity." And yet this hint from without, this "Guilty", he felt was to mean something; a return to the highway from a bypath, who could say?

At the end of another two months, after visiting clinics, having sessions with Trickcyclists (who recommended drugs) he knew that there was no hope for this way of life. A great apathy had seized him and reluctantly he threw in his job and returned home to a second defeat.

. . . .

Ben leaned across the counter of the Cocktail Bar in the Caledonian Hotel. He looked like any other tourist, a bit smarter than the natives maybe, but not till he opened his mouth and released his transatlantic drawl did you identify him.

"Can I get you something?" said the barman, doggedly Scottish.

"Say George, would you say I was mad, if I said I just saw a fellow out there, a fellow I was at High School with?"

"Dinna ken. I suppose it's possible. Did ye no' speak to him if ye knew him all that well?"

"I just couldn't believe it. Here I am thousands of miles from home. I walk out after lunch and the first person I see, or think I see, is this chap I used to be in school with in Madison, Georgia. I was stunned, but by then he was gone. I say, do you know of any Americans who live round here?"

George polished a glass and considered. "In the town, no. I've no' heard of anyone like that coming here to live. What did he look like?"

"That's just it. He was the right size and appearance from what I could see and he was dressed in oilskins and these big rubber boots . . . and he was carrying some parts of a generator or something like that."

Four men, vaguely seafaring, had been sitting at a table nearby. George directed Ben to them.

"Are you on holiday here?" asked one.

"Yeah, I have one of these Rail passes; I just go as I please and I arrived here from Glasgow just before noon".

"And you saw this fellow in oilskins carrying a generator?" He looked round at the others. "That could be any of twenty people."

"Maybe I'm just going crazy," said Ben. "Probably the chap just had some similarity to Eddie . . . Eddie . . . I don't remember his second name".

"Masters," said a weatherbeaten-looking type in his thirties.

"Masters . . . yes, Eddie Masters, that's it. How do you know the name?"

"He lives . . . ", and he pointed through the curtained window, "about two miles that way on a godforsaken island in the Sound."

"Oh, him," said the others in chorus.

"He's a Yank, I believe . . . or he was," said one.

"They say he came from Benderloch or Appin or some-where when he was a boy."

"I heard he was in Vietnam and got shot up."

"Nobody knows him. He comes over in his motor-boat for supplies and building materials but beyond the folk in the stores nobody really knows him."

Ben emerged from a dream. "That's it, that's it, that's him. He used to tell me about Appin. And he's here again?"

One of the four had gone through to the next room and brought in a big bluff bushy-haired man in his fifties.

"Jock, tell the gentleman here what you can about Eddie Masters. He was at school with him in some wee place in America."

Bushy-hair laughed and shook hands. "There's none of us can tell you much about him. He appeared in March and seems to have got the tenancy of Sgeir nan Fadh, not much more than a few rocks standing out of the sea . . . eh, two miles or so across the Sound. The island has a building on it dating from the war and a navigation light nearby, though it's not really in a navigation channel. It belongs to some big English Company . . . Glass I think and they were probably glad to get some odd soul to look after it."

"He must be a funny bloke," said a younger man, "to go and live all alone there."

"I think he's been working hard all the summer on the buildings and the installation to get it right for the winter. Rather him than me."

"Is he a holy bloke?" asked one.

"More likely running away from something."

"I would say," said the superior authority of bushy-hair, "that he's a perfectly normal fellow. I've spoken to him and he's only a wee bit American now, but we got on fine. Do you want to see him?" he said turning to Ben. "He's not on the phone, you know."

"I think he comes over on a Friday for supplies," said one. "You could maybe waylay him then. Maybe he wouldn't want to talk to you."

"What I can't understand," said Ben, "is why he's here

and what he's doing." The others agreed that they couldn't help him there. "But I'll look out for him on Friday."

Ben stood on the south breakwater at nine on the Friday morning. The son of a Federal judge, he too intended to follow the law; his trip to Europe was by way of celebration for a University graduation nobly accomplished. His repeated attacks of asthma when he was a child had easily excused him from the draft and he felt no bad conscience about that. Vietnam had lacerated the soul of democracy in the States and had left people confused about the nation's claims over the individual, especially thinking young people whom the politicians were ready to sacrifice for principles that were increasingly suspect. Ben and his friends at Harvard had often suffered acutely under a sense of obscene betrayal. Some had avoided the draft honestly enough . . . he had; others were dodgers in varying degrees. If you had any integrity you avoided the vulgar shouting demos, you maybe tried not to think of it at all. For nothing was as clear cut as it seemed to the shouting rag-tag on some campuses. But Eddie, he thought, had been in it, probably had no valid excuse to escape, was too simply honest to try and so was caught up in it. And he had been shot up, that's what they said. What might that amount to in physical incapacity or psychological damage? "And here I am," he said to himself, "lost in a sea mist on the south jetty, waiting for a motor-boat that may never come . . . and a fellow who may not want to know me."

He mopped the rain drops from his hair and drew his coat collar around him and waited. Suddenly he tensed, as though contacting something and a few moments later a motor boat puttered to a stop below him. The yellow oilskins on board threw up a rope for him to secure round a bollard.

"Not that way," said the voice, " round the other side," and Ben with his thumbs up knew that he had found his target. The yellow oilskins clambered on to the breakwater.

"Sorry," he said, "I thought it was someone else," then after a pause "so, it's you."

"Yes, it's me . . . after how many years? But what are you doing here?"

"Same question to you. Mine would take more telling; yours is probably straightforward."

That voice, thought Ben, the same, not the same, older, more confident but subtly different. Then, as though it was the most natural thing in the world, the two of them made their way through the dripping haze past petrol tins and fishboxes and old iron crumbled by the sea air, past the fish salesmen's stances and the canopy of the station, binding together their two worlds with each step. There was business and shopping to be done . . . Ben shared in that: Eddie had lunch in the Caledonian Hotel (too grand for me!) and when, by three o'clock, the *Da Nang* cast off and headed through the mist to the open sea, there were two of them aboard.

Through the silent mist they kept a steady course; silent they were too, Eddie from a habit he could not easily break, Ben wrapt in wonder of a totally new experience. He sounded a fog hooter when Eddie told him to, but did not realize that its echo off the rocks signalled that they were nearly home. Ben wondered where the companion of his schooldays had found all this navigational skill, wondered too at the deftness with which he stowed the boat in his sea garage. All furred with rain they climbed the glistening steps and came on a low concrete building. "Home," said Eddie, "hope you like it." Home, when they later explored it, was a living room with windows on three sides, a bedroom with two bunk beds and storage, a kitchen with Calor gas and a rain water supply. Outside were two storage sheds, the generator which supplied light to the house and would do for the navigational light . . . "and all the usual offices", said Eddie with a wry smile. But the mist had not lifted, so they settled in the comfort of the living room with its modern decor, curtains, light and a Music centre powered by batteries. Ben had not begun to emerge from his dream; but somehow they made an end-on junction with their lives and filled the information gaps. Beyond telling of his injuries and . . . as he put it . . . the sculpture that the phosphorus mortar had carried out on him, Eddie hardly mentioned Vietnam. Ben with an intuition beyond his experience was careful not to probe the sensitive areas. Before turning in that night they emerged from the one door on to the rock of the island. The mist was departed and in its place a fitful gleam illuminated the fretful sea around them. Two miles away the lights of the little town gleamed along the water-front; here and there single brighter lights indicated homes on adjacent land; car headlights swung round the curves of a tortuous road and over there lay the red and green riding lights of some boat at anchor. Lights! Above them the stars lay enmeshed in the sky's co-ordinates. Ben swallowed hard: it was so improbably beautiful. Back inside, Eddie strangely shook hands with his friend. "Thanks, Ben," he said, "for coming."

The Saturday was clear, cloud-covered but with distant views. They spent the morning tidying, completing some construction work and painting. Ben thought he had never been so care-free. They saw the mail boats on their way and all sorts of small movements on the sea about which Eddie seemed quite knowledgeable. At midday they called a halt, ate and settled in the living room. It had begun to rain and the gusts slashed across the windows, heightening the feeling of comfort within. The conversation started somewhere, but it was bound to reach its destined track before long. When he felt confident, Ben said:

"You haven't told me, Ed, why you're here."

"No, I suppose I have to do that. The trouble is, being sure about the truth, Why am I here? . . . I suppose you could say, because a friend of my mother's who has a lot to do with a glass manufacturing concern in Britain, suggested I return to Scotland, away from America and my problems. He obviously thought a lot about it, for he suggested my taking over Sgeir nan Fadh here as a caretaker for them. Is that why I'm here?"

"No," said Ben, "back a bit in time!"

"Because I was a poor unsmiling wretch hanging about my mother's home in Madison, virtually unemployable, fit for nothing. That?"

"No, further back yet!"

"Well," said Eddie, "I'll tell you. But you mustn't ask me

questions—ask me to say more than I want. I'm not in court, you know, and obliged to give evidence. And, as I said, I've a kind of unreal feeling about it all . . . I don't know what's truth and what's made up". (Here he smiled to himself, maybe remembering the kind-hearted Cathy and her solicitude.) "I think this is it."

"When I first came away from the battlefield, I cried inside myself . . . I've never admitted it to anyone, but it's true, I cried silently for the friendships and living a day at a time, the faces . . . the memories of simple noble things in an artificially simple life, the colours and the sounds of that lovely country. But then the photos began to fade: I didn't know if the faces were faces, you know . . . or decomposing back into the soil. Then I began to have dreams of ugliness and fear, treachery and abandonment and the bestiality of men caught in a trap. It was frightful. I kept looking on helplessly and wondering if it ever would change. Then one night in very strange circumstances I was confronted with the whole episode and felt myself pronounced somehow guilty of it . . . no, that's not quite right . . . something gave me a hint in that word 'Guilty' . . . that was where I should look."

Ben studied the face that was essentially young still, normally serious, disinclined to give itself away in a smile. Now there was a peculiar intensity in it. Eddie went on:

"I tried to work during the day to keep the thought away from me but it was always lying in wait when I went to bed. I think I may have been going mad, whatever that means . . . probably the others thought that too. The psychiatrists (the wry smile again) they offered me tranquillizers! I came home and must have made everybody's life there a misery."

Now it was the hopeless smile that Ben could see, the one they had known long ago in Vietnam, in the hospital, in Atlanta.

"You see, I couldn't talk it out with my mother, you understand that; and I couldn't get away from this accusation of 'Guilty', though I did not quite know why. It was after three or four months that I agreed to go back home to Scotland, to cut being an American . . . for this was always my home, I never forgot it deep down. The moment I decided, the pain began to ease."

"And where does that leave you now?" asked Ben.

"You could say back at the beginning, I think. There was all this hard work to do here . . . that was different, I worked with my hands in squalls and sunshine and bitter cold weather too . . . but it was something that did not need conscious thought all the time; and I knew that something was going on at a deep level in me. I came here in March; I had to learn about handling the boat, then got on with making this place habitable, with some professional help of course. Finance hasn't been a worry: the firm has provided well. I think they intend to test new lenses here sometime. I'm really very lucky . . . and extraordinarily happy compared with what I was."

The stillness in the room, punctuated by the lashing rain and the confused hiss that was the angry swell blowing up from the south-west dominated both of them. Two minds were ranging free and some time passed till they confronted one another again.

"But where does it get you?" asked Ben.

Eddie sat silent, his lips just apart, his eyes on the ground, wondering how much to reveal. Then he spoke quite decisively (and Ben would remember this hour all his life and be influenced and changed by it as by a new access of wisdom).

"I think a marvellous thing has happened. Work is a great way to get on with the thinking, you know. Yet I don't say I've done it, it has just happened to me. The more I devalued what I thought I knew, the more a sort of revaluation took its place. That's a way of putting it: maybe it's too philosophical. I wonder, do you get me?"

"Casting everything overboard to prevent the boat sinking? Is that what you mean?" said Ben.

"You've got it. It's as though we take on so many ideas and theories and opinions and beliefs, that we threaten to swamp the boat. Then when you have the courage to jettison them all . . . and out here in the Sound they just don't matter . . . you find, if you want it so, that the empty space becomes filled with more worthwhile goods. I don't know where it all comes from; not from reading, for I have not time for that yet. Maybe I just want it to happen . . . terribly want it to happen . . . Can you sit quiet and not break my train of thought too much. I'll try and show you a picture, but you've got to see it my way, not try to use it for other purposes. If I was really clever . . . maybe a poet, I would just speak so that the whole thing would be easily understood."

Ben nodded, wondering at this vital urgent Spirit that sat burning in the seat before him. Momentarily he heard the rain and a ship's siren far in the distance.

"Well, as I see it," said Eddie, choosing his words, for he had never stated it before, "all of us, free moving bodies, you would say, and independent of one another, have one thing in common : that at our birth, the half turn of the screw, so to speak, we take on board a bit of what is eternal and indestructible . . . life, God, call it what you will . . . And it's this common bit that calls out from me to you and you understand me far better than my words could make you. It's brother greeting brother. Now, if we have a bit of luck in our way through childhood and as young men and women, not too many crushing disasters and deprivations . . . we just know that . . . even if we don't heed it . . . we really only have one mode of operation to bring to the life ahead of us, be it long or short, and only one way basically of meeting those around us. I'm simplifying terribly I know. I don't mean to lecture you like a kid or a first year student, whatever it was that you called them. The Must, the absolute must, is to strip down all our pride and self love, which really is our greatest danger . . . simply have no conceit at all and meet every situation just as it makes a demand on us. Of course, I know in a more mainland way that it's personality or conceit or acting a part that makes life in society so attractive . . . and so dangerous. In a kind of two-edged way, like real people acting on a stage, we play our part before the world as we must, but in private we must strip ourselves down continually to basics. In a way we're like good runners, not Olympic but just determined to do our best at all times. And to the people we meet, have to do with in any way at all . . I expect I sound quite potty . . . we should really want to love them and serve them. That's my newest discovery; I certainly didn't believe that a year or two ago. The embarrassment comes from the fact that we don't have a right word for it. Love . . . well, it had other meanings in Okinawa and Da Nang and even in Madison and that's not what I'm at. It's what happens when you face someone else . . . and accept and want to help and don't even begin to think about yourself. I know, I've got to learn to put all this into practice. And you see, if anyone gets set on the right way and the right behaviour, it really doesn't matter if its at 25 or 35 or 65 that the moment of death comes . . . you'll be thinking I'm getting morbid living all alone . . . But it really doesn't matter when the second half turn of the screw comes. The body goes . . . and I've seen enough of that . . . the eternal part returns to store, positively charged I guess. The Life experiment has been worth while. Yes I really believe that now, 25, 35 or 65 it makes no difference . . . whether you do a morning's work or a day's work or a day plus overtime. It's all the same."

"My, my," said Ben, "I'll need a sabbatical to catch up with all this. Seriously though, it makes me wonder what I have been doing for the last four years at Harvard. And supposing you don't cotton on to the attitude and the Behaviour in good time . . . ?"

"If you don't cotton on but use your eternal part to kick merry Hell out of life, to act big and knock over the weak, well . . ."

Ben took him up: "When your second half turn of the screw comes and you look back . . . ?"

"You maybe see that it was all a ghastly failure. You were guilty and no excuses can be accepted. And maybe, who knows, you realize that it will all have to be done over again."

"My God," said Ben, "what a thought! Mind you I've been lucky, socially favoured, pretty well off, University education." He stopped, sensing the comparison with Eddie who was looking at him with a lop-sided smile on his sober face.

"Go on," he said, "I understand, present company excepted."

"Yeah, I was going to say, all that asthma when I was a kid, and both my aunt and my mother died of cancer and the heartache when my best chum crashed his car on the Western Highway and killed himself. You know even I don't think I would care to go through it all again, not even for the sake of the bright patches. What about you?"

"Man, so far as I can, I'm going to see to it that I don't have to. Life's great . . . but once only."

"So that's why you are here?"

"I think so. I've been tipped off a wee bit early about this 'Guilty' business and I am altering course. I'll stay here till it's time to go on to something else."

"And you'll know when?"

"Yes, I'll know . . . and probably have a quite new destination and goal."

These intense episodes cannot last too long. Eddie made some coffee and they listened to music, Shostakovitch 5 and some Richard Strauss, and Eddie thought the hours rich as they ranged through Civil Law and Scotland and his plans for a radio link. Sgeir nan Fadh was a magic crucible where they could meet one another face to face and understand, bypassing eye and ear.

On the Sunday morning, while Eddie wrote up the log which he kept, Ben scrambled about the rocks and mini cliffs, disturbing indignant seabirds which noisily rose from their perches and wheeled on unmoving wings over the dark water or stared with a moronic round-eyed dislike. Thus sun shone warm through the sea wind and etched sharply the configurations of land and shore all around. Great mountain masses reared up in a blue intermediate to that of sea and sky. A Sunday calm rested on the waters. Ben thought: "If only I could be conscious of the happiness in each moment here, store it up and enjoy it slowly later. I suppose that's why we want a cine-camera and a tape recorder. But you recollect only a small part of the experiences." He scrambled down to the water's edge where a tiny movement of waves slapped against the blackened rocks. He wondered at the strange debris cast up, weathered wood, bleached sheep's bones and the gifts of Man, indestructible plastic containers.

Then he heard his friend calling and hid like a youngster till Eddie found him.

"This isle is full of noises and magic," said Ben dramatically.

"That makes me Prospero," said Eddie solemnly," without a Miranda." Then, changing the subject, "Come up and I'll show you where I was born." He made a rough map and pointed out hills and islands, sea lochs villages and distant peaks."And that ugly lump just beyond these hills is Ben Nevis . . . Appin over there."

For a while they were silent, each circling his own thoughts like the gulls out on the skerries. They were paradoxically together and infinite in distance from one another; but their nearness among the thyme and the thrift was happiness indeed.

"I say, Ed, have you a time scale?"

"Don't know. I refuse to decide. The days will darken, the winter will blow its worst and I will be here . . . while the pattern inside me rearranges itself. You can think of me when you're in Washington."

"But I can't quite get it. You don't mean that your life is over . . . that there are no more decisions to make, no dreams and hopes. You're like me, in your mid-twenties, you can't want to throw up the sponge."

"Man, no, not at all. One of these days it is going to begin for me. I suppose back in Madison they are thinking what you could be implying: the poor nut that cracked his shell and has gone to hide. Maybe I saw it that way at first, but no more. I tell you, one of these days it is all going to begin. Your life story with any luck will be continuous from beginning to end. Mine has two chapters and only a long silence will connect the one with the other."

"And somehow you will know when and how . . . and where you're going?"

"I sometimes have the fantasy that the Ed who started in

Appin and went to Madison was programmed all wrong for the task in hand, whatever it is. It was going to take the Marine Corps and a paddy field south west of Da Nang to set the adjustments going. After all, I might have cracked up, done myself in, gone down the heroin trail . . . but it didn't happen that way. Instead something short of the miraculous happened . . . and without having a philosophy or a faith about it, I'll bet you it's going somewhere."

Ben looked down at the sun blanched rocks, not sure that he understood. Then he stood right in front of Eddie and said: "You'll promise to write and let me know when the . . . the great development occurs. Ed, in a funny sort of way, I feel responsible for you. You'll promise?"

"Yes, I'll promise. After all you're the only one . . . and it's almost open ocean between here and Georgia."

The halcyon weather never lasts long in these parts. By the time they had eaten and got the *Da Nang* out of its dock, the eerie mist had closed on them and it was eyes and ears and the compass that brought them across the Sound. They hardly spoke; Eddie kept his eye on his bearing and listened. For himself he would never have ventured out on such a day, but Ben had to be back to continue his journey early on Monday morning. After an interminable tension sea marks hove in sight and soon they were nestling in by the south breakwater.

"Man," said Ben, "I don't know how you do it."

"No more do I," said Eddie.

"Bye then, and you'll promise to write and don't be too long. I have not your faith: I might fear the worst."

"Right then . . . bye! And thanks again for coming all this way to see me."

Ben in his raincoat and carrying his grip stood on the glistening stones of the breakwater as the *Da Nang* turned and made off on its 170° bearing. Eddie did not look back.

. . . .

Correspondence: Ben to Eddie . . . March
. . . have been wondering how you fared in the January

storms. I keep asking about the British weather and naturally no-one knows why. In your Christmas letter you sounded surprisingly confident, but I am waiting for an account of what has happened to you. Were you marooned for weeks on end? I'll never forget that trip back to the mainland. I'll confess now, I was quite scary about it . . .

Eddie to Ben . . . April.

So was I, but I did not want to worry you by admitting it. I've been fine. I have been allowing my sense of my own significance to die away (I am not significant anyway in the way that most people think). The days of fog and storm suit my present stage. I stand on my Quarter Deck . . . you remember that platform high above the anchorage . . . and look in all directions into darkness and fog and I think: this is how it is, this is what we must come to alone, pretty unimportant and worthless, with no claim on anything, no demand that we should be heeded. I go inside and exercise myself to try to continue this awareness. Doesn't always work though. At times I have panicked a bit and wanted a TV set, anything that would give me the illusion of contact. But I sort of knew that I had to hold on. And so often it comes, just like a pair of buoyancy tanks clipped to my side: I just lose the panic and float in a great sea of confidence and contentment. I doubt if you will find any of this in the burblings of the psychologists; at any rate I'm just like a child learning to swim and confident that I'll reach new shores sooner than later.

I'm glad I have no ready made ideas, no philosophy, no religion, . . . did I ever tell you that my mother never went into a church again after listening to a sermon on the Damnation of Children . . . it was probably in her Appin days. It's my guess that I have to do it all from first principles, and that means no organized thinking, no picturing of what is going on or happening to me, just a warm sort of striving and push to break through the fog and reach some working understanding. Can I say that again in case you get it wrong. There has to be no thinking, no theorizing, no attempt to make pictures or imagination out of it, just a push of the will to get there . . . like crossing the Sound on a fixed bearing in an

impossible fog. At times I am endlessly grateful that so much
opportunity is given and that I can start on Chapter Two.

I'm all right; you need not worry. But I look forward to
spring winds and summer seas and they are slow in coming
this year.

Ben to Eddie . . . September

. . . when I returned from Montreal to Washington for the
Law term. You know, you have set problems for me. Ever
since I left that godforsaken fogbound lovely island of yours,
I have had something nagging at me, something that doesn't
bother the others here. You see, if you have individuals one
side and organized society the other, you sort of need Law in
between: we don't know other ways of holding the gloves.
But Law, instead of being a sensitive two-way bond between
them, tends to harden into something in its own right, serving
neither individuals nor society properly. You set me thinking
and you keep me thinking, that we don't try hard enough. We
just do the Pontius Pilate (sorry, you don't know about that!)
and wash our hands of the delicate responsibility . . . and
apply the law like the blunt end of an old Shepton. Then I
think of you, surveying the oyster-catchers and the gulls and
saying more or less that there's nothing else to it but living
your life with cast-iron determination and turning your ego
down to a low peep. You haven't convinced me, neither by
logic nor a priori nor prima facie . . . but I know in advance
that I'll find you are right, though I'll probably go on for
years kidding myself that I know better . . .

Eddie to Ben . . . November.

It's a Friday and I am marooned on the island, surrounded by
foghorns and an oppressive sea mist. I didn't go across today,
but I have enough food to last for a week . . . and I'm not
expecting visitors.

Friend, if I am not always intelligible, don't fear the worst;
rather that something in me is aching and groaning to a
rebirth. I followed your letter very exactly. By the way I
know that character with the washbasin and towel . . . I have
read the (shall I say) available documents and don't always
find them helpful. But the experience concealed behind all

that propaganda and special pleading must be closely related to the one my hands are reaching out to.

Reaching out . . . into the oppression of the silent fog (TS Eliot?) where one can only wait to be hauled through at the right moment. My situation is in all ways quite unique. I came here without hope . . . and I wait with longing and excitement to see . . . no that's the wrong way of putting it . . . in the hope after all, that something will be allotted to me. The journey through the dangerous forests lies ahead, that is, when I have to return from my Hermit's cell to the real world. I'll be more vulnerable because I have lost my hard shell. But if it gets as far as that, there is no apprehension: I will be under protection as I will be under orders.

The strangest thing is to deny intellect. The whole developed world puts its faith in reasoning and as far as I can see it's about a break-even whether the outcome is evil or good. You can concentrate on hospitals and welfare and literacy and choose not to notice starvation or chemical pollution or greed with its persuasive tongue. But reasoning is all most people seem to have and no doubt they try to make their poor best of it. And if after twenty-five years I've been lured on to this island to learn otherwise, I don't delude myself that I'm the only one. I'm sure there is something to be done with it all. Maybe I'll have a vision some foggy day and just glimpse how things really are . . . or maybe I'll not be given that, not be considered worthy of it. But I must not speculate nor think out a Geometry or Algebra of the Infinite (not to call it God or a First Principle or a Logos); there must be no imaginings, no descriptions of what is or isn't possible, no dragging in of human legal or democratic principles. It will be so terribly absolutely what it is that no words will signify.

The strain is considerable all the same. I can only think that in losing as much as I did, I was given the gift of endless endurance in its place. Home is now very much a going concern, much better than when you saw it. Lately my elbow was nudged to start reading again and I have plenty of time for it. It will of course be part of the final wash up, everything is. I'll let you know when things start moving.

Ben to Eddie . . . March

For Heaven's sake, Ed, reply to me. I wrote you in January; now it's March. If I could phone you I would. Are you still there? I'll admit it before you find out. I wrote to the Caledonian Hotel to see if they had news of you. There was some word of you having gone away and that you had returned, but no one knew for certain.

I hardly like to bother you with my news seeing I don't know in what state you are to receive it. I went and got myself engaged . . . to the daughter of a Senator. Rosalind is her name and naturally she is everything I would want my wife to be. We met at a ball given by a select Law Society without ever being introduced or knowing anything about one another. By two in the morning, as we walked together in an upper gallery, I just knew that this was it and the long search that men expect to have was over before it was begun. I guess she feels just that too. Of course I'm not a kid nor is she at twenty-five: we agree that it has all to be worked out but we know we can do it and make a success. I've got one friend I'd like to be there the day we are married . . . but I don't suppose he can give a promise. It will be November . . . maybe the sea mists would make navigation impossible? Well, that's it blurted out the way I would have done to my Mother had she still been with us.

But you, what are you up to. Write, Man, write or I'll have to cross the pond to see for myself.

Eddie to Ben . . . April.

Sorry, Ben, to have kept you waiting. I got your January letter but I could not reply then. Can I say, first, that I am very happy at your news and wish . . . oh, just everything . . . for you and Rosalind. I don't know her, but I expect she will be the making of you; perhaps a driving force to make you more practical and less inclined to poetry. In a way she will negative the bad influence I have had on you. I don't mind that at all. And after you've got your world built around you, some day I'll breeze in and find what you have made of it.

As for me . . .

I could never quite believe that it would be a straight run and it wasn't. Up to Christmas it was marvellous. I regularly got up at six in the pitch dark and had to take the Tilley lamp to check the generator and the water supply and this and that . . . you could really fall off this island if you were not careful. I spent times each day doing my 'exercises' . . . my reading had brought me to some books that were helpful in a practical way. I could spend a half hour completely separated from everything, concentrating on being nothing and longing . . . urgently . . . to be remade. The days were wonderful and open, snow on the higher hills and colours that left me speechless. Fridays I went across to the mainland as usual and felt strangely happier in meeting people but always had to be away by three to get home before dark. I think all that spell was a gift, building me up so as to have resistance for what was to follow.

It's a funny thing: I sometimes feel it goes right beyond our power to grasp. What is and what will be are both at times here and now, just as though something is preparing for a bad day which it knows is coming. Sometimes too I have a picture of myself as a piece of wood on the spindle of a lathe . . . and all I have to do is to be happy at being ground into shape. But analogies are never quite satisfactory. I'm sure that what has happened to me doesn't happen to most people. Does that make me special? Have I been chosen? I don't want to be special . . . that's not me; but I do also want to be chosen . . . for something, and at times I have been so elated that I felt like walking across the water to the mainland with half a dozen gigantic steps. Not literally, you know, but in the brilliance of my growing confidence.

I wish something could have warned me though about January. Now that I look back I see that I could have taken a hint from my reading. Those who have taken this road before me know that the darkest part of the forest is just before a clearing. Well, just before New Year I went to pieces. I gave up caring about myself, just mooched about, wallowing in self-pity. I lovingly toyed with death wishes . . . not very seriously, as I now see, not seriously enough to do anything. Then after two weeks, when the storms subsided at sea, on an impulse I left my island and went to Bristol . . . twenty and more years before my father had been said to be there. I stayed in a cheap hotel and roamed the streets and the docks trying to make casual friendships, trying to talk to somebody, anything to destroy the loneliness that was destroying me. There's no use dwelling on it; it was totally negative and unproductive; and you know in all that mass of people I only felt the emptiness . . . emptier. I had nothing to say to anyone because . . . there was just nothing to say. What can one do in Bristol in January if your home is not there.

To be sure, I can see now: it was all arranged: it was designed so that I would clear myself of the shreds and rags of the character who inhabited Chapter I. After about three weeks, one Friday, I reached the end of the clearing. I hadn't spoken to anyone all day . . . not what you would call a conversation: I felt rough and broken down. But in the afternoon the skies cleared . . . my skies, that is, and I was filled with a terrible longing for Sgeir nan Fadh. I could see in the mind's eye the waves on the broken cliffs, the stab of light from the four light-houses on the horizon, the wind in the grass and my own front door. It grew on me and I had just time to go to Temple Meads and get the night train to Glasgow. By midday I was starting up the engine of the *Da Nang* and then . . . home.

Home! It was the same, the gulls and the bent grass and the rubbish of civilization fringing the water mark. But I was different; I had been through something. AND IT HAD BEEN PART OF THE PROCESS. Sometimes I think this demand on me is impossible . . . but there is always the great magnanimous provision, encouragement when you need it, beauty around if that's what's wanted, the feeling of Physical well-being . . . even a chance meeting or a conversation on a Friday. Just after I got back there was a glorious storm and I had two unexpected guests when a largish boat put in with its engine broken down. It was a blown gasket or something wrong with the carburettor. The men were lawyers from Edinburgh in their late forties. I welcomed them of course and we had an interesting though lop-sided conversation: I wasn't saying anything about myself. I wonder what they thought of me; but in the course of the conversation said to me several things I just needed to be told so that I felt that they were in a way visitors from outer space. They were with me while the storm lasted for two days . . . then I took them over to the mainland where they got what they needed and brought it back. Next day they were gone. I'm sure they wondered about me; but then so did I about them. Who was it who entertained angels unawares?

Now everything is going forward again. I can't know, but I guess that sometime I'll be needed somewhere. This isle is too lovely to lose but I have the feeling that the last condition is that everything must be lost. I can't really promise about November; where would I get the fare anyway? You must send me some pictures of yourself and Rosalind so that I can keep you in front of me. I'll try and not let you down again . . .

Eddie to Ben . . . June

. . . and I'll treasure the photographs. It will be a great day when I do catch up with you both. Keep me posted with all the details.

To answer your questions. It's a strange experience to be and not to be. I'm sure first of all that my experience could not be a universal law: it's not meant for everyone. But where you are dead cold serious and sober . . . and no one is more painfully sober than I am in all senses . . . and see your shadow on two walls at once, I think you must just accept that as your lot. North to South I could have hopes and plans and desires. I have got to be practical, think of food, oil, wool to darn my socks. I suppose I might be all sorts of rotten things too if I loosened my grip on myself. But East to West I am reduced to what I basically am and have only time to train and prepare and keep balanced and far from frenzy (I was reading old Yeats). Attentive too to every influence that bears on me. For I know that the demand will be total as the support is total. It defies intellect to know how your words in your letter can be yours and at the same time uniquely designed to impart something to me that maybe even you did not realize. I don't try to think it out any more than I do how my batteries power my record player. Science is all right in its place (what presumption on my part!) but extended beyond what can be perceived or measured to some degree, science is a bad habit.

I suppose one can be battered into submission by these powers beyond intellect and maybe this does happen. In my case I know that I simply have to consent joyfully to being used. You remember the lawyers who were shipwrecked here? We had great conversations and they could quote poetry better, maybe, than they could quote law. One of them recited by heart a sonnet by John Milton which I had never heard . . . one written when he was blind; and in that strange way, as he said it aloud, I knew that he and something beyond him had said it just for me. I suddenly realized the continuity of it all through the ages: "thousands at his bidding speed" . . . of whom I will be one. I think that what we in blindness and conceit call chance is often an incomprehensible contrivance . . .

Eddie to Ben . . . September.
All of a sudden the summer is over. Early storms soaked me in blown spray whenever I went outside. I intended to make the weekly trip on Friday last but thought better of it as a Force 8 gale was expected. I'm ready now, I think, happy, standing on my own feet, physically and every other way. I have had some strange meetings during the summer with people who seemed to me like terminal points of futures. Strangely enough, August with its long sunlit evenings brought me an odd twinge out of the past; I suppose Vietnam is almost tattooed on my soul. I thought it was all gone; but it returned night after night to haunt me, the nobility and the worthlessness side by side, Man the predator hunting down others of his kind to destroy them, often to gratify only a lust for power. No animal could behave like this. I heard the pitiful ghosts of the guys I knew, wailing disconsolate in the shadows, because they were lost, rejected, abandoned, and had no more time to put it right. These were fearful nights: I could smell the earth smells, the rain smells and the strange

human emanation of fear. We were all scared down to our boots but we had to act as if we were not. As you know I insist on not getting things wrapped up in a orderly theory and this is more a determined act of will than something which just happens beautifully. On one of these nights I had to relive that mortar in the paddy field and waking in the dark. Before I could stop myself I was wondering

a) whether the mortar was designed to do what it did just so that Sgeir nan Fadh would follow, or

b) whether that had not been the original intention but an eternal improvisation made the best of it and assigned me to a new role at that point. However with daylight I put an end to the unprofitable speculation. All this lasted for nine days on and off then dropped from me like an irrelevance.

Meanwhile you have two months to go and I trust that neither of you is repenting of it. I want to hear all about it, down to the last detail, whether I'm here or elsewhere. By the way I had a guest for a week at the end of August, a young art student whom I met in the town one Friday. He was tremendously full of his subject and I was happy to learn so much that I did not know. He would be about 20 and no doubt thought of me as an old man . . . well, I am looking a bit weather-beaten and need some smartening-up. He kept telling me to sit still while he drew me, which I thought rather quaint and he vowed he would make a first-rate portrait of me one of these days. I'm sure he didn't begin to comprehend me . . .

Eddie to Ben . . . October.

The summons has come. One of the terminals I met during the summer suddenly wanted me. I'm to go to the south of England next Tuesday for an intensive training course before going off to Africa, what part I'll not know for a month or two. As I told you long ago I just know that the whole thing is just going where it must: I need have no particular apprehension nor make special preparations. I will swallow hard and work like a fury all weekend to get the days behind me and put everything in order for the Firm to take over after me . . . with my endless gratitude for what they made possible

But oh Ben! how will I ever leave it? When the *Da Nang*
heads to the open sea it will be the final loss ... before the
New World that I must start to gain. I can see it will need
self-discipline and a lot of support which I know will be
forthcoming. I will write to you from my new address and tell
you what I can. By the way, in the three-dimensional world
one cannot opt out and have no connections. I'll need to
quote a next of kin ... and as things are, that will be you.
Right?

Story Number Eight

THE LIGHTED ROOM

IT MUST HAVE BEEN the bell. . . some bell. . . no bell that he recognized in his weakness. . . merely a stab of sound across the infinite regression that enveloped him as he lay. The flight had already begun through impenetrable dusks, forests whose giant trees were his personal failures, crowding around him as if to witness the consequence of choice and blindness. The forest was brooding, alive with silent judgment, but there was no obvious track through it. To K. it was a unique experience, a powered regression so different from the fleeting memories of daily life. He had no experience of it, otherwise he might have recognized in it a reverberation of consciousness. And the screening was like a dream, but it was none: for recognition, identification, involvement and guilt tingled in every moment of it. The way down and the way out was the way nowhere.

It must have been the bell. It stimulated the overtones vibrating above his inertness. K. lay still; and for a moment when the flight stopped and the trail whipped back to the here and now, he remembered that this was hospitalization. . . intensive care, the voice had said. . . a fact, not the cause of anything. At an infinite distance he could detect pains and pressures, the entanglement of drains and drips, but this only with the lightest recognition. He made no attempt. . . or maybe no attempt was made in his state of thingness to conceive them, to locate them or to feel any wholeness. There were feet. . . identifiable where they touched the sheet, a stomach seething and draining. . . there were arms too and a

166

tiny breathing movement, unclear whether his or the machine's. Round him he imagined the busy apparatus, which maintained in him the alchemy of life.

With complete inconsequence he was of a sudden on the Flannan Isles a few years after the war. But it was not the sights and sounds that commanded his attention; it was the separation, the isolation, the distancing from human contact that provided the ground bass on which the harmony was built. Blue sea. . . puffs of cloud on a smiling Atlantic sky, cormorants and kittiwakes and the intrusive arrogance of the lighthouse. . . these were all there but not in focus; it was the solitary smallness in a sounding blinding world that thundered in him. He felt he was lying outside his tent as the summer wind dallied with his hair listening to music infinitely lost in the distance before or after. As now, he had only remotely felt hands and body; here he lay listening to sounds that did not identify themselves, hospital sounds.

Time, what is it? When you run with the wind, row downstream it isn't. Between decision and conscious change of direction it isn't. Is a dream time? Or memory? He swung into the past, to wartime, the Normandy bridgehead, the gloomy devastated villas and gardens above Sallenelles. At night you slept six feet down in a slit trench; an hour before dawn you were wakened for the Stand-to, men shuffling out of a dead sleep, putting aside the matting of brushwood as they hoisted themselves into the dim world. They eased sluggish muscles and shrugged off the cold at this least human hour of the morning, when the fog hung about the trees and the blackness of the perimeter was seething with possible attack. Many, he knew, longed to return to the death of sleep, but he did not. This was the magic hour of the day when the world of nature stood a tip-toe in expectation: small eft things rustled in the grass: the flowers of the hedgerow poised motionless, waiting to burst into the colours of the daylight. Men round him stamped the ground, lit cigarettes, gathered their jerkins around them in the morning damp; but he. . . he stood and thrilled secretly with expectation, waiting for the golden trumpeter on the horizon to sound the advance and call the day into activity. And the day came, another day, unlike any day that had been before in which they would all advance along the trajectories they were repeatedly choosing for themselves.

And now all these shifting luminous things were enclosed like x or y within the brackets of the bell's ringing, all of them out of time. The thought of the weariness of effort came over him. "But I must make an effort"... the voice was sub-vocal, somewhere among the neurones and stored memories of the Input. "I must make the effort this once to gather up the tangled ends of life. Here I am for the present in a hospital bed, like a huge Gulliver ridiculously tied down by puny inquisitive doctors. These tyrants have bound me with cords and left me with no movement to left or to right. Hospital bed? What comes before through the yellow fog of incomprehension? Why have I no identity here?" Momentarily he remembered the foggy mornings of his youth when the handkerchief was black with soot and the acrid taste clung to your lips... when the buses to the city followed men walking in front of them and the trains were a better speculation for the journey to school... till they ran over a fog detonator and the brakes seized on... Bang! went the detonator... K. convulsed as the bang took on a meaning; a great sound and a light broke on him and a cool voice within him said: "This is a terrorist bomb". So! That was the connection; that had brought him to intensive care through the never-to-be-recovered hours. This too was not cause and result, it never was, only an event then a void then a state, as now. A floodlight of great brilliance switched on within him. "I wonder which terrorists arranged this one... why the bomb was there timed for that moment... timed irrelevantly for me?" England was full of these people, the whole world was full of them; they claimed to be idealists, high and holy patriots, religionists, lovers of men, dogs, seals. So much of this idealism is only a fatuous ego-trip, an aspect of the clamour for recognition in an over-populated world that does not know you. Ruthlessly, recklessly they must be allowed to establish their identity...

"I am sitting with my murderer in a chromium-plated bar; I am asking him why. . . why the bomb? . . . why me? I look earnestly at him the way one human being is prepared to take another on trust. I will be happy to hear his reasons, maybe a cold, maybe a blurted statement, but reasons all the same. He with a face screwed up in hatred of his father. . . his mother. . . some people. . . all people and an enormous glowing phallic obsession with himself, blazingly answers, 'Because!' 'Because?' I ask. But there appears to be no cause, none that he deigns to communicate. . . or maybe one beyond my understanding. . . or one that glows in some secret chamber of his brain like a Host perpetually elevated."

Now the yellow fog was clearing. K. felt that he had driven that morning along South Gower Street, right into Albemarle Street and right again into Kencott Avenue. That was where the brick and plaster facade of the terrace, Number 10 or maybe number 12, blossomed out over him, a complete catalysis of brick, plaster and dust; when Up and Down and Dark and Loud and Over rolled him in a mat of incomprehension, stuffed him in a tunnel which surfaced in the hurrying lights of a hospital which illuminated his moments of near consciousness. BECAUSE OF A THEREFORE B! "Never", he shouted and the voiceless decibels echoed sycophantic in his brain. "There is no cause and no effect: That was eliminated from my catalogue of errors years ago. Only sequence: FIRST A THEN B. I know, I know; Physics and Chemistry and the rest reduce human awareness to the simplicity of the jig-saw puzzle on the carpet on a wet October afternoon. Simplicity. . . the difficulties reduced, so to speak, to two dimensions only. . . " and for a moment he saw the S.S. *Rawalpindi* off Hong Kong, a jig-saw puzzle of 500 pieces that he had played with as a child. . . and half of them sky. "But real life has no blind results that link hands with earlier acts. This for certain, only a sequence of moving vectors from moments of choice. . . and even the choice may not be free but infinitely manipulated." K. lay still as the clouds rolled over him and the whole tiny room of his existence was filled with the brightness of tearing pain.

Then the assize of agony was tholed and he was once more

briefly acquitted. Where was the point of choice that had swung the vector to Kencott Avenue? He almost had it but it eluded him; then it came again. He was in the austerely elegant office of Sir Alan Cohane on the fourth floor of the Addex Building. . . Addex Finance, one of those concrete and glass monuments to the success of International Finance. The Interview. . .? He could not now disentangle truth from fantasy in his memory of it. There had been eight candidates for the post. Problem: why had he landed it, why had he commended himself over the others? This was old ground which he had gone over repeatedly. If he had been Sir Alan, he might have chosen the one from Eton and Cambridge. . . or the one with a family connection to one of the great Finance Houses. . . or even the handsome ex-Guards Officer. Why had *he* been chosen? What does the choosing? The Candidate with his unique bouquet of life experiences which have brought him to that confrontation: the Interviewer with his unique life-bouquet too but, in addition, an imaginative blue-print of the bolt to fill the hole. K. recalled the night before the interview when he could not sleep; he had yielded to the temptation to live over the interview in advance; had sat in imagination with others (whom he did not know), in a waiting room (which he did not know), heard his name called to return to the interview room and meet again the Interviewer (whom he did not know): "We are happy, Mr K., to offer you the post". He had stopped the fantasy there, thinking it a kind of Greek *hubris* to go farther. Yet it had worked out exactly. Why? Which forces in the interviewer had selected which qualities in him to offer him the choice post. . . and incidentally, Kencott Avenue, the Hospital and the Life Support? Or was it the jig-saw on the carpet again where chance was half of it, the ill-fated *Rawalpindi* anchored off Hong Kong. . .

Hong Kong (he blew like a rag years backward into the past). Hong Kong. . . the years there all a flicker of light and moving faces. . . his service there as specialist accountant had been successful, all that he had wished in terms of freedom, available cash and a throbbing world external to him, uninvolved with him, that had made of each day an 'absorbing adventure. Best, they had advised him, to go there encapsulated as a British resident, homeward bound after three or five years. That had been the lure; that was what he had wanted. . . no involvement; but you could not avoid it everywhere you went, the awareness of a humanity like a spectre of your own, struggling, squalling in the intolerable business of surviving, each in his own square metre of space. The correct Briton would programme himself not to notice it, as he might do in Johannesburg or Lima or Poplar. K. had even blamed himself sometimes in his five years there for a cowardly flight from responsibility, as though his relationship to Hong Kong had been a lie. Yet it had seemed a good idea at the outset, experience, seeing the human world (staring at the poor?); we have an infinite capacity and need to justify what we do.

At this point some dis-ease in him made K. urgent to leave Hong Kong and get back to the hospital. . . it was as though there were no time to lose. Hospital was the most recent frame in the celluloid story. . . but he could not get back, for the ropes, that they threw, were always wet and slimy. . . he could not hold on to them and felt their spiral structure slip through his hands. He rested, singing and bright-eyed with certainty in the dark water where the ferry had been stoven in aft. He was suddenly in the cold water, intensely alive in the dark, clutching to a torn-off door. He regained peace and reviewed the facts: he had been returning by ferry from a visit to friends on one of the smaller islands: for some reason it had stopped in mid-channel and he was standing on an after deck to watch the trails of reflection in the darkness of that cloudy night. Suddenly the forepeak of a freighter was towering over them in the dark, to sheer the stern of the ferry clean off. It must have been a hideous crumpling of metal but his memory was soundless. Came a total silence and he was in the water; then the lid was off Hell and the Damned were all wailing. He was fortunate to be near the freighter and helped three women and an old man on to a scramble net that they lowered. He saw others by the light of the searchlight, weighed down by the heavy packs they were carrying on their shoulders,

threshing and groaning and drifting to death. These were minutes, hours out of time. He clutched to his door and in his
turn was hauled up the net to lie on deck and vomit water like
a stranded whale. But with incredible fidelity he remembered
the appraisal of that moment: I will survive, I will not be
drowned, this is not the moment. As he lay on the deck he
was intermittently conscious of the Chinese voices with their
peculiar fluctuating pitch. But it was his magnificent re-entry
into life.

K. lay still and the voices dimmed to a rasping unintelligible
sound of four whisperers speculating. . . he could hear them
as you listen in to a crossed line, objective voices as if they
were discussing the form of a computer input. He listened for
some modulation on the word 'He' but it came over as
metallic and ordinary as the clack of a keyboard, as if he had
ceased to exist and was become a statistic. Then the voices
blew away. Hong Kong and Addex. . . there was something
before his meeting with Sir Alan, or was it before he went
East?. . . something that might describe his route through
life. For a moment he was staring at morning fogs in damp
hollows on a summer morning somewhere between Bristol
and Wells. . . they never ceased to fascinate, these fogs and
you watched them drift into nowhere as the sun came up. . .
Pensford, Radstock, Maesbury. . . Why did he go to Hong
Kong?. . . what was the connection between the post-war
years and International Banking?

YOU CANNOT SERVE GOD AND MAMMON.

Now he had it; it was after his thirtieth or thirty-first
birthday when he was a promising young accountant in his
first post, that the Call had come. What was the strange
alchemy of the times that had changed the structure of his
awareness? He felt that he smiled at the fleeting memory of
himself, best student of his class, the model image of rolled
umbrella and pinstriped trousers, the small moustache carefully cultivated, that lent something of the reliable, the precise. Old Neffersen of Smith & Neffersen would have held on
to him with airy talk of an eventual partnership. That was
when the Call broke on him. . . "forsaking all other". He saw

a world yearning for peace and the love of Man for Man in the
Saviour, the ineffable consolation in His enduring presence.
He had called it the Will of God, given his all to it, first in his
spare time, then for two and a half years as full-time Evangelist. Even now the whole thing came over him in waves of
sweetness and agony : his astonishing success as a speaker : the
crowded meetings in middle- or working class districts ; his
own agonies of uncertainty as to his true worth as Mediator
of Christ. There was the ringing call to repent (Jesus possessed
or Jesus in person ?), the crushing devastating surrender of souls
to his appeal ; the generous glow as he picked them up bruised
and broken and forgave them their sins (in the name of
Jesus). The memory was all sunlit days and flood-lit nights,
the happiness in that post-war world of infinite promise. His
mind roved back and forward in time. Once he thought : "I
am dead", as he lay back still ; but the drone of the voices
beyond the machinery anchored him to the hospital. He
thought : "To die on these sunlit holy heights, that's when it
should have happened". But with the next oscillation of
memory he was older and wiser. Did it happen suddenly ?
Was it all the time slowly breaking in on him to reveal itself in
brutal reality with one disastrous collision ? Even now he
recoiled from the agony of the moment when he faced
himself truly ; cast off the delusions of grandeur, the renunciation of the world, he the surrogate of Christ. That terrible
dream when the Mother of God (strictly for him as a Prot-
estant she wasn't anything) smiled a little cynically at him and
blessed him and fondled his hair . . . and the smile was the
smile of his own Mother ! There were shattering blows which
followed . . . he could not now recall them . . . which made
him reach in terror for his Gospels. For the first time he read
them with an objective eye ; and he hated every word that he
read, the arrogance and presumption that here history took a
new course, the cheap miracles that achieved nothing, the
teacher's appalling lack of skill, even of humanity, the failure
of it all which two thousand years of slaughter and devotion
and cathedrals and superstition could not uncall failure. These
had been the most agonizing moments of his life, far worse

than anything in the war or anything since. He had written down : The death of Life is not going to be half so bad as the death of Illusion. Even now he felt racked with the thought of it. . . and wondered if it was maybe accomplished. But the objective voices clicked on in the silence, varying only a couple of tones in pitch.

In and out of Time. . . for a while nothing at all, then music passed intermittently over him. Gratitude like a cold sweat broke from him as he remembered his early days in the Concert Hall, his introduction to Brahms, to Wagner, later to Mahler, all of it an experience that could compel humility before objective greatness of utterance. During the Crisis music had come to his aid, had held him steady as the terrible tremors of the withdrawal racked him. "I have eaten of the insane root that takes the reason prisoner" : he had said after emerging from the cleansing agonies of Mahler 6. The crisis over, he had decided, some said, to serve Mammon after all, which was accountancy and Hong Kong. But privately he had never lost sight of God. . . he had never tried to explain this to anyone, for most people don't begin to understand. . . yes, he had laid every move open for inspection from that day. It was only the irrelevant theological pages that he had torn out and consigned to the flames. Without any passion he could now think of the decision to accept the offer of a post by the Bank in Hong Kong. Was it his decision? Is a decision ever a decision? Maybe only a profile of pressures that eases us this way or that? Had God after all understood his predicament. . . and made the way straight to Hong Kong. . . and the ferry disaster. . . and to Addex Finance, to South Gower Street, Albemarle Street, a girl crossing the road unsteadily on a bicycle, into Kencott Avenue, then that, then this?

Now Noah was sending out doves, which brought back parts of the world's past, his present. Faces drifted past him, faces and photographs the perpetuated moment of relationship to the photographer. . . eyes dull and responsive, hiding from a too penetrative glance. . . eyes that mirrored the bubbles on an effervescent personality. . . eyes that spoke the moment of love. They passed too rapidly to be named though

he would gladly have stopped and questioned them; sentimental to talk of forgetting. He saw the fellows in his accountancy class in the years before the great Illusion struck him, the
tall and the short, the stale and the ones with glasses as they
appeared in a college photograph. Where were they now?
What havoc and roses had they involuntarily scattered as they
rampaged through life? And he thought of the faces that were
not in print, the faces of the war years when cameras were
forbidden. These years, whatever they had been in reality,
were now the golden years, all their grossness and brutality,
fear and cowardice filtered out as unmemorable, and simple
heroic beauty left as the precious ore. This would not be true,
he felt, but he preferred now that it should be so. . .

Sitting with Ivor on a perch overlooking the moonlit estu-
ary of Orne, the Bren on its mounting pointed down the road
to where an enemy would come. Nations were making huge
endeavours against nations and every endeavour was noise
and destruction and death; but here in the palpable moonlight
shining indiscriminately over foolish friend and foolish foe,
Ivor and he talked of home, of their own patch of reality, of
the life that would be, at times falling silent in a community of
thought, at times staring down the road to the enemy lines
until the watch was up at two in the morning. . .
. . . two miles down a freezing stretch of road in a Dutch
January where his greatest wish was not to encounter anyone,
stepping into the shadows if a vehicle approached. . . for they
were not always British. . . then the turn-off across the railway line and on to the marshes to where A. troop kept warm
in an eerie farmhouse and waited for the news of the outer
world that he would bring them. . .
. . . crouching in a slit trench in a deathly frozen night on
the high banks of the Maas, George at his side, George the
hundred per cent reliable, who was doubtless as scared as
everyone else but never showed it. When you peeped over the
parapet between explosions, you saw the limitless black water
of the river, silently rolling on in the darkness through the
Biesbosch to the open sea. They had huddled together for

warmth and courage and to keep clear of the shells, that kept falling on the parapet... two babes lost in a magic wood...

... and the faces of the dead visited him too; Peter with whom he watched the light come up over France on that never-to-be-forgotten morning of the Norman Conquest:

"Bliss was it in that dawn to be alive
But to be young was very Heaven..."

The river of infinite possibilities was enchanted. K. drifted back down it like a twig pushed from bank to bank by a physics of infinite complexity which may have been chance by another name for all that we can know. Something was trying to push its way up through all this minutely-remembered experience of past life... something was breaking out into life in him as a defenceless raw perfect bud from the dead wood, something that had to do with your outgoing to others, your generosity with yourself... it had little or nothing to do with morals or manners or sin or guilt... these were the static judgments of people stranded on an island, going nowhere... it was the unconditional question: Did you use yourself in an outgoing way or did you consume yourself for your own satisfaction: no caveats, conditions, consolation prizes for bad luck, just that, using yourself up in a way that pre-empted moral judgments... if you transgressed, it was error, human frailty, stupidity at worst and you worked your way out of it by a change of direction.

And the whole thing, was it a huge multiplication sum that started with the fertilized egg and ended, for him at least, as he turned into Kencott Avenue?... powers, influences, turning you over and over, making of you something marginally different at each turn? Was there ever choice? Or was choice a name we gave to personalize cause and effect, itself illusory? Was there in fact only a kind of fate and predestination that absolved you from the Hell and Judgment that Christians peddled so enthusiastically? Free choice or fate, was that the balance on which human action swung? Free choice or fate? Yet not that either. Not Fate, nothing so blindly stupid, so limited, so intellectually of the people. Free choice... or surrender to the Call of the moment, not every moment,

willing surrender, perpetual loss of the power to choose,
amor fati truly understood. When he reached that point he
felt he had won home.

K. lay still (he had in fact been still for a good hour now
with no awareness of time). In the infinite distance he sensed
his body, so far away that no voluntary decision could reach
out to it; aware of the faint action of the machine's breathing,
breathing for him life on borrowed time; unable to hear the
irregular jog of his heart beat which had earlier echoed
through his ruined structure.

Then suddenly, like a camera swung to a bizarre angle, he
saw himself as he imagined he must be, lying on the bed,
mummified and roped together to keep the various parts in
place. How grotesque that thing seemed, a great alembic and
filter and drain. Round it foreshortened with bleak and indifferent features, four persons stood dressed in light and dark,
achromatic in the world of the black-white camera. They
conversed in flat tones.

A. glanced at his watch, appeared to sigh wearily and
looked at B. and C.

B. checked with the clock in the room and made a remark
to C.

C. signed a form, made out and awaiting only signature;
handed it to B. who countersigned.

A. slipped two levers into vertical position and flicked
some switches.

A., B. and C. left the room

D. folded the sheet over the mummy and followed them
out.

K. may have felt himself smile as the incrustations left him,
warfare and accountancy, the saving of souls and the dark
water. . . and the red pullover of the girl with the bicycle. He
would feel that they all now meant nothing at all in themselves; they had been means to the end about to be revealed.
Not error and judgment, he would think: I used the thing
positively as I could along each vector as it appeared: I did
not try to understand, to theorize, to give myself certainty.
And that is it: that is right. To be sure he felt that something

unspeakable was happening to him. . . then came like a child into the lighted room where he would know as he had always been known.

Story Number Nine

THE PENDULUM

IT HAD TO BE May that year, a blue diaphanous afternoon in late May, and I was questing northwards from Lochinver. I remember that it was May for all sorts of reasons, but chiefly that I wanted to stage my arrival before that of Scotland's sorrow, the midges. Happy that I had no timetable to keep to, no planned itinerary, my tent and equipment to care for basic needs, I could drive on and stop and turn aside. On these occasions I am never quite certain whether I decide where I am to go or whether I am whistled down the wind by some ultrasonic call and suddenly find myself where I am to be. Anyway I turned down a dirt track towards the rocky coast and spied a dream of a camp-site in a hollow out of the wind, scarcely a minute from the scenario of blues and greens and greys that was the summer Minch and the low line of the Long Island on the horizon.

There was a croft maybe a quarter mile away set down. . . who can say otherwise. . . among outcrops of rock and low bushes and streaks of gravel. I went over there first and knocked. The elderly woman, in her late sixties perhaps, who answered the door, assured me that I would be no trouble at all. Did I need anything? And when, in the course of three minutes' conversation, she discovered that she had been a nurse in her earlier days in the town where I now live, she would have me into the parlour and plied me with questions.

"But you don't live here alone?" I asked, fully prepared to hear that that was so.

"No," she said with a voice that took me back to my years

179

in Glasgow, "my young brother lives with me. If I say 'young' you'll be thinking him a boy. No, it's as you might say relative. . . he's sixty-four."

And there it might have rested: I would have crossed to my camp-site and they pursued their ways in Ardvarlich, or whatever their cottage was called. But it wasn't to be left at that.

"My brother Stewart," she said, "has gone blind, you know. It was some infection he got in Italy during the war and it was never properly cared for. When he was fifty he began to know what was coming and by fifty-five he had to retire. He was with the railway," then with a little dry laugh, "we were with the railway and between us we provided signalman, station-master and porter at a wee place in the Highlands." (It was a stretch of line I had travelled on with its three trains up and three down each day and goods trains to order.) She went on: "I had made nursing my career but when his eyes began to weaken I came out of that to look after him, you might say, and share his work. It was lucky there was such a post available for us both. I used to laugh and say that I could see if the signal was up or down when he wasn't quite sure. But it could only go so far and he had to admit defeat. So we came here."

"You must have been close to him to give up your own life. Wasn't a bit of a sacrifice of yourself?"

"Och, I don't know," she said, spreading her fingers out on the table and looking at them. She thought for a moment, then said: "In our family days when my father and mother were still living in Springburn in Glasgow, I was the big sister and Stewart was a wee wayward boy who had ideas of his own and would not be steered by my mother into a safe job. I started nursing, did my training in Stirling; I know he quarrelled furiously at home and when he was sixteen left school and ran away to the railway and eventually became what was called then a signalman-porter. He lived completely on his own and I hardly ever saw him."

"Where did he work?"

"Somewhere down in Galloway, I don't mind the name.

Then the war came on. . . were you in the war too? Then you'll have to meet Stewart; he doesn't often have the chance to talk to anyone other than me. I tell you what: you go over and get your tent up. . . do you need any help? . . . no, no I've got time enough in the afternoon. Right, you do that and come back in an hour, say, I'll take you to him. You'll have supper with us tonight?"

Not now for the first time but often, I have found it rewarding, necessary even, to give up small private plans for the urging of the moment. I returned to the car, assembled the framework of the tent, got it right the first time and in forty minutes had it all looking like an effective dwelling, much more to my liking than a Cocktail Bar and a Hotel Dining Room. Two gulls kept me under curious surveillance. For ten minutes or more I sat out on a rocky ledge, looking to sea, allowing the winds and the memories of history and fiction to strum gently across me. . . nothing systematic, rather a feeling of the richness of life and hope and human awareness that generations of McLeods or Mackays had programmed into the soil and rocks of this inhospitable terrain. Fantasy, you say? Whimsy? Why should one sell every moment of one's soul to Science and deny these nearer things? Awhile I watched a small vessel make infinitesimal headway against the detaining crispness of the Minch; and when I looked again it had moved and was running, perhaps for Ullapool. Back at the croft, I was hospitably asked inside again. The woman. . . Mina, her brother was to call her, said:

"I thought I should maybe tell you a couple of things. Stewart, my brother, as I said, is now almost blind. He wears dark glasses because the dazzle on the sea hurts his eyes and, I think, like lots of people, he hides behind them. I didn't want you to get the idea that he had been a failure or anything like that. In the thirties he was good at his job and got on well, I think: but he had a completely private self that no one ever knew about; he had ideas, but he seems to have kept them all secret. He told me once that he had books and books of writing, some of it poetry and he seems to have developed into a very individual young man. But he never tells me about that. What's that? The books? Yes, they were black note-books locked in a box and when he went to the war he stored them at home but told his mother to let no one read them. We had to move home suddenly because of some wartime damage and they got lost. When he came back from Italy he just shrugged his shoulders, but I think he was vexed.

But, of course, I was away myself all these years. I went into the Forces as a Nurse. . . I was in Normandy and later in Germany. When I was demobbed I became a Health Visitor in one of the developing Housing areas in Glasgow."

"That, I could believe, was a job and a half."

"Maybe. You know there's a bit of the same thing in me as in Stewart. Neither of us, how can I put it, bear a certain kind of fools gladly. So we have to have our sort of independent command: I had my Housing Scheme and later we had our remote station."

"And that would be part of the reason why you came out here to the wilderness?"

"I think we both took the war in our stride. . . we were different people then because that's the way it had to be. . . just like a play we had parts in. When the play was over we had to become our awkward unromantic selves again. I found the uphill struggle with women who couldn't quite cope with rents and families and feckless husbands. . . well, at times it was an unrewarding struggle, but it was one to one, me and one of them with nobody much looking over my shoulder. With Stewart it must have been different; he was in some ways changed by the war, he learned to get on with all kinds of people and be sympathetic and understanding. But there seems always to have been the secret bit about him, the great struggle going on within him to free himself from things he didn't want to be a prisoner to. I find it difficult to say, for I'm not quite sure what it is he fights so mightily with."

"Has he maybe come to terms with it?"

"Maybe. . . or maybe just swept the whole thing away as no longer relevant. One thing though: he's not the least wee bit sorry for himself as you will see. I think he has won through to a secret happiness. But, there, I don't know and the two of us don't expect to trespass on one another beyond certain gates within us."

"You have secret gates too?"

"Aye that. . . aye that. I work about the house during the day, mostly in a silence that's open to the winds and the birds and the sea. I have hens and a cow. I think long thoughts. . . what it would have been like if some poor soul of a fellow had taken a notion of me and there had been a home and children. . . I think all women feel that deep down. . . what it would have been like if I had had another nature in me. . . or if there hadn't been the war. And then I think that's all romance and unreality, for I am what I am and followed the thread that seemed inevitable. Where it goes I don't know; but I never talk of it to Stewart, nor does he to me. Yet we live warm and considerate for each other, as though deep down we were joined as one."

"Will he maybe not find that I am an intruder?"

"Not a bit. I went over and told him and he was real happy that you had come". . . she laughed. . . "as if he had been expecting you."

She led me over the short turf, here and there eroded by the winds down past ancient sandstone rocks like worn teeth protruding from the soil, until we came to the rock ledge with its deep angle of depression to the sea, soundless as this height to the ear, but with its onward sweep of wind blown wave resounding in the mind. Stewart was there, wearing his dark glasses and, just as we approached, putting down a tape recorder. He could still see something, for he rose and greeted me warmly; and I wondered where I had heard that sort of lilt of voice before.

"This," he said, "is my one concession to modernity. I can record my thoughts and play them over and get them into some sort of shape. See the clever device for telling which tape and which side of the tape."

"I put little dots on them," said Mina, "like braille, and he can feel them."

"And you are up here on holiday," he asked me, "just a chance visit?"

I told them about it, about my experiences of the last week. Then Mina had to go and, as I suspected, bake and prepare a meal: but nothing less would be allowed. Stewart told me of the view out to sea and of the changing kaleidoscope of the weather; I had to remind myself time and again that his memory, not his eyes, did the seeing. And all the time, the roundness of his voice and the flatness of some of the vowels reminded me of someone I had known in the distant past. . . or maybe it was just Glasgow folk I had known.

"I expect Mina told you about my eyesight. It was one of these inevitable things that happens in our lives. I was captured on one of the landings on the Italian coast and kept prisoner near Genoa. I must have caught some infection there but just thought it was the dust or lack of washing water. Then I escaped and was on the loose for months, working my way south to meet our oncoming British forces."

"And they took their time about it, I seem to remember."

"Mind you, it was a tremendous formative experience, that; I've never stopped thinking about it. And my eyes did not really bother me, not for another twenty years, and by that time I was just another delayed war casualty and not near as bad as many. I returned from the war to my job with the LMS Railway and after one or two changes of location, took over a tiny place on the Wick line. . . it was a crossing point on the single line, two small platforms, a signal-box with a dozen levers and a neat little booking-office and waiting-room. I was happy there."

I thought desperately: Where have I heard such a voice before? I scanned the phantom ranks of my schoolfellows, of University friends then I said: "That would be where your sister joined you?"

"Aye, she would do that. There were two shifts, you see. When the old fellow who worked the other one retired and they had difficulty in finding someone else, she applied. They looked sideways at her for being a woman; the Inspector got her to demonstrate her physical and mental skills. He could not think why a Nurse wanted to change over the single-line staff with some of these smart alecs of drivers. He sneakily told her to pull off the down distant signal. . . it was quite a distance away and needed a hefty tug. . . and she managed it first go with just a smirk of triumph. So they let her have the job, under my supervision. I could still see well enough then, but at times my eyes were sore and watery."

"So, you made a go of it together?"

"Surprising how well it worked. We're both individuals, but quite alike too. Knowing myself, I would say that she is the bigger. . . the stronger character of the two of us."

"And that was your life?"

"All day and every day, bar Sundays, when nothing ran. The box was open from seven in the morning till ten at night. . . the freights ran south in the late evening. But there were long spells in between when the breeze off the moor or the north-east wind kept me company. I managed to read a lot."

"Any special type of reading?"

"Science and philosophy mostly. You know, in the days before the war when I was my mother's sorrow, people thought me as prickly as a porcupine; but at heart I was soft and romantic and wanted to like people and to be accepted. But so many of the people I met seemed to live programmed lives. . . have you noticed? . . . programmed along their prejudices and their class traditions. Like the trains they ran on rails, in case they risked getting into unpredictable situations. You'll have noticed how security and unchanging routine is most people's secret desire. . . for all they say to the contrary."

"But your war experiences would alter that?"

"Completely. These fellows round about me were jerked out of the groove and faced change small and great every day of their lives. Especially on active service. . . in the Desert and the Landings. . . and you know it's as though they became real people, not men toiling in a graveyard. Of course you lost your friends, dear friends. . . you could lose bits of yourself too. . . but all the time it was ten thousand times life. And at the end of it all I knew I could never go back to a graveyard situation. I wish they had not lost my diaries. . . and the poetry from the Galloway years. . ."

(Suddenly the doors of perception began to open in me: the hints and guesses began to fall into place.)

". . . If I had had them I could have measured the difference between my earlier and my later work. Of course it might just have been the difference between a young man and one sadder and wiser."

"And you wrote poetry and read between the down and the up train. Not the average signalman or stationmaster, for that part."

"The Down and the Up and the light engines and the freights and the track tamper. . . oh, it was almost as bad as wartime: no two days were the same. I used to pride myself that ours was the most efficient station on all that line." He was looking away, thinking back down some sunlit corridor of memory. "I always wondered," (here I almost knew what he was going to say) "if I would ever meet that old academic problem of the two long freight trains arriving simultaneously at each end of the section." (I felt the scales fall rapidly from my eyes and knew that identification was imminent.) "You know that old chestnut of a problem. Each of the two platforms can hold an engine and twenty trucks. Two trains with an engine and twenty-five trucks approach from either end of the single line. You know? Question: how to get the one to pass the other?"

"And it really happened one day?" I asked him quite incredulously, but not because of the problem.

"Just once."

"So," I said deliberately out of a dream of the past, "you told one driver to leave five trucks behind and the other to do likewise. Then the first went right through the station and pushed the five trucks ahead of it as far as the distant signal. . ."

"Stop, stop!" he said excitedly, how do you know this? It hardly happens to anyone? Were you on the railway too?"

"Stewart Anderson, I know because you told me. . . but you were David then. Do you remember a long thin school-boy who spent a holiday in Galloway a year or two before the war?"

"And it's really you, Andy, and I can't see you? Have we changed all that much?"

"I've been trying for a quarter of an hour to put a name to a voice but my voice was attached to a David. . . but, yes, I was David S. Anderson in those days, right? I suppose between the 22 when I knew you and the 64 you are now, you've changed, we've both changed."

"I never knew if you had survived or not. So many didn't and I was not inclined to enquire. But I can't believe it. Oh, I mind you so clearly. . . we met in Glasgow once didn't we? But down there it was summer and the week when I was off in the evening we walked round Drumlaken Loch and recited poetry to each other and watched the midges dance above the water-lilies. You'll have to tell me all that's happened to yourself."

"Later, man, later. Let's stay at Drumlaken Loch."

"It was a strange summer that, full and lush, and though you wouldn't know about it, I had sort of blotted my copy-book in the neighbourhood and the good folk pointed the finger of scorn at me. And I so much wanted someone to care a wee bit about me. I wish I had not lost my diaries and my poetry."

"I wonder if I could remember one of them. How was it? Yes, it went like this:

Inside the couples come and go;
Melancholy saxophones
Manipulate them to and fro
Turning fast and stepping slow
(and he continued)
While at the door I stand,
I darkling and alone,
Alone and aloof from their happiness. . .

"Man, Andy, it's a voice out of the past. Can you remember anything else?"

"Maybe not at this minute. But I am sure I have one or two at home that you wrote in your letters."

"I thought a lot of you. . . I must have to trust my poetry to you. You feel so sensitive about it. Maybe that was unfair of me, seeing you were. . . what?. . . . five years younger? You remember the last night before you went home from your holiday, there was a great thunderstorm and we both got soaked."

"But it was great to be out in it together. Mind you, I thought you were going to ask if I remembered the trial you set me."

"What was that?"

"One of the evenings when you were on shift. The boat train was due; you pulled the levers and I could see the green light winking in the gathering dusk. You said it was difficult for the boat-train driver on the leading engine to see you holding out the single line staff. So you stationed me farther along the platform with a lighted paraffin flare held at arm's length, while you gave and received the staff in one wild movement and the boat train swept through at 50."

"These boat train drivers had no respect for difficulties; it was supposed to be 35 but they always took the straight stretch at speed."

"I was quite terrified with that flare. I thought you did it just to prove me."

"I'll not say no. What was I like then?"

"I can see a stocky chap, smaller than me, with a bullet head and black hair and arms that could have fitted a boxer. And your face was always lighting up with enthusiasm. I think I admired you because you were everything that I wasn't. . . working, independent."

"I bet I don't look like that now?"

"I'm not so sure. Stand up and take your glasses off. Oh yes! Turn the hair black again; take off a stone or two. . . or three; ask for your eyesight back and there's David Anderson I knew, signalman-porter at Drumlaken."

"So, it comes full circle; my past catches up with me and isn't entirely lost, eh?"

For a good half hour we were in the past as Stewart tried to
disentangle the shadows he had been fighting in those days.
His mother had been the strength in the home, trying to keep
a working-class family's head above water during the lean
years. Her sights were set two levels above the Springburn
housing scheme where they lived. Everything had to be
proper and respectable; you took your standards from surroundings higher than your own. But Stewart was her own
son and just as determined as she was, but along a different
track. Why should you model yourself on other folk, who
generally made a poor best out of their slavery to circumstances. Better to keep to yourself and listen and watch with
shining eyes while Nature crowded round you, as living as
yourself.

"You mind, we sat under the lime tree at the entrance to
Drumlaken park and tried to think ourselves into its ponderous growth, the water going up and the sugar coming
down. . ."

"And it was thinking too and watching us and trying to
influence us as we passed."

"I never spoke about it to anyone but you; the rest would
have pitied me, which is the usual response when people don't
expect to understand you. It was a vibrant world that summer. You see, I was wanting to be a real person, not a
programmed dummy. Man, Andy, I haven't remembered
Drumlaken for years. I must be more of a sentimentalist than
I thought."

"And after that it was into the army?"

"Yes, quite soon after the war started, but I wasn't in
Europe for Dunkirk. . . I missed that. We trained in various
parts of England; then one day we had a move, a long rail
journey by night and ended up. . . guess where?. . . in Galloway. I felt I had come home again. Once in the early hours of
the morning we passed through Drumlaken, coming from the
harbour station. I hung out of the window and smelled the
cold sweet air as we swept through at fifty and some old
fellow did the trapeze act with the staff. Must have been
difficult; there was no flare. After that it was Egypt, the

Desert, right along to Tunis. I reckoned I lost six lives on that excursion; I wonder, did you find the same: if you survived without loss of any of your working parts, it was the greatest experience you would ever have in your life. . . the nights, the early mornings. . . the pettiness and magnificence and sifting of human character, your own included, all around you. I sometimes think a world dedicated to peace would perish with frustration. "

We went in and had a meal; then sat the long evening out in the lee of the house, piecing the tumbled jig-saw of all our lives together.

Before I went back to my tent, Mina said:

"I'm so glad that you came. Isn't it strange that you met Stewart all these years ago. You know things about him that I don't know. " And then, more reflectively :

"I think it's a good thing to have a year or two after your life's effort. . . just to think it all over and come to terms with your lost hopes and abandoned ideals and your memories. . ."

"And, " said Stewart, "to repent of all the wrong you have done wittingly or otherwise on the way through. . . to re-pent. "

We had after all only got up to date and I was curious to know the new ventures they were both involved in. They had hinted so much. The next day I was led into a strange track, the sort of track from which, once you set your foot in it, there is no reversal. I picked up a little plumb-bob lying on the mantelpiece and asked Mina if they used it to dowse for water.

"No, not that, " she said with her little laugh, "we have enough water hereabouts to last us all year. No, I use that to explore lines of force. I learned it from Stewart, who learned it while he was on the loose in Italy. He can't see what it tells him now. . . and anyway, I am sometimes very sensitive with it. "

"Sometimes?"

"Well, you see, we're in a different world when we are working with that: you're not in a laboratory where things must obey your self-imposed principles, for we really don't know what it is we are cooperating with. Stewart will tell you: he'll go on for hours about it. The fact seems to be that I pick up lines of force running across the countryside. In some cases where the Underground is solid, I don't always get a good response; where there is Underground water, my pendulum responds. . . but we don't believe that it is recording water. . . rather powerful invisible forces radiating across the surface of the land." Here she looked at me and burst into a laugh. "And you're just incredulous, aren't you? Well, we are going to show you this afternoon. But on you go out with Stewart and not get in my way while I tidy the house and feed the hens."

Stewart had been at work with his tape-recorder. I told him about the pendulum and quickly realized that here was the new focal plane of his existence.

"You know," he said, "it's all of a piece since the Drumlaken days and the war and the Highland section of the LMS till now. . . until now. . . I mean, it's been growing together with a drive of its own all these years. I see it thus: Man has been thinking far too hard, overvaluing the process of deduction and theorizing; and most of the theories will turn out to be ridiculous fantasies, mark my word. Democracy, Theology, Logic, the structure of the Atom, Science. . . all of them fantasies where mind-activity has been allowed to oust the patient will to experience with our whole being, not just the boxed-in mind, the world around us. Of course, I know we are so far gone in the scientific and technological drive, that we have to go on. . . improving things, as we say. There's a level chance that we will end by destroying our material civilization, not just with a bomb: and the people who are left in odd corners of the world like this will go back to watching with bright eyes like the birds and listening and feeling for the great forces as trees and plants do."

"Man has alienated himself, you mean, isolated himself on a dead end?"

"Alienated himself from Nature and from God. I have often been struck that the effective god of the religions is in nearly every case God made in the likeness of Man. I'm referring to the official religious negotiations, not to personal experience."

"And you in this place are trying to go back, trying to force yourself back. . . ?"

"Well, I don't put it that way. It's not an intellectual exercise or discipline. In that case it would just be a system like any other, human wits unthinking what had been built up over the centuries. No, it's the evidence around us. And the terrible thing about that evidence, the terrifying thing, is that it just won't be played with as you play with a computer or a system of equations. It is in its own way as alive as we are, as the birds and the trees are, as God is. I first sensed this a number of years ago when I played with dowsing techniques. . . and it was playing with them at that point. . . and I came to know, what no scientist wants to know, that Mind can contact things without the need for sense or intellect : no need to hear or see, no need to apply mathematics or logic, just contact. Did Mina tell you? She is my pendulum now that I can't see it ; but in fact I can sense a lot just through my hands."

"What do you sense?"

"Lines of force running across country, sometimes four feet up above the ground, sometimes right on it. And some places, like relay stations where the direction is changed. And some places, stone circles and others where the power is concentrated."

I did not break his vision. We sat silent and I tried to imagine the world we call inanimate ringing in my ears and the power all about us.

Stewart took up the thread :

"What this power is, or these powers, I cannot tell you. I suspect we are to use them and not theorize. That they can be good for us or bad for us, I do not doubt. Up here where the human population has largely departed, the Power seems purified, uncorrupted and beneficent. I'm sure it is Man the Destroyer who corrupts these powers and makes them hostile. I try to see an interpretation of Adam in Eden and maybe this is a universal memory which the Hebrew priests got all muddled up with theology in their own best interests. A man might know God up here. But I have heard it said, where human vileness has surpassed itself, there is a sort of evil in the power that does not clear for a long time. It's not just fancy that makes people uncomfortable in some of the glens; people, even sophisticated ones, can sense the unwholesome unwelcoming powers. I expect these places that have been desecrated for the building of oil-rigs will be a long time in healing, long after the bushes and heather cover them over."

I took them out in the afternoon, a crackling dry breathless afternoon when the heather and turf smelled good and the small indigenous inhabitants of the turf, tormentil and thyme and lady's mantle had reasserted their immemorial claim to room and existence. Here and there the light green rosettes of the butterwort were unfolding but the bloom was not yet. We visited several standing stones, one of them tall and sinister. Mina and Stewart speculated on them as transmission pylons for energy.

"People," said Mina, "have been too ready to see these in a religious context. But away in the third millennium B.C., five thousand years ago, people hadn't come to moralized stories of salvation and sin and a God personally interested in the small details of their lives.

"I think,"said Stewart, "that people, ordinary people like us, were more nearly aware of their place. . . their humble place in the Creation. They were aware of birth and life. . . like the plants and animals, they were that too. And without having any organized thought about it, they knew death as the most natural process in the world, natural and necessary, and in that sense good."

"I have often thought," said Mina, "often been angry to think how smug theologians of the latter day referred to these people as pagans, as though that was something so pitiable and contemptible compared with people obsessed with moral salvation. These people, like all people would be good and bad, but they would be a sight more natural, because they had not suffocated themselves with intellectual conceit. My guess is that they lived aware of their kinship with growing things and with powers that reside in the Earth and in all creation. That is : Man as part of the creation, not the usurper who long ago has in any real sense ousted the Creator he talks about."

We were silent awhile, content to feel bound by deep ties and subterraneous forces. I felt that if I had allowed myself to speculate, I would have identified this as the Love that courses through the blood and marrow of things, beside which the love that fills our stories is a sentimental thing, the garment of self-pity turned inside out.

"What is this force," I asked, "which invests these stones and flashes across the land? Do you realize, we can't transmit electricity without wires. . . we've never solved it, clever as we are. But this travels across country and... KNOWS where it is going!"

"Come up first and see our Stone Circle. Circle of fire was the old Gaelic name for it, possibly inherited from even earlier peoples. But later folk who came and knew nothing of it, would no doubt cross themselves in fear and called them the Devil's Teeth. . . at least, that's what they were on an old Ordnance Survey map."

We went up on to a grass moor and there it was, twelve or sixteen huge stones more or less upright, a circle flattened at one side.

"Their geometry was good," said Stewart, "but because they had not a number system, they never quite arrived at the value π which was needed for circles. You see, they probably wanted the circumference to be an exact number of megalithic yards. . . you know about that? And the flattening of the circle was the way to do it. Don't ask me why! But I'll be daft enough and say this to you : if I sit quietly amongst them some day, feeling myself a part and no more than a part of it all, maybe they'll tell me : maybe the unique thought will just come into my mind."

I looked at the grey weathered stones of unimaginable antiquity, sealed with circular patches of green and orange lichen. You could say that they were stones, ordinary stones, some sort of metamorphic grit maybe. . . but ultimately the scientific mind would say 'just stones', the word 'just' illustrating their infinite distance from the intellectual inventiveness and cleverness of Man. Just stones, curiosities, ancient superstitious markers if you like. But the one that stood near me, caught in its age-old silence, seemed to utter something that I could neither understand nor escape. Mina intrigued me with her pendulum performances; I could make it work a bit, but she had so perfected the unthinking of herself, that she became strongly receptive. The thing located bands of power and round the stones this strange force zipped along.

"Could it ever escape?" I asked.

"You're better not to tamper with that," said Mina. "Once I accidentally released it and it took me some hours to recover. I think you did it too, Stewart?"

"Yes, it hit me in the stomach and the head: I realised I had interfered with something that is completely objective. . . I mean, if I did that, it had to respond that way. After that I was careful."

"We think the energy travels in bursts to the south-east, to that big stone we showed you, and there it is probably deflected south. . . but that's not our business."

From the high moor the land sloped downward to the western sea, blond and brown where the grass and bracken had not yet covered the ground with new life. But here and there I could see spots and slashes of colour, chrome green, italian pink, burnt sienna. It is an empty country now; in places you find the stone outlines of small fields and gardens where people took up a natural habitation before the greed of Man and its inhuman science of Economics changed the pattern of occupation. Some were driven away as unprofitable economic capital; some were lured away in the search for wealth unbounded of the plugging of basic material wants; some wanted the freedom to make a kirk or a mill of their own lives. But always it was the loss of the tenuous bond that linked them to Nature and the soil and the live forces that energized their humanity. An old walled graveyard nearby with almost indecipherable stones records the passing of those who chose to stay and remain one with Nature. Perhaps it was all inevitable: perhaps it is a circular motion after all

that will one day bring back sensitive people to live where
Man might live fulfilled and happy. It won't be in caves or
smoky huts, of course: technology insists on ever better
standards of material living, but it will be something sensitive
and considerate, a feeling that you are part of Nature, not
there to dominate and exploit it. I looked at range upon range
of mountains and outcrops, valleys and ice-formed slopes. I
had a vision of forces, energies, leaping across them like
unperceived light, forces that would not be denied, not even
in the human holocaust.

"I ponder it endlessly," said Stewart, "more intensely I
think because of my one faculty lost. You can't turn history
back, you can't stop history. I try to think what sort of people
inhabited these valleys, these seaward slopes, when the ice
withdrew and made room for them. There's no use idealizing,
for life would often be cold and painful and uncertain. But I
wonder too, would it sometimes be intense and in a sense
secure, more than we know, when the wonder of returning
Spring was wonder indeed and there was a nearer identity of
hands and leaves, blood and sap. . . when there was a need for
life and growth and a need for death so that young growth
might supervene. Nowadays we would take it hard without
soap or car tyres or paper. . . or the ability to write and read.
We don't expect to reverse civilization, and shouldn't want
to. . . and probably won't have to. But how to clear ourselves
of the grime of thousands of years?"

"The grime?"

"The hard crust of attitudes and delusions and everything
else that makes it easier to live without effort. . . live without
really living, if you get me. As far back as history extends
Men have been dominating men, often with intolerable savagery unknown to the animals. Men have also been content to
submit to men, for that way there was always less effort
needed, less discomfort, less need to be alive and kicking. It
was physical domination at first; then it was ideas and ideolo-
gists, often priests, who defined the limits of what was acceptable belief or not. The Christian church suppressed Science
and those who thought in non-religious categories; the

church in its turn was ousted. . . or nearly so. . . by what called itself rationality and enlightenment and millions in the over-developed world are content to let Science have its way and sink into grinding slavery to industrial civilization and technology. Once governments might have had a hope of being free. . . of taking free decisions. Now they too are enslaved to international business, nuclear progress and mutual fear. In all that horror, organized religion, the churches, Christian, Moslem, Hindu and the rest have no valid comment to make, because they stopped effective history so many hundreds of years ago."

"Stewart, it's as well you are north of Lochinver and mostly out of the poisonous cloud of it all. You know I had a sudden memory of that little wooden house you had in Drumlaken on a wet evening. I met the ancestors of your present thoughts then."

"But don't go away and think I am buried in mourning for the past. Quite the opposite. I have an enormous belief in the future, in the circularity of things. We are hopelessly encrusted at the moment with beliefs we don't really believe in. And these prevent us from walking simply and free across our world, free of the conceit that we are. . . that we are different from, superior to. . . masters of Nature. . . and Nature is there to be defeated, harnessed, exploited. That we must lose. We've got to look at the gulls. . . the milkwort. . . the rowan trees, with kinship: we too must respond to the great wind out of the west that summons life to the annual festival; we a part of it."

"But I ask him," said Mina, "can you have cities like this, great urban areas where people are caught in the mill-race of expectations that others have designed for them. . . you know, material goods, pleasures, salvation, instant love?"

"I think of that one too," said Stewart, "and sometimes I do not see any change of course short of disaster on a large scale. . . disaster, that is, for all those who have to lose everything. But then, by another way of reckoning, I could see it as the next loop in the coil. Who knows, may be it would be the beginning of a better and wiser attempt. It has happened several times in the world's history; only false philosophies make us believe that it could not happen to as fine a species as we are."

"But," I ventured, "you have to sweep away the picture of a beneficent God brooding indulgently over the sorry antics of mankind. People, even irreligious people, will cling desperately to that."

"You know, if that fellow in the New Testament ever did ask that ultimate question: What is Truth?. . . and if he meant it, not just flippantly, he was probably a more penetrating observer than all those who have heaped their wrath on him since. Truth? Is it more than a cry of human despair? Well, whatever we say about it, it will never be defined by Councils of the Church or by the British Association. It may take another circularity, many circularities before Man stumbles on it."

We waited in a silence broken by little aromatic gusts of wind and the small drone of brown bees questing for spring flowers. We were at one, and Stewart spoke for us all:

"And meantime for those who can, whether they live in the Torridonian sandstone or the Green Belts round cities or in the detritus of crumbling civilization, there must be a new sort of courage, the courage to strip off all the comfortable illusions. . . you know. . . the illusion of progress, the illusion of the uniqueness of Man, the illusion that we have at our command a God made to suit our needs. We have to strip these off at all costs and be as naked as the first leaf in the northerly wind. It grows, for it has its roots in soil and rock and seepage and who knows what else charges the Underground. We would have more material protection than the leaf, but need too the beneficence of these forces, we a relevant part of the creation, taking our place, claiming our share, not blinding ourselves, deafening ourselves to it with the adoration of our own achievements."

"Are you saying then that in what you call the overdeveloped world Man is effectively lost? The thing is irreversible: there will not be a short cut back to the high road?"

He said reluctantly, as though it was beyond his remit to

say anything, "I think so. But that doesn't mean we should sit in gloom and pessimism. I think. . . " and he stared away across the landscape, seeing nothing, but maybe smelling hillside fires which the other two of us could see blowing blue and tenuous in the inshore wind. . .

"... I think, Andy. . . and I'll say it to you, for Mina knows what I think without my saying it. . . maybe the really important thing, apart from the business of living which we can't avoid, is to be seeking our true salvation every moment of our lives, not in intellect, not in religious systems, but in unthinking ourselves into the created Beings we really are. So we may find the Holy, that which is set apart. The stones and the circles and the forces, like Nature are all a part of the true Ground of our Being. To be there in utter humility, to sense them vibrating with life around you is immersion in the Ultimate. I think a man might have a new sort of vision of God and the creation. . . and tremble with a sort of terror and joy, to know how much he is part of the beginning and the end of it."

Story Number Ten

RADNOR FOREST

AS WE WATCHED, the evening festival of clouds transmuted itself to silver sunlight behind the powerful outline of Radnor Forest. It was a time for no words. The eye and the mind were intimately involved with the change in the blues and the golds, the intense outlines of the hill silhouettes, the reticent curves of the lower slopes now settling into night and darkness. From half-minute to half-minute the ratchet in the perception clicked as the detail of active day settled frame by frame into the generality of night. I looked at Nick, head on the supportive palm of his hand, staring into the West, the planes of his face contriving for him a greater intensity than you see in the daylight.

"Cut!" (I said). "Where are your thoughts?"

"Nothing new," (he replied), "we have discussed it all before." (Then softly, for the hefty fellow he was) "But it comes over me again and again at the day's end. You know the strange illusion you have in the morning and the afternoon when illumination is maximal, that you are securely on your own feet, know what you are about and settle your own purposes. Everything is vertical and direct. . . you yourself have your assured place. But as the shadows thicken around you. . . look! there's a creature on that wall, a stoat, I think, getting the last rays of the sun. . ."

"But as the shadows thicken around you?" (I prompted).

"Your place in things seems less assured; your fellowship with others becomes ghostly. I think evening always did bring on fear and loneliness, the feeling that despite all your efforts, you have no human companions or guide. But you know what I mean."

We had discussed it often before. Now this twilight moment when even our outlines were falling away and only imprecise memories of each other remained... now this moment tingled suddenly with insecurity. We had watched somewhere on our travels a child run desperate to its mother; we came on two teenagers at a turn on the path somewhere embracing, oblivious to us, kissing as though they would merge into one another. Some people, out of insecurity and terror of aloneness, fitted their unconformity to that of someone else and called it Love; they sought sexual union and called it love only to realise sometimes in their disillusionment that their love was the savagery of mutual domination. "I should be a builder of bridges. . . ", so began one of Nick's poems. . . but the bridges were the slender constructs of experiment and hope over the infinite abyss that separates one from another. Must it be so, this endless separation, we had often asked; but no philosophy, no religion, had approached an answer. And the grosser theories of politics and Socialism brushed away abysses and bridges together and laid as their substrate the Togetherness of Man.

"You see that notch to the left of where the forest is?" (said Nick). "See the light streaming down through it, a perfect man-made notch. We'll go up there tomorrow and look back down."

It was time to return to the tent, brew up some tea and prepare for the night. The air with its September chill made us glad to return to the security and warmth and the hissing gaslight that hung from a roof pole.

Twelve days afoot in Hereford and Radnorshire. . . they are probably called something else now. . . had served to deepen a friendship that had long passed the superficial. Nick's way had by chance (as they say) crossed mine and he had been my care and responsibility for quite a while. So far as bridges can be built over the void we had done so, and we had reached such an acceptance of each other and our different orientation of attitude that when the crossroads was reached and Nick would go one way, I another, we knew that there was no cause for sadness or recrimination: each man's evolution of his life is implicit within his own unique complex of circumstances. We had traversed the quiet valleys during these twelve days, out of time almost, you might say, greeting the rare countryfolk who crossed our path on the little twisted hedgebound ways, or at a field's top under some elder trees where a tractor paused at the turn. . . people going about their ancient business with modern tools in their hands. Inevitably we had honoured old Alfred Watkins who had pioneered the ley line hereabouts in the 1920s; the topic like so many had uncovered in us both the underlying attitudes with which we faced the Unknown.

We had stood that morning on a hilltop marked 'Camp' on the survey sheet, and taken bearings and checked the imaginary straight line which joined two other hill-tops and an ancient crossroads and a thirteenth-century church. You could draw just such a line on the map; it took the eye of imagination to see it on the ground. Yet that too was possible. Sweep back the centuries of what we call progress, repel Norman and Saxon and Roman, imagine the land heavily forested, the valley bottoms wet and marshy, the people on the ground as scarce or scarcer than what we had seen today. Yet the fact seems firm: they were probably no less intelligent than we, even if they had not the implement techniques of writing, counting and measurement. Could you imagine a productive intelligence without these props? Could you guess at an intelligence looking out through eyes like ours on a paradoxically same-but-different landscape of Bache Hill or Creigiau and the valley bottoms, where castles and mills and tracks of old railways denoted Man's playthings of his growing-up. What would ancient people with our standard of perception and response make of it as they observed and saw their problems of living traced on a terrain wilder than this on just such a September morning? We err if we imagine their response a brutish acquiescence.

"You fundamentally want to believe in progress," (Nick had said).

"I don't. You want to find things organized to some better end and that's why you're concerned about social welfare and religion and things like that. But somehow my set of data doesn't predispose me to think that way. I see vast detours and diversions in which we get ever farther away from our essential humanity."

Of course I knew his point of view. I had tried so often to station myself there and look down through the futile centuries. It was no occasion for dispute, rather the endless restatement and approximation to understanding. I played into his half of the court:

"I just can't think that all the organization and application of human wisdom to the problems of Living, the love of one's neighbour, the care for the sick, the mentally retarded, the handicapped. . . all this amounts to no significant gain. And what about science and technology, improved amenities, labour saving. . . "

"And," (he added, head to one side, question mingling with statement), over-population, maldistribution of wealth, the toxic environment, you know?"

"Yes, it troubles me. But I can't think that to go back to the raw simplicity of Stone Age man would be any solution at all."

"That troubles me too. Human life has to be tolerable, not a pitiful disillusionment after youth and a longing for a speedy end. I always remember that thing you told me about the old Sibyl's reply to someone asking what was best in life. 'The best is unattainable,' she said, 'never to have been born; and the next best thing is: soon to die.' I wonder if I could ever come to think in such a hopeless way as that. Or is it the reverse side of the Truth? Yet I'm sure it must have been so for lots of the people who built these mounds and so-called camps. I wonder if it was implicit in Man's Nature that he would come in the end to worship his own indwelling principle of Intelligence and make that his god. Did the mistake have to be made?"

"You know the popular phrase, using your God-given intelligence to solve your own problems. God-given! That's the other assumption. Even yet we are at sixes and sevens between a Creation story of the genesis type and one of the evolutionary type, which may after all be just as improbable as the other, if you have the courage to take off your scientific blinkers."

"I think that's what I mean. Though a few people nowadays, a very few people will really build their faith on an Act-of-Creation beginning, the big battalions unthinkingly worship evolving human intellect and have long ago put that in *loco dei*. I mean, that's their faith and they will stake their working life on the truth of it. . . and the Old Man in the Sky is left for the Sunday Schools."

Up on the hill top there, on the short-cropped turf, there was a marvellous sense of freedom. You could just gaze at the ridges and the hill-tops, blue upon blue with forest thrusting from the slopes; you could scrutinize almost with the eye of God the human world and its organized purposes. . . a Post Office van stopped at the roadside; a tractor ploughing the furrows of winter, unseen a circular saw whining along tree trunks, cattle motionless beside their shadows in a meadow. Sometimes I could sense it but not with the clarity of my companion.

"Why," (I asked suddenly out of my well of thoughts), "why would neolithic Man want to survey and fix routes across the land? It would be trackless, I know, but why go to all this trouble? Even if we agree that the ancient tracks and the Marker stones, the tumps and the tumuli were located where they were and nowhere else and for a purpose. . . still, why go to all this trouble?"

"Isn't it possible that Man was fundamentally different then. . . far more sensitive to all sorts of natural things than we are and only as intellectually developed as he needed to be. . . that he felt his roots mystically, though really enough in the soil. . . he had not yet been seduced by intellect to reconceive and fashion the Earth after his own heart. Isn't it possible that the sons of Earth of that time had to be in contact with the soil and never allow themselves the conceit that they could do without it?"

"You want to class Man firmly with the plants, trees and other animals? . . . and forget in its literalness this son of God business. I think the Western world has too readily taken over the speculations of desert peoples when they allowed intellect and imagination to raise them to the status of the likeness of God."

"Yes, I begin to think so. I wonder whether Man's self-exaltation and his eventual destruction are implicit in his nature. . . like a soap bubble that just has to burst some-time?"

"Or did he take a wrong turning somewhere?"

We had sat atop the hill on the crisp turf facing south-east along one of Alfred Watkins' ley lines. But a great spinnaker of cloud came bellying across the sun and reminded us of our lowly earth-bound status. We thought: Rain. And began to make for the low ground.

"Do you think, Nick, that Man, before he let himself be cut adrift from the rest of creation. . . do you think he could sense things . . . I mean, forces within the earth, purposes calling him from a distance. Could knowledge have transmitted itself by direct awareness, and not by reading or symbols? This is the point where I find the leap still too great to make."

"I'm more rash than you. I like to make a great leap and imagine what it would be like from the other side. I would say: Yes. Let's agree that Stone Age living would not be to your taste nor mine. But then neither would life in Darkest Africa today be to our taste. I think that there could be more than superficial evidence that the suppression of the specula-tive Intellect means a heightened awareness of. . . oh! lots of things. . . evil behaviour, malevolent destructive things, I mean. . . and communication and objective sorts of know-ledge. I often think that the collision in Africa, say, or South America, between a ready-made intellectual moral system such as Christianity is, and a civilization rooted in the rocks and the soil, has produced an irremediable disaster. You'll not agree; but I don't think that the Christian theology even begins to make contact with the peoples there, and I don't care how many Rock Gospellers and Communist priests you quote at me. The thing is a fundamental violation of slower peoples by arrogant Northerners."

"Yet Christianity at its best will always claim that the Holy Spirit will accompany it on its journey and see that everything works properly. I say so with some diffidence. . . and knowing what you will say."

"Yes, inquisitions, massacres, tortures, brainwashing. I believe in the Holy Spirit all right. But not that way. Where was it during these innumerable hideous episodes? Or like Zeus in Homer, had it gone off conveniently to visit the Ethiopians?"

We laughed and had to agree that for all our perplexing speculations it was good to have a world of literature ready for recall to level out the score. But we agreed that these were the poets, the Creative Folk, in whom survives the essential fire, no matter how far away its origins.

The September nights are long. We had time after supper to sit and read a little so far as the illumination allowed; and to have our quiet half-hour together, when from different points of the spiritual compass we freed ourselves from Ego and rededicated the night and the coming day to such service as would be apportioned to us. The night was quiet with only the occasional rustle and squawk to indicate acts in the ceaseless drama of Nature around us. Nick went down to the brook below, gathering who knows what impresssions for later poetry; I turned the lamp low, went out and did up the flap of the canvas and made my way up to the little hill behind our camp. The night was dark and the star-grid changed as clouds blew over from the west. At the top, in a little hollow out of the wind, I stopped. I set about loosing from myself, prizing away all the incrustation of care and speculation for the future, the thoughts about others and the lichen of worry about the world in general which grows on us unbidden. At that moment, I thought, all over the world, individuals were doing likewise, turning their backs on circumstance and homing-in on the receptive simplicity which was theirs for the effort. I do not now remember the sequence of my thoughts. I had left my watch in the tent and was untroubled by time. But to be sure I reached a state of abstraction where even the impact of sense was unfelt. What happened? I do not know. But later when I emerged from it and told Nick, he confirmed it: it had happened to him too. I knew that I had contacted some other order of experience.

I felt a tingling in my hands and feet which seemed to guide me about a landscape like a blinded man with a white stick. I imagined I walked prodigious distances and did not become tired, being sustained by some input of secret energy. Here and there stones set in the ground glowed invisibly with recognition and were the guide points for my way. I thought that I met a man... but his back was to me... who carried two staves and searched the land with them planting one and moving the other. People passed me in the quiet dingles, small swarthy people moving in the starlit darkness as though they knew where they were going; but I seemed not to exist for them. At one point below an ancient forest of beech and oak, where a man could have despaired of direction in the dark, I was caught as it were by a wind, though nothing moved... as it were by a force to which I responded. I passed into the forest and moved obliquely through it and was soon toiling up last craggy outcrops of the hill beyond. I paused there and was suffused... how can I say... by a strange security beneath my feet and up through me, so that I looked out and up on to the stars, I the highest thing in that landscape, with a happiness and a sense of greeting and of kin. Below me, here and there points of dim light shone for me; I had to remember later that the age of towns and villages and lit homesteads was not yet. And I wondered, perhaps as I returned from the distant past to the Present, whether it might be that earth and stone and water were alive in some physical way and the trees and plants and mosses drew their life from this, and animals and Man, just a shade more sophisticated, moved in measures to them as the poet said 'like a dancer'... but only so long as his feet were in the grass and the soil and the rock and the underlying force.

It was with the swift passage of a meteor in the south-east, I think, that the spell broke and I was recalled. After staring long at the stars and into the darkness, burgeoning with unidentifiable shapes, I picked my way down the stony track and came to the tent where the light was turned up and my companion within. I asked if the bank of the brook and the autumn hedgerows had thrown up any original combinations of thought.

"No," (he said), "we've been talking too much of these blessed leys and old Watkins' theories. I think the interpretation of his evidence could be different from what he proposed. I saw a man with two staves plotting a route. . ."

"And little swarthy folk hurrying along, knowing, it seems, where they were going."

"You saw them too? I wondered if you would."

"Perhaps our imagination was just projecting something of what we had been talking about."

"Or perhaps, when you create a mental vacuum in yourself, you can contact a memory of what has been. You remember that time at Funtington near Chichester?"

"Or the deserted Almond valley in Perthshire? I never could give a satisfactory account of that."

To be sure, we did not know what to believe or whether it was a matter for believing or just accepting on another level. We doused the light and slept.

A shower in the early morning hours ushered in the day, the last day of our pilgrimage. I listened to the determined patter on the canvas, coming in gusts as the wind orchestrated it and dying away. . . then I fell asleep again. We woke together to sunlight and silence. The air smelt good, refreshed by the night.

"It's only fusspots like us who insist on washing and shaving first thing in the morning," (said Nick). "Maybe that's the ultimate secret why we get on so well together."

"I couldn't begin to dig out the reason why I must shave before anything else. Maybe just a damned determination to be different."

We ate, packed everything away but in a different order, for I was to take much of the camping equipment home in the train. Nick said:

"I dreamed I was walking straight across a desert, straight for endless miles and somehow I never deviated. Then I met a man with two staves which he held up as if blessing me."

No dreams had visited me, at least none that I had rescued as I came awake.

"In a scientific age," (said Nick), "it's perverse, I know; but it's great not to be able to explain things, to be left with the mystery."

"The man with two sticks?"

"The little swarthy folk hurrying past in the dark? You realise that we both had the same experience though half a mile apart last night."

"But in our rudimentary knowledge of things that matter. . . that's just another mystery."

"We're an unpractical pair," (said Nick pausing as he fastened up outer straps on his rucksack.) "The sophisticated world would laugh us right off sheet 148 and on to 149. Shall we set off up the straight track to that notch on the skyline and make across to Bleddfa?"

We did that. I passed the place of my night vision and found the mystery dispelled by the light of day. Sheep were cropping the grass noisily; they looked uncomprehending at us as we passed. At the notch in the skyline we stopped momentarily, then headed north. It was a marvellous day, late summer heat mingling at these heights with the first admonition of winter cold. I thought of the world of Nature around us, the bedstraw and the thyme and the other tiny plants which patterned the turf. For many of them, for birds and insects as well, winter must mean a suppression nearly to death, but never quite. They come back, with prodigal efforts they come back and flaunt the success of their survival. Do they have any awareness what happens to them? Does something akin to a deep faith drive the root and the seed and the multiplicity of free moving creatures?: they will survive no matter how hard the winter. Only Man can put paid to their titanic efforts with his bulldozers and poisons and heedless arrogance. They survive. . . but at what a cost! Seeds sperms eggs a millionfold that only a few may break into life. And if we interfere, if we out of pity or the desire for profit, enhance the survival of one species, we upset the balance and prepare for ourselves who knows what horrors. So I communed silently with my own thoughts as we surmounted these bare hills, surprising ourselves with the ever-widening views of lovely Central Wales. I kept thinking: in the slow upward march to civilization we have worked out our own system of values and are determined to impress them on Nature whether they are appropriate or not. Religious folk, Church folk, Tom or Dick, the average decent person around us would have it that each of us is uniquely valuable, has a destiny, if we like to work for it. Each one of us! The teeming over-populations so rudely suppressed by famine or flood or pestilence! The luckless folk, crippled, debilitated in mind, the Hopeless which the overdeveloped countries keep alive at prodigious expense! Is that from principle or sentiment or a complete blindness to the natural order of things?

So with the thrust of my knees and the grating of boot soles on gravel or rock I find that useful exploratory thinking goes on, particularly on the upward slopes where poise and balance come more easily than on the descent. We paused below Rock Dingle where the little road tumbles awkwardly to Bleddfa. We had chosen this way because a mile or two farther on we had a visit of obligation to make, a visit to the two Miss Wrights who some years ago had with exemplary kindness come to our rescue in a deluge.

We found them at home in a cottage sadly in need of repair but beyond their strength and resources. The garden in front was just such a charming small wilderness as two elderly ladies cherish. We spent an hour and more just listening to the saga of their lives. Miss Jane had had, surprisingly for her age, a kidney transplant a year or so ago. It had been successful; but she conveyed the edge of a querulous uncertainty about it. Miss Millie with her robust health attributed all to the love of Jesus who so meticulously provided for the small needs of their lives. Nick and I were the Greek chorus, making suitable comment so far as we could judge it, and trying from out of our different world to contact them on the level. They were so kind and generous; but I felt now, what I had just guessed at before, that their life had fallen into a most delicate equilibrium, so delicate that I wondered how it would cope with the disasters that lurked in the future.

"Janie just grew worse and worse, but we hardly noticed how far it had gone till a new young Dr Tuplin took one look at her and set things moving. A clever young man he was, from Newcastle in the north I think."

I wondered how Miss Jane had faced the transplant at her age and asked her.

"We prayed about it of course; some of our friends said Yes, some NO. But in the end the Doctor had arranged everything. So I just took my case and went to the great world of Hereford."

"We felt that it was the Lord's doing, you know, that Dr Tuplin saw Janie and recognized what was wrong. God would want her to live; I'm sure I could not do without her."

Nick asked her about the hospital; that would be a new experience for her?

"Well, not quite. I had been an out-patient years ago when I hurt my back. But this was different. Everybody was so kind and considerate, the nurses so smart and attentive. I had three days to wait before anything was done, before the first tests. I just used to lie in the ward and go over in my mind all the paths from here to Llangunllo and up to the camp on Wysin Hill. It kept me from thinking about anything else."

I said to Millie that she would feel lonely.

"I endured it for three days on my own. Then I packed my case and went to live with a cousin outside Hereford. So I went in and saw Janie every day."

"You know," (said Janie), "some people are just terrified of the anaesthetic. Somebody told me to say some rhyme over to myself while they were preparing to do it, so I decided on that old Housman rhyme, you know

Clunbury, Clunton, Clungunthlet and Clun
Are the naughtiest places under sun.

I don't think he said 'naughtiest' but we do."

"And how far did you get with it?"

"I think I got to 'naughtiest'. . . at least next thing I knew, I was coming to with someone else's kidney in me."

But then a strange thing happened. I went into the kitchen

with Millie to help get something to eat, and she talked to me of her fears and her faith.

"But," (she said), "and you mustn't say it to Janie, I am worried that we did wrong. I know there's all this science and medicine; but we are also in the hand of God who decides our own end and how we go. We must believe that or we believe nothing at all. And, you see, maybe I was so afraid for myself that I encouraged her to do something wrong. Do you understand? Something that is available. . . but quite wrong."

I tried to allay her fears, but neither she nor I was convinced. I helped her in with the tea and the light meal which she insisted in putting before us. I had promised that I would write to her about her problem once I had had time to think of it carefully. We interrupted Nick and old Janie in a very intimate conversation. The matter was dropped and we moved to sunnier things. They stood in their porch as we left, framed in clematis and a convolvulus that had long since got out of control. I will remember them with a pang: they made no secret of their heart and their Faith. I did write to them, twice, at some length, and I hope that it helped. But they died, it seems within a fortnight of one another and Janie was the first to go. I hoped that they had both found their way through the dark wood to some understanding.

The day had clouded over when we left and somehow other things had diverted our attention. Or maybe it was that we had each our share of the story and wondered what the other part was. We toiled up through a little wood, then over open heath, gaining height rapidly; still we said nothing to one another. It was as though the episode in the valley into which we had intruded one noon in September had split into two mutually uncomfortable stories. Just before the slope turned away and blocked the extensive view to the south-east, we stopped and eased our backs awhile. Still we said nothing: the clouds were gathering from the west. I looked at Nick, always in the search for a new portrait format. I don't know for certain about landscape painting; but when you are ever on the search for the essential in portraiture, you are always storing and filing impressions. Some people, particularly younger folk, have such a natural way of inclining the head, stretching out their legs, clasping their hands in strength and registering an incipient smile at the corner of their mouth. I find this exciting; now Nick was doing just this for me without realising it. Then quite unexpectedly he said:

"I feel we intruded into something in that little house and will have to do something about it, but I don't know what."

I kept my hand concealed and said merely:

"Meaning?"

"I was talking to Janie while you were in the kitchen and I was appalled. . . yes, that's the word. . . appalled to discover that she felt she had done wrong in having that operation but did not want to mention it to Millie. You know, she talked to me in that sort of way that leaves you feeling you were just put there to listen. She talked a lot about it and then said. . . I remember her words. . . 'I'm sure God has his time for people like me to go and we have no business interfering. But, you see, it was Millie. I didn't know what she would do without me. And somehow we couldn't talk about it.' I was appalled that two people who have been so close to one another, who have lived their lives in that small valley, couldn't build that last bridge."

I looked at him, feeling the implication of it, then told him the other half of the story.

"Strange, isn't it, that civilization and modern science offer a temptation and when we accept it we know we have finally destroyed the innocence of life."

"But," (he said) "we will not have strayed into that house merely to observe. I expect our services will be needed. . . you know?"

"Yes, I was thinking that too. We must keep Millie and Janie in mind; I'll write to them quite soon."

Then we resumed our way. This is a land where Nature with the hand of an artist has adjusted to the slow centuries; Man has intruded with his structures and metalled ways and an ecology not too far removed from the masterplan of Nature. Elsewhere in a turbulent world it would not be so; here it was a pleasure to feel the wise adjustment untroubled

by the hurtling motorway or the eddying millions. You have
to stop though, stop and gaze not too intently at the pattern,
the natural order and the arrangement that centuries of mind
have imposed on it. We had time that day, and other purposes
than covering set distances. We had reached our last ridge, the
one that overlooks the youthful Teme, high above Knucklas
with its viaduct, and bearing towards Knighton, the parting of
our ways. The clouds had withdrawn to give us a benison of
afternoon sunlight. I had withheld a thought for some days
now but it urgently needed an airing.

"Nick," (I said) "are you sure you know what you are
doing?"

Nick had many smiles; this was his tight-lipped one.

"I mean, are you prepared to take the future on trust? At
your age it could be a long one."

"Well," (he said), "I know how you feel. The whole
pattern of your upbringing looked for security and firm
footing. And you have made it with training and a career and,
I would guess, great opportunities ahead. But I. . .? I don't
have to go over all the details of my troubled years and my
lack of security. I just don't feel the same way about a secure
cut-and-dried career."

"I know that. I appreciate that out of your box of pieces,
you pick another way. And I have no business at all even
implying that you are being rash. You don't really think that,
do you? Maybe I just wonder if there is something more I
should have done."

"For me? No, no. You've done everything, more than I
could ever have had the right to expect. The opportunities,
the financial backing for my training. . . I'm endlessly grateful
and you can be sure it won't be lost. Maybe someday when I
am older and wiser, I'll know that it is time to fit into a slot
and anchor myself. But not yet."

"I am sure you know what you are doing."

"Maybe I am incurably romantic. . . maybe I'm at a stage
you got over so many years ago. I see the world of human
events, the stage as it were, offering endless possibilities. Do
you know what I was just recalling? About three years ago in

our Dramatic Club we were given the skeleton of a play, and the players had to work out the moves and the dialogue and the development for themselves. It was enormously perplexing but in the end we wrote the play. I remember while we were on stage, those of us in the wings waiting to go on, were going about with shining faces: we were Creators not just Players. And just for now I want to be a bit of a creator, not just a performer."

"And your immediate plans again?"

"When I leave you at Knighton this afternoon, I'll head for South Wales where I know somebody. I have quite a lot of talents and minor skills and I'll use them here and there. Particularly in the winter. You can't really be moving round the British roads in the middle of winter."

"Will you go abroad soon?"

"Yes, there are places there that really call me, Canada, Australia. . . and I have contacts there who could help. I think I just want to find out what it would be to. . . trust my course to Higher Direction."

"I should understand you there. I quite agree there's no particular moral credit in following a career structure, unless you have others dependent on you. You would need to be sure you did not have dependents or any commitments at all. It's like a man defending himself in Court: if you choose to do it the hard way you have to know the rules and responsibilities."

"Yes, I think I am plain cold sober; I usually am. And I am happy in that loneliness is not a problem. For most people that would make my course impossible. Somehow a semi-detached in the suburbs with a hedge, a garage, a wife and two children isn't my way; I just know it. But I appreciate that it is most people's way."

"What do you think you'll get from it?"

"I hope to be able to say from farther on: I have lived. . . as conformably to Nature as possible. . . as free from the spurious drives of modern Man as possible. . ."

"So long as you have good health and a bit of luck?"

"Yes, that too. Health you've got to look after but the

unexpected is always there. Luck? Well, I suppose so. It always seems such pagan meaningless term; and it may be something else, a real feature of the cosmic world that we do not begin to understand. Yes, I want a bit of luck too. And I'll not be on my own. You know?"

And I did know, for we had talked so many miles away and brought to each other an ever clearer exposition of our world as we each knew it. I had a feeling that it turned on something structured perhaps. There are those who need the scaffolding from the messy foundations up to the clouds; they need to see that it all fits together and really fronts the clouds with a certainty. I was brought up to that, and with my studies and training had probably taken the whole thing for granted. The structure spelt for me my limits and my duties and that is comfortable and behovely... I used the word but do not quite know what it means. But the circumstances that brought Nick into my orbit had altered all that. Nick with his ability and perspicacity no less than mine, and a strong resilient character and youth on his side, had challenged my structure.

"It's secondhand, that," (he had said in the earnest way I could never mistake), "it's secondhand and we are called to make ourselves respond at first hand."

I guessed he was right for I too was steadily approaching that view.

"Maybe I'm too vehement and no philosopher... I am no philosopher and won't be one. But I basically don't believe that we are born to respond differently to the rest of creation. We don't need any spiritual bureaucracy to deal with our cases, nor any theology either. We get down to it and go it alone."

That had been our way for two years now, though I with my function in organized society had continued to comply with the demands. Were they just demands of propriety? Meaningless gestures to allay alarm? I had realised, too, that it very much depends on your education whether you concede a ready validity to tradition and the wisdom of the ages. In me it had meant that; in Nick with his fantastic emergence from a veritable sea of bad fortune (in which to my secret joy I had been allowed to play a part). . . in him attitudes had not crystallized: he felt no pressure from the "done thing." The confidence was his; the courage was his; mine was now to wish him well and murmur his name with a blessing.

We came down to Knighton, a little town in which I have never been at home. We had tea in the only place we could find open, of which I remember. . . nothing, except a wild sort of evangelist who asked us urgently if we were saved. I saw Nick wanting to argue with him, then thinking better of it, he left well alone; for the question must be rhetorical. We found our way through the streets at close of shop to the station, which has survived several threats to its existence. I took the camping gear and would contrive to get back to Birmingham with it. Nick said:

"I'll be thinking of you till next we meet. What a world of interest we have between us; one life would never be enough to explore it all. I'll keep you posted, never fear. And if I ever need you badly or you need me, I bet we'll know. . . and know what to do."

The conversation drifted away to practical matters, loose ends that needed tidying up.

"I say," (he said suddenly) "will you write to the old ladies and try to bridge the gap. I'm not sure I've lived enough years to be able to do that properly. It has been the one cloud on a lovely day."

People were gathering on the platform; I was pleased to see that the Central Wales line sustained a fair traffic.

"There's just the chance that I may go abroad quite soon: depends how things work out. Of course I'll see you before that. . . unless you happen to be abroad at the time. I hate waiting for trains, don't you?"

"When I was young I used to wish that my mother would not come to see me off on long journeys. I hated pulling out into an exciting future and leaving her in a static past full of memories."

"I think I am doing that to you—"

"Except that I understand and am one hundred per cent

with you in your decision and adventure. Nick, always be a builder of bridges!"

At which point the dark green diesel multiple drew in having come all the way from Llanelly. . . and drew out two minutes later. There had been nothing more to say. After that there was a varied and exciting correspondence, phone calls now and then. But as Nick had prophesied I was abroad when his sudden chance came some months later. So we did not actually meet again. And that was four years ago. . . or five.

MARTIN

MARTIN lifted the pen from the vellum and surveyed it critically: the big I of "incipit", black with authority but breaking out in a fantasy of reverse curves on a pale straw grid. He looked at it, head to one side, teeth lightly clenched, reading the fantasy with a care born out of the few years of his apprenticeship . . . length to breadth, thickness of the back-strokes. It seemed adequate to him, Martin; would it be adequate to the Glory of God, in whose name every activity in the monastery was undertaken, from the vilest to the most refined. He wondered momentarily about the Glory of God, not sure that he really knew what it would be; then he looked through a narrow lancet window to a grey sea, idly fumbling and splashing round the drab rocks of that coast. His small horizon was that and no more, nothing free-moving, nothing that delighted in its will and wantonness. He looked again at the big I and decided that he must grind down some more black pigment. Then likely as not, from the sombre colour of it he would think of the morning's events, a rare change in the prescribed running of an abbey: how they had stood in two rows at the strand where the boats left and, wind-blown in the grey cold, had chanted the "Obiit" as the mortal remains of Brother Aelfrid were carried aboard the flimsy craft and two senior Brothers had rowed him across to the burial island to inter him and lock him fast in a circle of prayer and waters, lest anger should bring him back. They said that the Dead raged there sometimes but could not overcome the frustration of the moving waters. And as he was borne to the Strand, they had chanted Obiit, obiit . . . he has gone to meet it. Somehow the Latin was ceremonial, impersonal but when you took it back to the vernacular meaning there was mystery and terror, "Gone to meet it". After the Office Martin had strolled round to Brother Comlech, the mason, to warm his hands at his brazier and rid himself of the bleakness that had wrapped about his heart.

Martin at eighteen and Comlech at forty-six were only two of the life histories that played themselves out on that wind-swept spot. Idleness was not encouraged; but if you knew how, you could warm your hands and feel momentarily in your veins the life of Man, that was ever at variance, as it seemed, with the Service of God. Comlech was a shrewd observer and could be persuaded to say more than he meant. He knew the other Brothers charitably, yes that, but with a particularity which always had the effect on Martin of stimulating questions.

"Now this Aelfrid," (said Comlech) "had reached sanctity, but not without a struggle. When I was a boy about the place and just learning my trade, he would be in his twenties. There was something . . . I am not sure what it was and would not care to sin by guessing; the Reverent Abbot of that day would have had him put dryshod on the Mainland with a staff and a cloak and nothing besides. But several of the Brothers besought him in God to be merciful: it would be to thrust a pigeon in the way of eagles or a carp in the slow stream where the pike abide. So the Abbot kept him but put him under a vow of silence for three years. In all that time he could only speak to his Confessor and he endured the sentence. I think he gave up the fight within himself, settled down and allowed himself to become sanctified."

Martin listened to him with the young interest of one in whom the struggle still lurked in the fold of the future and sanctity was no certainty. His thoughts were confused; where he might have put a question, he chose to stay silent.

"I think it cost him a sore penitence," (Comlech continued), "but he would weigh his chances in a desperate world against the safety within the Church and so would come his surrender."

"Do all men have a struggle to accept the Rule?" (asked Martin, checking a too great forthrightness in his voice). "Did you have a struggle? Will it come for me?"

Comlech drove his chisel to the corner he had marked on the stone. He laid the mell down but the chisel remained an extension of his hand. He said:

"I did not find it beyond my power. I came here at sixteen and took the easy vows of my prime. As far back as I could remember I had been hungry and here there was food in return for work and obedience. At eighteen years and a half I was to accept the Great Vows and the tonsure and it all seemed just a part of a life in which I had little say. My parents were dead and our house burned by some marauding Earl in his power lust. What would I have gone back to? I loved this struggle with stone and the wresting of beauty out of the grain and the stubbornness of it. What else would I have done?"

"But the vows," (said Martin), "the Great Vows . . . you give up your freedom . . . you have nothing and are nothing. Sometimes I panic at the thought. Did you not so?"

"Boy, you fear most what you dare not mention, the fire in your body, the hunger in your limbs that troubles you in loneliness and the night. No?"

"Yes, that too. Was it nothing to you?"

"For some weeks before my acceptance I was troubled. I was afraid I could not do it. I spoke to my Confessor and he assured me that this was every man's trouble; but Grace would be given and strength so that wicked rebellion would be stilled in me. I suppose it has been so . . . largely so."

Martin looked at him, looked at the serene careworn face; but the years between eighteen and forty-six were a lifetime and he did not wish to think of it.

"And Aelfrid," (he asked), "did he joyfully surrender to God . . . or was it the surrender of a man to an all-powerful lord, given but without gladness. I did not know him, for with his failing eyesight and his pains he gave no access to one of my age."

"Yes, I think he won through to sanctity. It is a great act of

Grace if it comes to a man unbidden. Most of us need an iron will to fight temptation and rebellion and the heat of the body; and if you fight long enough and hard enough you find acceptance at length. When do you take your Great Vows?"

"Between Beltane and Midsummer," (said Martin).

As he said it he could feel the fear that already gnawed at him.

The Abbey community was shrinking. Perhaps the great days of the monastic life were on the wane. Perhaps, since the dangers from foreign shores had ceased, the challenge and the glory were less. A hundred years ago, he, Martin, might have prepared himself for the bright agony and bloody martyrdom that awaited those who laboured in the Abbeys by the sea shore. He had often thought of that as his pen deftly shaped the elegant letters, as the eye paused between words and calculated spaces. Perhaps the danger that came out of the sea mist nerved you to the Act of Faith, to the surrender: you wanted to be complete when your time came and die a man, as soldiers die, not a squalling brat, silenced with a thrust of the sword. But now? The world was changing and the heart of Man less inclined to submission or surrender.

He had run about these Abbey buildings almost as long as he could remember. He could just recall the day when his father's servants had delivered him into the keeping of the Abbot; they had wanted to call him Samuel at first, after some story in the Scriptures; but the curly-headed boy would have nothing of it, so he remained Martin and grew up cherished and beaten by turns, making himself useful in return for the food and the small chill chamber off the Dorter which had been allotted to him. For the Brothers would not hear of him sleeping with the community, sharp-eared and unsanctified as he was. And they had put him to Latin and the writing of the spoken language, for he spoke with more than usual fluency for one of his age. Then, because he was always in the Scriptorium and watching the two Brothers who prepared pens and inks, drew designs and worked out strange apocalyptic beasts, it was natural that he got small tasks to do there; and, showing an aptitude, he replaced first the one Brother,

when his hands were crippled with pains, and took over the job when Brother Clement was drowned crossing from the mainland one February night.

As a boy he had rejoiced in the friendships and society of the place, a joy that always seemed to make light of the cold everywhere and the chill First Office long hours before the winter daybreak. For Brother though he was not, they fitted him to the discipline of the place. One day when he was eleven or twelve a great Earl visited the place bringing with him his sons and the Lady, his wife. Martin made himself inconspicuous, for of a sudden he felt ashamed of his poverty and unkemptness before these magnificent people. But they sent for him and the great Earl had spoken to him like King Solomon in the Bible: he had asked him what he learned, what trade came to his hands, whether he was obedient. And the Lady had given him a pair of fine boots, too fine, but they fitted him alone. The Earl's great sons were disdainful and bored and could not wait to be gone. Only later as he pieced words to words, did it dawn on him that he had been deposited here out of harm's way, the Earl's love-child by some country woman, not to be reckoned in the succession. He could still remember the disdainful faces of his half-brothers.

When he was fifteen they had prepared him for his Prime vows, which at that moment seemed a reasonable enough projection of his present life: they said he was now man enough to take this decision. He was also shrewd enough to sense that of alternative there was none. At that moment the hunger and curiosity for the great world on the farther shore had not begun to ache in him; unlike Comlech and all the others who had known that world, such as it had been for them, and renounced it, he had only distant childish memories. To handle a boat, to work at his lettering, to labour at building or ploughing or reaping, all these skills he had more or less. The life of the place was self-contained, changing its aspect as the days darkened to winter's funeral, as the sparkle came on the sea again and the cuckoo called, when life was more relaxed and the chill gone. Under it all, imparting form and continuity lay the Rule, the Offices, the tasks, the cheerful sharing of the nastier parts of the routine. Martin took his share of it at fifteen as one who could not imagine the world ordered otherwise. But here and there barbs of conversation, unexplained things that men did were already preparing him for the agonies of doubt.

He caught himself once, twice, thinking uncharitably about some of the Brothers; little more than thirty they were in number, yet all their dignity as men tended to dissolve into a trivial silliness. Where a man should say: This I do, or that! they would say with a giggle that maybe St Benedict would come to them in a dream or St Christopher help them repair the haycart. His Confessor had told him to pray unceasingly that he become simple and childlike and he had tried; but he knew full well that there was nothing valid in his prayers. He had overheard what he should not, two of the Brothers resting in the shade of a wall in the afternoon and their conversation was sensual and unsanctified, filled with fantasies and imaginings that he could scarce understand. Not, you will know, that things like these were unknown to him; the society of men leaves nothing unmarked with crudity and ribald humour and he too had been the butt of that as he came to manhood. But this, his Confessor had told him, was the Devil in his most subtle and alluring form; only with heroic endeavour and savage repression could the thing be stilled: it was also helpful to take the Discipline now and then. But the simultaneous contrast between the Love of God which pursued them relentlessly hour by hour and the lapses of surrender to silliness and gluttony and the pricking of the flesh. . . that must be the condition of Life, he thought, and must be accepted now in others as perhaps later in himself.

Then there was the day when with eight of the younger Brothers he had crossed to the mainland and travelled on earthen ways to the Nunnery of St Hilda where were a relic of some antiquity and several books to be conveyed to the Monastery. The nuns had prepared some cart-sheds with bracken on the floor and blankets, that the men might sleep the night; and because the weather was good they had supper in the open courtyard before the nuns' chapel. To Martin it was all excitement and the Great World. The lay sisters who attended to their wants were the first of women whom Martin had seen in ten years other than the Earl's great lady. He felt awkward before them and aware of his clumsy manners and tongue that could not find the right things to say, as the others so easily did. It was summer and a long easy day, for they were absolved from Office till they returned. Towards evening all had disappeared somewhere from the cart-sheds except Martin and a Brother named Stephen. Martin wondered at the silence and said so; Stephen, a young man of twenty-four looked at him with a slight sneer of superiority.

"Wait till you've been under vows for a few years and you will know how to enjoy a holiday."

He said this with more resentment than superiority in his voice.

"Why not you then," (asked Martin). " You've had four years; is that not long enough?"

"I'm not made like them. I had bad luck. Why don't you grow up and find what the world is really like?"

Martin did not understand him; but sensing his bitterness, he diverted the talk to something else. Before long they had found new common interests that would make good friends of them. Then a servant-girl came and bade them cross to the Speaking Room: the Reverent Mother, she said, wished to see them. They went, slightly alarmed at this bidding, and for a while were left alone in the silent room. Then through the curtain came three of the young lay sisters, who spoke to them. Martin felt uncomfortable as their eyes devoured the two young men, roaming excitedly from head to toe; he did not understand what their oblique remarks signified. Stephen, who knew full well, turned on a cynical bitter tone, as it were repelling them and mocking them. Then more came in, perhaps half a dozen others or more. Martin thought momentarily of the eyes of owls or lynxes that he had drawn. The women stared impudent, triumphant. . . then with a shriek they fell on the two of them, frenzied with the rigours of their tormented lives. What happened was too humiliating: Humanity was stripped to the Beast. . .

. . . Suddenly they were gone, their baying laughter silenced as the curtain fell; Stephen and he gathered themselves from the floor and put themselves to right before slinking back to the cart shed. They were both mortally angry but for different reasons. These furies had uncovered Stephen's incapacity and he was humiliated to the death (but Martin did not know this); with Martin they had made merry and he had felt himself caught in irremediable sin, for he had responded physically to their lustful play (but Stephen did not know how he had felt). When it was dark and the others not yet returned, Martin heard his companion sobbing quietly and rather awkwardly put an arm round him. Stephen turned and wept on his shoulder.

They returned next day, as merry and pious a set of Brothers as you could expect to see. Martin was not slow to guess at their merriment, but he had to come to terms with his own problems, he who had not even made his great vows.

Now as he looked back at it with the understanding of life and men that two more years had given him, the episode seemed trivial enough. How would he respond, he wondered, were the thing to happen to him now? The Beast is in Man and will out after his own kind. Is it surprising, is it a sin? But this Love of God for which these men gave up all, gave up the Beast and the Angel, what is it? Is it some great thing like the wind or the sea or the thunder, of which you become a part when you surrender? Or is this a dream of Man, no more than that, a vast tower of Babel which is the Church, demanding the surrender of ever-increasing numbers of men and women, yet remaining for ever an experiment? The weeks were pressing on; Beltane would come and they would demand of him that he make his Great Vows.

The spring days brought warmth and greater comfort in the Scriptorium as it faced south. As his pen moved deftly over the writing surface, Martin compared the fuller, more fluent curves of the summer with those of his gloved hands on the dim afternoon of a frosty winter's day. Even the fantasies of his artistry moved more nimbly now and replaced the more angular geometricisms of the year's end. Mostly the work proceeded apace as he set himself a measured task for each day; only occasionally would he cross the courtyard to confer with one or other of the scholar Brothers about a reading or a gloss or some unexplained marginal mark. These were the good days when work seemed sufficient to contentment and genuine pride in achievement sent him happy to bed in his little cell. But there were other days when all the demons rose against him and he had to fight to suppress rebellious feelings. With Poverty he had no great quarrel: possession of the world's goods only brought on envy and greed and competition, fear too lest it all be taken away. Martin was not sure but he felt that this was no great issue. With sexual purity, sexlessness he could only imagine. You controlled the heat of the body so as to become more spiritual, live closer to God, be simple, have visions. Some of the Brothers who came in as men must have known what they renounced and many made light of it. He, Martin, could not know what he had not experienced and maybe that was a blessing. But twice, maybe thrice his dreams were disturbed by the vision of a man with his back to him and the sunlight ahead. He said: Your renunciation is all for a straw: get out and live! The Dream and the words had come to him but they made no sense. Concealing it from his Confessor, he said that he was not ready to make the sacrifice. The old Brother looked at him strangely and asked, Who talked of a sacrifice when the loss was dirt and vileness, the gain a step on the ladder to Heaven? But he gave him another month and counselled prayer and disciplined thoughts.

The Abbot was a rare visitor to the Scriptorium but he had been known to call at times when some special letter or document was to be prepared. This work was confidential, but Martin had long ago been trained by his mentors never to open his mouth regarding what he wrote. One afternoon when he was wrestling with an involved and beautiful superscription of Celtic design, the sun with its warmth enfolding and giving meaning to a Cross, he became aware of a presence behind him and knew from the silence and the faint smell of mint that his Ghostly Superior stood by him. He worked until a question from the latter about the design obliged him to stop and answer. Martin's first impression was astonishment that this reserved man with hands and knuckles distorted by cold and privation should speak with such authority about this lay-brother's work. . . and with such appreciation. He missed nothing: an alternative reading in the Luke Gospel: the geometric designs of winter: and this. . . a man with outstretched arms against the rising sun.

"Christian or pagan?" (he asked Martin). "It will be well if you quickly take your vows and become one of us."

Somehow the gentleness of his voice invited courage and a manly statement.

"Reverent Father, I have found uncertainties in my Faith and have delayed for a few weeks."

"I know."

"Besides. . ."

"Speak with no fear!"

"I am not sure in my heart that I have a vocation for this life. The lettering, yes, of course and the general labour and goodwill and fellowship. But there is in me something stubborn that will not make surrender."

For a moment Martin saw the grey eyes look at him with who knows what compassion; maybe he too had a memory of how it felt to be eighteen years. But when Martin glanced again at him a hard steely glitter was drawn over the eyes. The Abbot said, too gently to be comforting,

"You will make your vows. There is no other course for you. In this case surrender is required, regardless of scruples. You will see it as I see it some day."

The effect of this apparition was to cause Martin to omit a word; which in its turn cost a deal of effort erasing and smoothing. He turned aside, as he had been taught, and apologized on his knees to God. He could not miss it: there had been a threat in the Abbot's words. But as there was no

way of asking for an explanation, and he could not discuss it with the Brothers on principle, he turned it over and over in his mind and sat up at his little cell window in the night watching the sea that fretted on the moonlit rocks and the wind blowing where it listed.

In the next few days the question of responsibility for his own future had become important. Strangely. . . or maybe it was natural enough. . . Stephen had become a close friend. They did not let this be known in the daily work of the Abbey and sought places as far removed from each other as possible. Friendships were not encouraged; they impaired a man's single-mindedness to God. But in the leisure hour which Martin often passed in his workplace, he was frequently sought out by the older man. . . and how old you become at twenty-six. . . and together they took flight in fantasy from the trite comment and pious tomfoolery that cheered the common-room. Stephen always brought a Latin text which he was construing with difficulty; it could provide a pious excuse were someone else to call. Stephen had come to life once he knew that his secret was shared; he had also found it easier to capitulate and ran his life into a still groove. But with a bit of himself he wished that Martin would not do so. Without actually discouraging him, Stephen sought out the structural weakness in his attitudes and shed with a word here and there a doubt regarding the surrender. In the freedom of these hours they came a long way.

"Why," (asked Martin) "is it good for you and not for me? Why should I not prostrate myself and swallow hard and drive out the devil of rebellion? Here there is security; here I am needed; here is a hope at least that the uncertainty and waywardness of life on the mainland is exchanged for an ascent to the nearer presence of God?"

"You are the Devil's own advocate, Martin. You do not believe a word of it."

"Oh, I do. . . with one bit of me I do. You have taken mighty steps to win the struggle and you will get there."

"But you?"

"Stephen, if you make me do it, I must confess to you

alone, hardly even to myself, that it's all darkness in there. I am happiest when I am working or sleeping, for then his eyes are not on me."

"Whose eyes? The Reverent Father?"

"No, no. . . Stephen, it would be a shame to say it. . . and wickedness for you hear me and not denounce me."

Stephen laid his rough hand on Martin's finer one. He said, "I'll bear the sin. . . and I won't denounce you. Tell me. . . if you want to trust me."

Martin looked at his friend and trusted him; he made a quick move to the door to see if anyone were lurking there. Then he said quietly:

"It is not God. I don't know God. I don't know what it would be to know God. . . I mean, whether things would be clearer or more in confusion. But there is another one who has come to me in my sleep. . . strangely he looks like you. . . and he speaks to my heart as though he knows all that is stored up in there. I wonder, is it a son of God? And he says to me: Do not surrender. Flee rather, and take your chance in the world outside. In no wise surrender. You give yourself to a god that man has fashioned for himself. This terrifies me in a way. As I work I try to think how there can be contradictory voices on this side and that. And he looks like you, Stephen. I think that's why I am prepared to trust him."

Stephen looked at him, trying the impossible, to understand another man's problem from another personality. But it was difficult for him to keep at bay the thought of the immeasurable loss that threatened him. Then the hour was up and the bell rang for Compline. As they left the room Stephen said,

"If you are to do this thing, you will have a sign. Let us pray for that."

The summer days were on them once more. It was an easing of the Spirit to get away from the grey walls and work in the little fields of springing bere and red wheat. Patient toil, if not one of their vows, was the ethos of the place: hands and legs got to an easy rhythm and persevered through the long hours of daylight while the tide ebbed and rose again; the larks and the peewits rejoiced in their element and at dusk the swifts swooped and rose among the buttresses and gutterings. A sickness confined several of the Brothers to bed; it was for all the rest to turn to the field-work that would not wait. Little copying was done in that month. As he walked the long stone corridor and back again, Martin listened to his feet and imagined more urgent feet behind him. As it happens he had almost ceased to believe in a sign when it came.

We may well speculate on the incidence of mental disorder, neurotic or psychotic attacks in the monastic conditions of that century. The mentally-disturbed had once been an object of wonder, of god-possession in the pagan pre-Christian days. But the Semitic world had brought to light devils, encroaching spirits, things that clung to the life of the living and threw them into disorder. The Gospels contained many instances of these devils and their overthrow; but the wisdom of the centuries and a particular council of the Church had declared appearing spirits as no part of official belief. But when you were faced with threshing limbs and rolling eyes, wild torrents of animal sounds, in short madness, it was tempting to creep back and acknowledge the devils after all. This much was popularly accepted: devils hated cruelty, beating, starvation. For want of a magician to drive them out, you beat the sufferers, chained them, starved them. It probably happened but rarely and mostly with old senile men who could be confined in cold chambers and urged without cruelty on the way to Glory. But Brother Aengus was thirty-six.

His sudden absence from the Common Room and the gossip there soon enlarged some strange symptoms into devil possession. Martin knew little of it save that a room at the far end of his corridor was closed up and accessible only to two senior Brothers, one of whom knew what there was of medicine. After two weeks the wonder was growing commonplace and, while they missed the presence of Aengus, they were happy to ask no questions. As he recalled the event later Martin remembered that he had thought much about Brother Aengus. What is this madness? Is a man totally and irreversibly changed by it? Or might someone come along and say or do something so that he be turned back to himself? The Gospel stories suggested this; but the Church taught that these things were the credentials of the Founder and could not happen nowadays. Had they then in the case of Brother Aengus to wait for the improbable appearance of the Saviour of Mankind and a passing flock of sheep? He thought in a rash sort of way that this is not how God could have ordained things. But who would know what to do and who would dare to do it? Perhaps the Abbot? Perhaps those who had accumulated the greatest sanctity, for whom the Dark Cloud that hid the face of God was at its thinnest?

It was one evening in late May during the hour of recreation. Martin was in his workroom finishing off a letter for the Abbot. Of a sudden Stephen was at his side, saying:

"Brother Aengus has broken out of his cell. He is in the Common Room raging mad and everyone is paralysed with fear."

To be honest, Martin could not have described with certainty the events of the next half hour, had others not been present to attest to it. Stephen told him later that he turned from his work-bench, staring round-eyed at him and said,

"Why have you come to tell me?"

Stephen said to him, quite improbably,

"Because you will know what to do. Come, you are the only one who is big enough for this."

Martin had gone with him, his feet scarcely touching the floor, or so it had seemed. But he could remember afterwards being caught up into some thing and saying silently: This is the sign. God do not fail me now! He entered the Common Room with a great stride, all the six feet of him, and seeming to the trembling Brothers as if he were seven. He had no time to take in the horror on the stricken faces, the fear of the Beast broken forth from Man. In the midst Aengus now lay on the floor, now foaming, sometimes bawling, blaspheming with every second word. He beat the ground in a frenzy of frustration and made to rise on tottering legs but fell in a wild convulsing heap. Martin stood before him, legs astride and said with a thunderous voice,

"Let him be: come out of him: return to the half-world between life and death where ye belong!"

At this Aengus crumpled in a whimper and lay sobbing on the floor. No-one moved or uttered a sound. Martin stood commanding the situation. After what seemed an eternity he said,

"Brother Aengus, look at me!"

Slowly the heap of limbs and rags straightened itself out and turned round to sit, leaning back on one arm and gazing up as though hypnotised. He was a hideous sight, unshaven and foul with spittle and foam sticking to his beard. He held out his hand to Martin and shrieked "No, no!" then turned away.

"Look at me," (said Martin), "keep your eyes on me!"

And truly he did. All the others cowering round the walls were caught in the spell.

"Do you want to return to the man you were? Can you hear me? Do you want to return to the man you were, free from attaching spirits? Keep looking at me!"

Brother Aengus made to say "Yes" (at least the others all thought so) but at once there broke from him squeals and screeches, things half-human, like children about to be torn from their mothers. Martin stared, held out his hand towards the man's face, while Aengus stared back at him and gibbered and squeaked.

"See," (said Martin with a quiet and terrifying authority) "when I take my hand away they all leave you. When I take my hand away they all leave you. They will be gone and will not come back."

And he drew back his arm and let it fall by his side. Aengus was stilled and continued to stare at Martin, now with eyes of desperate devotion. What happened next was no less terrifying; no-one in that room could have remotely shared Martin's experience nor could know what he would do next. He was seen to say quietly and firmly as though speaking to a sleepy child,

"When I take you by the hand and stand you on your feet, it is all over. You will be well again. You will be Aengus once more. You understand; it is all over."

He grasped the left hand and pulled him to his feet. Aengus blinked, then smiled and said, "What are we all doing?"

"Brother," (said Martin) "go and wash and return to assure these others that a great mercy has been possible for you."

Then Martin, like one not of this world, strode out and lost himself somewhere in the Abbey precincts.

That was effectively the sign: it told Martin something that he alone could know. Stephen talked to him about it two days later while they were working at the far edge of the bere field. Martin said,

"I don't know what happened. Something possessed me as I entered the room and used me like a tool. It was all pressure to carry out a command and not let go for a minute. . . like holding the rope so that the boat does not swing away on the tide. Only once did I come to myself and hesitate, just before I made him stand. I wondered if I could dare to do it. For it came to me that maybe I was trying to do something too big for one who has not the courage to take the Great Vows. But the pressure said, 'Do it,'. . . and I did."

"And is it, as you said in the doorway, the sign you are waiting for? Will it decide you?"

Signs we may have if we are open enough and not strangled by our human intellect. But a sign will come from without. . . from out there; it will have a syntax and a grammar that we may not at first understand. I think that Martin was fortunate to live when he did, where he did, in circumstances that had kept him naive, ready to respond like an amateur actor on a stage, with no set moves. In the days following he spoke but little to the others; perhaps he did not notice that they made no attempt to speak to him. What had happened, should after all not happen; the ordered system that spelt Man's relation to God, structured by sanctity, study and long years of experience had been rudely wrenched aside. You could not say that it had not happened: you were there. Brother Aengus was known to be cured of his possession or whatever it was, though he was still confined to his room till some great Religious personage would confirm his normality. Something had happened; in your dread of the abnormal you would have preferred to think that it had all been a dream. The Gospel stories were a colourful episode of the past in an alien world; they existed for the Present only with a spiritual or symbolic truth: thus alone were they tolerable. The Brothers rehearsed the past in their daily Offices and lived virtuous lives in the present. Suddenly the past had become real among them, erupted with horrors and dangers that it was convenient to believe were not there. The human attitude to Martin swung precariously like some light structure in the wind. They looked at him with wonder (the youngster who had run about the place since he was six, the calligrapher who had not yet been received into the community); they looked at him with fear (for had he not commanded devils and freed a man from an affliction which God might have imposed on him for secret sin?); they looked at him with just the edge of resentment (had they not all cowered against the wall, fearing for their lives, so many of them, and this one Nobody had shamed them all). What neither Martin nor the Brothers knew was the perplexity that surrounded the Reverent Abbot and his Elders.

Pro: A great marvel had been performed.
Contra: It was performed within the Church by one not
            received into the Church.
Pro: The Love of God had been made manifest.
Contra: Or, as God had not been invoked by a ritual of
            exorcism, this could be the work of the Devil.
Pro: This calligrapher had performed a wonder which
            might echo to their credit throughout Christen-
            dom.
Contra: But if wonders were performed within the Church
            by those not of it, where would all discipline be?
Pro: This man, when received into the community,
            might be a great glory and strength to all of them.
Contra: Or he might feel himself greater than them all.

The Abbot reminded them of his promises to the Earl.

Martin could not be sent away or made to disappear. In the end with some perplexity a plan was made. Martin would be summoned to appear before the Abbot and the two senior Brothers next day.

Called from his work at a moment's notice, Martin had not time to prepare what he would say : the whole thing was too near and too perplexing. For the last two days he had felt stifled by the thick felt-like layers of predictability which surrounded the monastic life; he wanted to be somewhere far from the sight and sound of it to try to think out what had happened. But the time had not been given. In his working clothes, with ink stains on the sleeves, he entered the Abbot's chamber where the three men awaited him. He bowed his head and kept his eyes downcast as he felt appropriate to this unwonted occasion.

"The Grace of God be with you," (said the Abbot).

"And with you too, Reverent Father."

"We wish to know from your own lips what happened in the Common Room the other evening."

"Reverent Father, I find this difficult. Since that evening I have longed to be alone somewhere to think about it, but the life of the place goes on. *A Man is not Expected to be by Himself.* However, I will say in my rough way what I think happened. Brother Stephen called me as I worked, and told me of the terror in the Common Room. I first asked him why he came to tell me this; but I did not heed his answer. For, even as I asked, I felt the issues of life narrow to one small hole through which I could creep. There was something to be done; I did not know what, but I was not allowed to doubt that I could do it. When I entered the room, I, Martin, knew not what to do, but something greater had taken possession of me and drove me on. I could not now tell you what I said or did; you would have to ask the others. I was just aware that I was holding as it were to a rope and I had to find determination to do it."

"Did you pray to God for strength?"

"Reverent Father, every morning at the beginning of my work I pray that whatever strength or wisdom or patience is

needed, that will be given to me without further demand. I
often need it in my work. This was another such occasion:
I felt the strength and the wisdom flow to me."

"Where did this strength and wisdom come from?"

"Where else than from God?"

"Could it not have come from the Adversary?"

"In God I believe; the Adversary is an invention of the
imperfect thoughts of men."

One of the senior Brothers gasped.

"But if the Church teaches that the Adversary is as real as
God you must accept it?"

"But Reverent Father, as you know well, the Church does
not and cannot teach so. My experience I am sure was of God. But
why and to such an ignorant servant as I am, I can give no answer.
Perhaps you have had yourself had such an experience?"

For several hours the interrogation dragged on. Martin was
Child enough to remain insensitive to the sinister threat that
hung over him. Towards midday the Abbot said,

"We have no way of determining if this thing be of God or
of the Devil. In so far as Brother Aengus is now hale and in
his right mind, we are disposed to think that it is of God. But
we think too that it could have lain in the inscrutable purposes of God that Aengus be mad and a warning to us all."

Martin stared incredulous at him, but in the stillness of the
room it went unnoticed. The Abbot continued,

"The Church is God's kingdom on Earth. It is not appropriate that irregular events like this be allowed to happen. We
feel that, however well-intentioned, you were misguided in
trespassing clumsily on events greater than your understanding. Had God wished Aengus cured, he would have selected a
qualified and devout servant of the Church to do so, one in
whom obedience and discipline and sanctity were already
ripe. You were not able to do this thing and you did not do it.
By a great mercy God pardoned your intrusion and wrought
good out of evil. We invite your comment."

"Reverent Father, I have lived long enough in this place to
know when I may open my mouth and when not. Your
authority and wisdom and experience makes as nothing any-

thing I could say. But you invite me. I say, you are wrong, all three of you, even if you destroy me for it. I may have been used once in my life to act as the pen or the chisel or the mouthpiece of God. We may all be used so. But I cannot count on it that He will ever care to use me thus again so long as I live. There is, I think, no right of Sanctity or Wisdom or High Authority even in the Church. We are used as we are needed."

They showed no reaction to his words but were sore perplexed. Grace and sensitivity were not lacking in them but they clung to a rigid structure made by human minds. It is probable that each of the three knew in his heart that they had touched the well-spring of divine experience; but their honesty was in two compartments, and they never truly knew what was in each other's hearts. Martin was asked to wait in a side room while they discussed the issue and when he returned, it was to uncompromising demands:

You will take your vows and accept the tonsure forthwith.

You will take a vow of silence about this thing and never mention it again, so long as you will live.

You will never again intrude beyond your rank and station in matters in which only the highest councils of the Church have wisdom.

Martin towered over the rulers of the Abbey; they sat small and sunk in on themselves as though mirroring their wretchedness and confusion. The two Brothers stared at the ground, the Abbot studied a document that lay before him. Outside in the summer silence only a small wind echoed in the window openings.

"I require time to think."

"There is not any thinking and no time. You do as you are bidden."

"Do I understand that this is the instruction of the Earl?"

There was clearly embarrassment.

"I humbly ask again: do I understand that this is the Earl's instruction?"

The Abbot might well have asked what Martin knew about

the Earl. But he was old and tired and felt God outwitting him at his own game.

"I did not propose that there should be any delay," he said, avoiding the issue.

"Can you compel a man to make vows when his heart might be uncertain, or even against it?"

There was embarrassment and panic; one looked to the other for wisdom or support; the Abbot lost his grip and surrendered.

"You have a week to prepare yourself. A sennight from today you are received into the Church, to poverty, chastity and obedience."

Martin stood humble, as humble as six feet can be before old crumpled men. The Abbot made a gentle sign of dismissal and he left in a painful silence.

When he thought about it years later, or when he could be induced to speak about it to a rare friend, Martin was never sure of the truth of events, of his own states of mind or motives. He returned to his work-room and with determination completed a page near the end of a Mark Gospel. Sometimes it was comforting to escape from himself and his surroundings in a task that held a worth in itself, were he never personally to achieve anything. It might seem strange, if you had a problem to face away from it, deliberately not to face it; but this was a strange piece of wisdom he had picked up from an old and saintly Brother now gone into the shadows. Turn away, do not decide for yourself: allow the greater unseen movements of Heaven and Earth free room to play their part and shape your future. Rationally considered he was caught, a prisoner on an island condemned to the tonsure by the arbitrary fear of an Earl, condemned to submission and to renunciation just when he felt the dawn of something new within himself. The Abbot was wrong, yes! . . . but he was no free man one way and another. The Church was wrong, yes! . . . you might dare to think that but it would take courage to act on it. If the Church played a political game, if it bought and sold the Truth to serve its own ends, it

was doubly wrong. What appalled him most was the compul-
sion to make vows from his tongue outward, to live a liar and
a coward and a traitor, worse than any tin-pot Judas. But all
this came afterwards as he sorted it out in his own mind. For
the moment he turned away. . . for he knew that round the
shadowy side of his mind something was resolved in him to
escape.

Meals were a silent routine; he worked mostly alone: few
came his way. He walked up and down in the afternoon
behind the range of ancient ruined barns, trying to delight in
the sea wind that blew so blithely over this prison. He caught
himself thinking: Prison. Then: If I am to escape, the time is
short and something must happen to bring about the impossible. He strained himself not to think and plan; but loneliness
and desperation were round every corner. One day after the
interview, he returned to his room and made himself work; it
was an hour or so before he noticed that someone had taken
down a large Old Testament, an old but authoritative volume,
and marked Joshua I,9. With a shock he realised that the Latin
translated to: 'Be not afraid, neither be thou dismayed: for
the Lord thy God is with thee whithersoever thou goest.'
Martin's heart leapt to the words. But who had been in his
room? Who had dared to put a mark on the sacred book?
Next day when Stephen called to see him, genuinely wanting
help with his Latin text, he said simply: How can I help. . . as
though he had read Martin's thoughts. Martin replied:
"Your life is here: I will not get you involved. Pray for me.
I am too confused to do that for myself. Pray that if you can
be used, you will be. I dare say no more."

Two more days had passed and the slow movements of
circumstance were not apparent. Then instructions came that
he was to move his bed to his work-room. It would have been
easy to see in that a sinister foreclosing of doom; but thinking
of it afterwards, he was sure that he had seen it as a stepping-
stone to the future. Then he was ordered to keep to his room;
meals were brought and handed to him; it was given out
apparently that he was in preparatory seclusion. That was the

third day, a wild storm of wind and rain. The fourth day dawned grey but the clouds lifted and the sea ran glittering in the mud channels and the tide came in towards evening. At seven o'clock a strange and great certainty came on him; the hours were running out. Martin cleaned and tidied the scriptorium, laying everything in order, cleaning the pens and the brushes which he had used. He found himself thinking: This I am doing for the last time. . . but it seemed a strange thought in an unmoving situation. When darkness came, he did not go to bed, but held all his small possessions ready in a bag which he had found outside the door. He tried to pray, but was too full of himself and his crisis to make anything of that, unless it was the gesture that might be acceptable.

Before midnight, as he sat on his bed with sleepless eyes, he knew that he was waiting. When the door opened and a silent cowled figure touched his arm and drew him, Martin took his bag and followed. Earth things and Spirit things had moved to the initiative. He followed along the corridor to a back door, past the Dorter where all save one were asleep, out on to the rough land, up the track and over to where the bere fields stood stiff in the darkness; then down the gritty path and on to the ledges of rock that marked the shore. A little rude boat lay there which they floated and climbed into, he and his silent guide. They paddled out into the still water but they had to exert themselves where the current now beginning the ebb pulled them southwards. Then they came to still water again and the further shore, sandy with rough grass blowing in the wind. They stepped out and pulled the boat ashore; and they stood out of the wind as though irresolute what to do. Then the silent companion gripped Martin by both his arms, desperately gripped him as though he would not leave him; then fell and kissed his sandalled feet.

"Oh no, Stephen, not that; I am not worthy."

The other stood up and handed him a little leather bag with some coins in it.

"The Reverent Father bids you go on your way with God. So do I. Never speak of this night till the world has moved on and those concerned have gone the way of all the earth."

He turned and pushed the boat out into ebbing midnight waters and was lost to sight. We have no access to the wild confusion of his heart, however much our modern voyeur tendencies clamour for a minute-by-minute commentary. To be sure there was relief and gratitude that he was free, uncertainty too at his own inexperience in making a future for himself. He felt an awful responsibility that he had been loved; by the incredulous Aengus; by Stephen, whose best compromise for bad luck in an unsympathetic world had been surrender; by the Reverent Father himself who, laying the rigid discipline of his calling aside, had chosen, he too, to be the servant and the implement of something so great that no name should be found for it.

The chronicles of these troubled times are mostly lost. . . or maybe they were never committed to writing. Martin's name crops up in the early records of two of the tiny cathedral cities of England. Later, when he would have been twenty-five or twenty-six he appears to have toiled mightily in communities further south, overwhelmed by inroads of the sea and consequently by hunger, disease and despair. He seems to have worked as an archivist for some time in one of the Fenland abbeys where he was credited in some utterance or sermon (had he been licensed as a Friar?) with the remarkable statement:

"*For such as love God, Death comes neither too soon or too late, exactly at the right time to compass His purposes.*"

And that timely death seems to have recognized the finish of his achievement at the age of thirty-five, if we dare to rely on a verbal commentary and a broken stone cast aside by the builders when a community in the nineteenth century rebuilt and rededicated to some doubtful monastic use an abbey torn down in vandalistic glee in the times of King Henry VIII. One wonders whether he was ever again called to emergency service as he was on that day when he laid bare some terrible evidence of what we even now choose not to believe. But we know what he thought. Like most of us he emerged from an

indecipherable past and disappeared almost without comment. Not in stone nor in book does his immortality lie, but
there where he knew that it should, in the hearts and minds of
those who crossed his way.